Stories in the Stepmother Tongue

Stories in the Stepmother Tongue

Edited by
Josip Novakovich & Robert Shapard

White Pine Press • Buffalo, New York

WHITE PINE PRESS
P.O. Box 236, Buffalo, New York 14201

Publication of this book was made possible, in part,
by grants from the Lannan Foundation
and the New York State Council on the Arts.

Acknowledgments: Julia Alvarez, "Joe," from *How the Garcia Girls Lost Their Accents.* Copyright © 1991 by Julia Alvarez. Published by Plume, an imprint of Dutton Signet, a division of Penguin USA, Inc., and originally in hardcover by Algonquin Books of Chapel Hill. Reprinted by permission of Susan Bergholz Literary Services, New York. All rights reserved.

Andrei Codrescu, "Born Again," from *In America's Shoes,* City Lights Books, San Francisco, 1983. Reprinted by permission of the author.

Judith Ortiz Cofer, "Not for Sale," from *The Latin Deli: Prose and Poetry,* by Judith Ortiz Cofer, The University of Georgia Press, 1993. Copyright © 1993 by Judith Ortiz Cofer. All rights reserved. Published by the University of Georgia Press, Athens, Georgia 30602.

Acknkowledgments continue on page 253.

Cover art: "Mami, Mami," 1985, by Julio Galan.
Used by gracious permission of the artist.

Book design: Elaine LaMattina

Library of Congress Cataloging-in-Publication Data
Stories in the stepmother tongue
edited by Josip Novakovich and Robert Shapard ;
p. cm.
ISBN 1-893996-04-2 (paper : alk. paper)
I. Short stories, American—Minority authors. 2. United States—Emigration and immigration—Fiction.
3. United States—Social life and customs—Fiction. 4. Emigration and immigration—Fiction.
5. American fiction—20th century. 6. Minorities—Fiction . 7. Immigrants—Fiction.
I. Shapard, Robert, 1942- II. Novakovich, Josip, 1956-

PS647.E85 S76 2000
813'.0108920691—dc21   00-031996

*Thanks to
Jeanette Novakovich,
Revé Shapard,
Michelle Tyau,
and Kathleen Matsueda.*

Contents

Introduction

Last year in America the National Book Award went to a man who used to be in the Chinese army. Four of the eight Guggenheim fellowships for fiction went to foreign-born, non-native speakers of English. Writers like these in the past have made great contributions to English language and literature—we need only think of Joseph Conrad, for example, who was Polish (born Józef Korzeniowski), or Vladimir Nabokov, born in Russia. Now many more are entering the American literary scene. That should not be surprising since a million immigrants arrive in this country every year, and today one in ten Americans is foreign-born. Yet such writers have gone largely unrecognized as a literary category. Perhaps this is because, individually, they have been included under the very wide term "multicultural," and certainly they are that. Or perhaps it's because many of the new immigrants, writers included, haven't fit the old stereotypes. Strictly speaking, most, but not all, of the authors in this collection have English as their second language; most but not all are immigrants. So first I need to explain what is a stepmother tongue writer—and what is a stepmother tongue.

As for what it's like to write in English as a stepmother tongue, and why choose to write in it at all (the answer isn't always as obvious as some might think), Robert Shapard and I asked each of our authors for a personal statement, and we have included these with the stories.

What is a stepmother tongue writer? I will give you my own example since I know it best.

In the sixth grade in Daruvar, Croatia (then Yugoslavia), we had to choose a foreign language, and only two were offered, Russian in the morning, and English in the afternoon. To solve the shortage of room space, we had two shifts in the school, one ideal for morning risers and another for owls. In the morning I was listless, and it took me a long time to become alert. I would have preferred to take Russian, because as a Slavic language similar to Croatian it would have been much easier. But instead for several years I took two hours of English classes a week, although they were mostly in Croatian and I hardly paid any attention to them.

Then, at the age of sixteen, as a clumsy soccer player, I sprained my ankle and stayed in bed for two weeks. (I could have gone back to school sooner, but this was an excellent occasion for absenteeism.) My brother Ivo, aspiring to learn English in order to become a rock star, had bought a dozen Langenscheidt's books in simplified English, with vocabularies of 450, 750, and 1200 words. I grabbed the one with 450, Greek Myths. As a kid I used to read fairy tales, and now I would not have admitted that I still wanted to read them. Under the guise of learning English, I read the book in a couple of days, slowly, amazed that the meanings of the words came across, through a shroud of letters, from a long distance of memory and guessing, to create wonders of a drunken pantheon. I kept reading the books, and jovially I wondered whether I would turn into a half-man half-goat or a donkey, or, equally astounding, a foreigner.

The experience was so intoxicating that I grew obsessed with English. At night I listened to the Voice of America, BBC. In my walks I memorized English words from a dictionary. I gave all my friends English nicknames. Zeljko, coming from Zelja, or wish, became Willy. At school I took notes in history classes in English. I wanted the experience of being in the language—so I applied to American colleges. I got a full scholarship to Vassar (at the age of twenty), where liberal arts education, consisting mostly of writing papers, helped me develop a writing habit, in English. I enjoyed reading stories, and wanted to write them, yet when I sat down, I was sober enough to realize that Croatian was my strongest language, no matter what, and I wrote several stories in Croatian. Thinking that I had already mastered the craft, I mailed the stories off to a friend of mine, who ran a literary magazine in Zagreb, *Gordogan.* He replied: "What language do you think you are writing in? This is not Croatian—too many Serb words, too much strange syntax. First learn the language, then write in it."

In my absence, Croatian had changed under the political influence of national emancipation. Serbia had long dominated Yugoslavia, and forced much Serbian vocabulary and syntax upon Croatian, and the revision made sense, although any notion of nationalism made me cringe. I did not like the idea of ethnic cleansing in my mother tongue. Before going to the States, I had spent a year in Serbia (as a medical student in Novi Sad, Vojvodina, more precisely), and no doubt, I picked up some vocabulary there, and damaged my syntax by reading anatomy books and memorizing Latin terms. And in my region, Slavonia, we spoke in a dialect that had many more influences from Serbian anyhow than Croatian literary language did. I thought these slight deviations from any kind of standard would be colorful, regional, lived, authentic. But my writing in my real native language would be taken as a political statement of pro-Yugoslavism and anti-Croatianism. I didn't mean to make political statements; I wanted to write basic stories. The response from Croatia was a blow. For one reason or another, I could not be a writer there. Before, I was not a Communist, and my family was not an old well-connected Zagreb family, so in the old framework I could not be accepted. In the new one, with the nationalist strivings, I couldn't be accepted either. If I was to change my language and relearn it in order to write stories, I decided I might just as well write in English.

Of course I'm only one example. How many others among the million immigrants to America every year are like me, writing stories and other literature in English as a second language? Nobody knows exactly, especially since it isn't always easy to say whether English is a writer's second language. In some cases, there's no doubt: Mikhail Iossel moved to this country at the age of thirty, with a poor command of English, and several years later wrote *Every Hunter Wants to Know* in English and published it with Norton, though he still occasionally writes in Russian and considers it his strongest language. But if you immigrate at the age of two, and all your education is in English, is English your first or your second language? Chronologically, it may be the second, but in strength, the first language. In other cases, English may be the third language. A student of mine, Michael Benharroch, writes in English as the fourth language. He grew up speaking Arabic and Hebrew, later lived in Venezuela, and only afterward learned English, and now he is brave enough to write in it. How do we classify him?

And what about writers born in the States? Some experts claim that, even if at home the family speaks the language of the old country, for anyone born here English is their first language because of the surrounding, pervasive media in English. We questioned this, and selected two non-immigrant writers, one an Arizona writer, Stella Pope Duarte, who grew up surrounded by and speaking Spanish, the other a writer who also lives in Arizona and is a Native American, Simon Ortiz. Anyway, who is the native speaker? Simon is a native of this country, with roots deeper than anybody else's, yet he considers English to be his stepmother tongue, the language imposed from the invading culture. Even though he grew up speaking English more than his native Pueblo, English is his second language, in a spiritual sense. How would one classify Simon?

Considering such gradations and variations, Robert and I concluded that the term English as a Second Language (ESL) was inadequate for our purpose, and anyway it sounds cold and bureaucratic, especially compared with what people call the language they were born into: their mother tongue. So we came to prefer a term that should simply indicate an expanding family: stepmother tongue. In America the mother tongue called English has adopted many eager writers, and of course there are many cases of good stepmothers. But proverbially stepmothers can be cruel, and perhaps it is true English treats many newcomers harshly and unlovingly. If this is true, why write in English? And the answer would rarely be what seems to many people the most obvious.

Nearly wherever I go I run into non-native speakers writing in

English. Years ago I met a young man in Prague who wrote exclusively in English despite not knowing whether he could ever publish in English. For him it wasn't a practical question of reaching a large literary market—perhaps the most common reason for writing in English given by those who don't write in English as a second language. For some, yes, that enters the picture, for who does not want to make a living? But to me it seems there are nearly as many reasons for writing in English as a stepmother tongue as there are stepmother writers themselves, and I am often surprised not only by how many there are but by who they are. Just the other day, I had lunch with a Croatian psychiatrist, Feodor Hagenauer, who surprised me when he told me that he was writing mostly fiction these days, in English. It reminded me that Chang-Rae Lee (another non-native English writer whose fiction would fit here) had the courage to plunge into writing because of the example of his father, who, when he came from Korea to this country as a physician, not fearing the fact that he would have to master the language, did not choose to practice medicine as a surgeon or some other kind of medical specialist who might not need excellent command of English, but as a psychiatrist. Certainly English has liberated many people to speak their minds. For example, Nahid Rachlin, whose work is included in this book, couldn't speak freely in Iran; she experienced freedom of speech in English for the first time and still writes with that jubilant air of freedom. And internationally, we need only look at CNN to see that political graffiti and appeals are mostly in English—in Tiananmen Square, in Kosovo refugee camps—for English is the lingua franca, the language of computers and the first language of the United Nations. So no wonder that the language has an appeal of liberation in it, personal and political. One could of course see the language differently, as a language of oppression, exploitation, and international capitalism. From this standpoint a more revealing question than "Why write in English?" might be "What has prevented people from writing in English?" In the past, the idea in this country that foreigners could not speak up and write in English as well as "real" Americans stems from an exploitative attitude toward immigrants, who used to be mostly laborers, factory workers, slaves, service people, and so on. Many of those attitudes (and jobs) are still around, although we are also now getting more used to seeing foreign-born people leading in the sciences, business, and the arts (in fact, foreign-born musicians dominate the classical music scene). On the whole, incoming foreigners, if they are fortunate enough to have opportunities for education, may not be as doomed as they were in the past to being second-class citizens in English, but can be on a par with, or even surpass, native-born Americans in their mastery of the language.

Yet it is true that the pressure toward conformity in English is still quite strong. At the University of Cincinnati, where I teach English literature, in one of the cities with the lowest percentage of immigrants in the country, as I read my teaching evaluations I ran across several in which students complained that they had a foreigner with an accent teach them their language. To them, that was an injustice; to me it was an injustice as well, that I had to deal with their xenophobia! But even immigrants themselves frequently adopt the same xenophobic attitude toward foreign-flavored English: they are disappointed if in an English as a Second Language class they have a teacher with an accent. That is the pattern, that the person who is discriminated against adopts the attitudes and turns them into an inferiority complex. I worked for two years at Nebraska Indian Community College at Santee Sioux Reservation, and several people there told me that they have to fight the prejudices against their own people that they picked up from the whites. Many immigrants have faced similar prejudice, though sometimes it's less a matter of race and more of a linguistic ranking in favor of the "original" English speakers.

Social and political issues like these lead to another book, many books, besides this one, which seeks mainly to introduce and celebrate an important and growing area in American letters that many readers have been unaware of. As I said before, this may in part be due to stepmother tongue writers elsewhere being included (in a way made invisible) in broad ethnic categories where they have little in common with the other writers linguistically. (They may have very different cultural attitudes as well—see Bharati Mukherjee's comparison, following her story, of herself with Amy Tan and Maxine Hong Kingston.) Anyway, having an accent is not always a drawback. Take for example Andrei Codrescu, who has a heavy accent yet is one of the keenest observers of American culture and is the wittiest commentator on National Public Radio. I should not even use "yet" in this context; perhaps it is partly *because* of his multilingual and multicultural background that Mr. Codrescu can be so resourceful in English.

What is it like writing in English as stepmother tongue?

Simultaneous knowledge of two languages gives one a kind of stereo-perceptiveness, so that in either language one can benefit from the sub-liminal and liminal dialogue with the remaining language; in English, Codrescu can echo some angles from Romanian; in Romanian, no doubt, from English. Julia Alvarez, in her statement for this collection, has said that much of her verbal rhythm, her word choices, and her attention to the sound of her prose comes from her native language as spoken by her family. Bilingualism, psychologists have demonstrated, stimulates a child's intelligence, and I dare say, an adult's. In English, more than Japanese, Kyoko Uchida felt free to experiment, with "Letters like colorful building blocks" which she would "line up and rearrange to create phrases and sentences, and from them entire pic-tures, imagined countries, histories, songs, silences," creating some-thing more her own than anything else she had known. This stimula-tion of invention is also noted by Ha Jin, this country's most recent National Book Award winner. "English is an expressive language," he says; "It's quite common among Chinese immigrants that when they begin to write in English, they feel they have more to say...." Mikhail Iossel, on the other hand, says that in English he has less to say, but that's good, because in Russian there are too many word choices, he can lose sight of the story he's trying to tell "in a maze of complex sen-tences."

Emigration, with the gain of spatial and cultural distance, helps many writers to put their old experiences into perspective—or even to realize that their observations and memories from their home are worthwhile story materials. When we write, we translate our day-dreams, memories, thoughts into stories anyhow; writing in the foreign language, the aspect of translation is magnified. Every phrase from home can be turned, cliché examined, and repaired in the process. For example, when I got to the States, I didn't know how to order eggs sunny-side-up, so I said, "Make me eggs so that they look like eyes." The student cook in the co-op dorm thought I was being poetic, until I explained to her that I simply didn't know how to translate "jaja na oko," the expression in Croatian with the image of eggs as eyes. So a standard phrase and cliché from another language, translated into this, may result in a fresh image.

But while freshness in turning phrases is an advantage for a new-comer in English, the disadvantages are of course more numerous. For me, not having a childhood in English means not having the lullabies, the charm and ease of a child's ways; it also means not having a good ear, in most cases, for numerous dialects, and presents a serious handicap in dialogue writing. So there are many uncertainties to work against. Jerzy Kosinski said that sometimes he chose words in a sentence with his hand trembling like a needle on a compass: as a foreigner he was self-conscious and careful, for awkward choices could happen. In my own case, English words didn't carry the political and emotional baggage of a repressive upbringing, so I could say whatever I wanted without provoking childhood demons, to which Croatian words were still chained, to tug at me and to make me cringe. So, at least at first, I was a relaxed stepson, with an attitude of liberty: What do you expect of me? I am only a foreigner. I could allow myself to make mistakes. But now I have almost completely lost my original access to that kind of fresh imagery, for I no longer translate in my mind from a Croatian rough mental draft but write directly in English. This reminds me of Minfong Ho's statement, in which she says although she is most proficient in English now, the language she writes in, she still cries in Chinese, the language of her emotions, and she tastes in Thai. And Andrew Lam tastes in Vietnamese: "The word *chua*, for instance, which means sour, invokes a more sour taste to me than the English word sour. That is, I would salivate more if I heard *chua* instead of sour." Though of course for his readers for whom English is the first language the reverse is true.

Of course, this stereo-perceptiveness of two languages is not just a matter of words but can extend to world views and maybe universes. Shirley Geok-lin Lim says "Some of my characters speak only one language; they are limited in their ability to relate to others outside their language circles and also in their ability to imagine these others." Others of her characters can shift easily from one language to another and perhaps like stepmother tongue writers see a larger world. I hereby invite the reader to sample those worlds in the statements of the authors themselves, and especially in their stories in this book.

As for the stories, we attempted to select a range to represent different linguistic groups and immigrant populations, although, of course, we have far too little space to even begin to cover them all. Quality was the primary criterion. Quality needs to be qualified—what struck us as quality; there are different tastes. In selecting, we read perhaps a thousand stories from various journals, books, manuscript submission calls, and so on. These were the stories we liked best, and only later we found that all together the authors had won many high awards for literature, such as the National Book Award, National Book Critics' Circle Award, and American Book Award, and prestigious fellowships, besides the Guggenheim mentioned earlier, such as the Wallace Stegner and National Endowment for the Arts fellowships, and their works had appeared in annual prize anthologies such as *Best American Short Stories* and *Best American Essays*. Several are, by literary standards, best-selling authors. Two are regular essayists on National Public Radio's *All Things Considered*, and another's novel was an Oprah's Book Club selection. But others here have yet to be widely recognized.

Finally, I want to add that this anthology stems from a feature which my wife, Jeanette, and I edited in *Mānoa: A Pacific Journal of International Writing* and which Robert and I expanded to make a book. Several commercial publishers, in consulting with their business departments, concluded that they would not know how to market this book, and they weren't willing to take a risk, and so we are publishing with a non-profit press with a distinct interest in the global approach to literature. White Pine Press is a happy home for us, especially considering that the press has a Human Rights series and many other noble pro-jects, to bring forth neglected literatures to this country.

—Josip Novakovich and Robert Shapard

Stories in the Stepmother Tongue

Judith Ortiz Cofer

A Theory of Chaos

Having just turned ten in a new place, I was sent to find help for my sick mother. Ships and war planes were gathering around Cuba and my father was in one of them, silenced by national security, dead or alive, we did not know. I could not speak English and so was totally alone. Words in the new language were simmering in my head like bees trying to communicate salvation through dance. My life was chaos shaped by chance, biology, and either el destino or circumstance. I did not know or care then that I carried the coded message to make language out of pure need. But then, as I entered the too-bright drugstore alien as a space ship, sudden as Ezekiel's wheel, mysterious as the Annunciation—I could understand the speech of people, I could read the labels, and raised my head up to hear the voice over the loudspeaker. All was clear, and fell into place, even the blinding light. It had taken ten minutes of absolute dread, or nearly drowning in my own chemicals, and maybe of synapses folding into dams and bridges: a million butterflies lifting their minuscule wings as one, gale winds over Iceland. And the strange attractor this time dressed in aqua and pink robes, and feathers, called down by my mother from fevered dreams of Guardian Angels to aid me. Given the gift of tongues, my heart and brain synchronized their wing-beats, or cranked a secret engine just long enough to allow one small frightened girl to fly a little, to hover low over the chaos, and just above where meaning begins.

Not for Sale

El Árabe was what the Puerto Rican women called him. He sold them beautiful things from his exotic homeland in the afternoons, at that hour when the day's work is done and there is a little time before the evening duties. He did not carry anything men would buy. His merchandise, mostly linens, was impractical but exquisite. The bed covers were gorgeously woven into oriental tales that he narrated to his customers in his halting Spanish. My mother bought the *Scheherazade*. It was expensive but she desired it for my bed, since it was the year when I was being denied everything by my father: no dating like other sixteen year olds (I was a decent Puerto Rican *señorita*, not a wild American teenager); no driver's license (the streets of Paterson, New Jersey, were too dangerous for an inexperienced driver—he would take me where I needed to go); no end-of-the-school-year weekend trip with my junior class to Seaside Heights (even though three teachers would be chaperoning us). *No, no, no*, with a short Spanish "o." Final: no lingering vowels in my father's pronouncements.

She knew that I could be brought out of my surliness, my seething anger at my father's constant vigilance, by a visit from the storytelling salesman. On the days when I heard the heavy footfall on the staircase announcing his coming, I would emerge from my room, where I kept company only with my English-language books no one else in the house could read. Since I was not allowed to linger at the drugstore with my high school classmates nor to go out socially—unless my father could be persuaded to let me after interrogations and arguments I had come to dread—I had turned to reading in seclusion. Books kept me from going mad. They allowed me to imagine my circumstances as romantic: some days I was an Indian princess living in a *zenana*, a house of women, keeping myself pure, being trained for a brilliant future. Other days I was a prisoner: Papillon, preparing myself for my great flight to freedom. When El Árabe came to our door, bearing his immense stack of bed linens on his shoulder, I ran to let him in. Mother brought him a glass of cold water as he settled into a rocking chair. I sat on the linoleum floor Indian-style while he spread his merchandise in front of us. Sometimes he brought jewelry too. He carried the rings and bracelets in a little red velvet bag he pulled out of his coat pocket. The day he showed us the Scheherazade bedspread, he emptied the glittering contents of the velvet bag on my lap, then he took my hand and fitted a gold ring with an immense green stone on my finger. It was ornate and covered my finger up to the knuckle, scratching the tender skin in between fingers. Feeling nervous, I laughed and tried to take it off. But he shook his head no. He said that he wanted me to keep the ring on while he told me some of the stories woven on the bedspread. It was a magic ring, he said, that would help me understand. My mother gave me a little frown from the doorway behind El Árabe, meaning *Be polite but give it back soon*. El Árabe settled back to tell his stories. Every so often he would unfold another corner of the bedspread to illustrate a scene.

On a gold background with green threads running through it, glossy like the patina on the dome at city hall, the weavers had put the seated figure of the storytelling woman among the characters she had created. She seemed to be invisible to them. In each panel she sat slightly behind the action in the posture of wisdom, which the salesman demonstrated: mouth parted and arms extended toward her audience, like a Buddha or a sacred dancer. While Sindbad wields his sword at a pirate, Scheherazade sits calmly in between them. She can be found on the street corner, where Aladdin trades his new lamps for old. But he does not see her.

El Árabe spoke deliberately, but his Spanish was still difficult to understand. It was as if his tongue had trouble with certain of our sound combinations. But he was patient. When he saw that one of us had lost the thread of the story, he would begin again, sometimes at the beginning.

This usually drove my mother out of the room, but I understood that these tales were one continuous story to him. If broken, the pattern would be ruined. They had to be told all the way through. I looked at him closely as he spoke. He appeared to be about my father's age, but it was hard to tell, because a thick beard covered most of his face. His eyes revealed his fatigue. He was stooped from carrying his bundles from building to building, I assumed. No one seemed to know where he lived or whether he had a family. But on the day of the Scheherazade stories he told me about his son. The subject seemed to arise naturally out of the last tale. The king who beheaded his brides was captivated by the storytelling woman and spared her life. I felt uneasy with this ending, though I had read it before, not trusting the gluttonous King Schahriah to keep his word. And what would happen to Scheherazade when she ran out of stories? It was always the same with these fairy tales: the plot was fascinating but the ending was unsatisfactory to me. "Happily ever after" was a loose knot tied on a valuable package.

El Árabe took the first payment on the bedspread from my mother who had, I knew, gotten the dollar bills out of her underwear drawer where she kept her "secret" little stash of money in the foot of a nylon stocking. She probably thought that neither my father nor I would have any reason to look there. But in that year of my seclusion, nothing was safe from my curiosity: if I could not go out and explore the world, I would learn what I could from within the four walls. Sometimes I was Anne Frank, and what little there was to discover from my keepers belonged by rights to me.

She counted out ten dollars slowly into his hand. He opened his little notebook with frayed pages. He wrote with a pencil: the full amount at the top, her name, the date, and "10.00" with a flourish. She winced a little as she followed his numbers. It would take her a long time to pay it off. She asked me if I really wanted it—three times. But she knew what it meant to me.

My mother left with the bedspread, explaining that she wanted to see how it would look on my bed. El Árabe seemed reluctant to leave. He lit a slender, aromatic cigarette he took out of a gold case with a little diamond in the middle. Then he repeated the story of Scheherazade's winning over of her husband. Though I was by now weary of the repetition, I listened politely. It was then that he said that he had a son, a handsome young man who wanted very much to come to America to take over the business. There was much money to be made. I nodded, not really understanding why he was telling me all this.

But I fell under the spell of his words as he described a heroic vision of a handsome man who rode thoroughbreds over a golden desert. Without my being aware of it, the afternoon passed quickly. It caught me entirely by surprise when I heard the key turning in the front door lock. I was really chagrined at being found out of my room by my father.

He walked in on us before I had time to rise from my childish position on the floor at El Árabe's feet.

He came in, smelling strongly of sweat and coffee from the factory where he was the watchman. I never understood why sacks of unprocessed coffee beans had to be watched, but that's all I knew about his job. He walked in, looking annoyed and suspicious. He did not like any interruption of his routines: he wanted to find my mother and me in our places when he came home. If she had a friend drop by, Mother had to make sure the visit ended before he arrived. I had stopped inviting my friends over after a while, since his silent hostility made them uncomfortable. Long ago, when I was a little girl, he had spent hours every evening playing with me and reading to me in Spanish. Now, since those activities no longer appealed to me, since I wanted to spend time with other people, he showed no interest in me, except to say no to my requests for permission to go out.

Mother tried to mediate between us by reminding me often of my father's early affection. She explained that teenage girls in Puerto Rico did not go out without chaperons as I wanted to do. They stayed home and helped their mothers and obeyed their fathers. Didn't he give me everything I needed?

I had felt furious at her absurd statements. They did not apply to me, or to the present reality of my life in Paterson, New Jersey. I would work myself into a shouting frenzy. I would scream out my protests that we were not living in some backward country where women were slaves.

"Look," I would point out of the window of our fifth-story apartment in a building at the core of the city. "Do you see palm trees, any sand or blue water? All I see is concrete. We are in the United States. I am an American citizen. I speak English better than Spanish and I am as old as you were when you got married!" The arguments would end with her in tears and the heavy blanket of angry silence falling over both of us. It was no use talking to him either. He had her to comfort him for the unfairness of twelve-hour days in a factory and for being too tired to do anything else but read *La Prensa* in the evenings. I felt like an exile in the foreign country of my parents' house.

My father walked into the living room and immediately focused his eyes on the immense ring on my finger. Without greeting the salesman, without acknowledging my mother who had just returned to the room, he kept pointing at my hand. El Árabe stood up and bowed his head to my father in a strange formal way. Then he said something very odd— something like *I greet you as a kinsman, the ring is a gift to your daughter from my son.* What followed was utter confusion. My father kept asking what? what? what? I struggled to my feet trying to remove the ring from my finger, but it seemed to be stuck. My mother waved me into the kitchen where we worked soap around the swollen finger. In silence we listened to the shouting match in the living room. Both men seemed to be talking at once.

From what I could make out El Árabe was proposing to my father that I be sold to him—for a fair price—to be his son's bride. This was necessary, since his son could not immigrate quickly unless he married an American citizen. The old salesman was willing to bargain with my father over what I was worth in this transaction. I heard figures, a listing of merchandise, a certain number of cattle and horses his son could sell in their country for cash if that is what my father preferred.

My father seemed to be choking. He could not break through the expert haggler's multilingual stream of offers and descriptions of family wealth. My mother pulled the ring off my finger, scraping away some of the skin along with it. I tried not to cry out, but something broke in me when I heard my father's anguished scream of *Not for sale! Not for sale!* persisting until the salesman fell silent. My mother rushed the ring out to the living room while I tried to regain my self-control. But my father's hoarse voice repeating the one phrase echoed in my ears; even after there was the sound of a door being shut and the dull, heavy footsteps of a burdened man descending the stairs, I heard the pained protest.

Then my father came into the kitchen, where I was standing at the sink, washing the blood off my fingers. The ring had cut me deeply. He stood in silence and, unmoving in the doorway, looked at me as if he had not seen me in a long time or just then for the first time. Then he asked me in a soft voice if I was all right. I nodded, hiding my hand behind my back.

In the months that followed, my mother paid on her account at the door. El Árabe did not come into our apartment again. My father learned the word "yes" in English and practiced saying it occasionally, though "no" remained NO in both languages and easier to say for a non-native speaker.

On my bed Scheherazade kept telling her stories, which I came to understand would never end—as I had once feared—since it was in my voice that she spoke to me, placing my dreams among hers, weaving them in.

ANDREW LAM

The only English I knew up to the age of twelve was "No money, no honey." I think I learned it from the Saigon prostitutes who walked the tamarind tree-lined boulevards near the Independence Palace—across from which stood my school where I was taught Vietnamese and French. Back then I thought English was a rather terse and rather ugly-sounding language—you don't have to say much to get your points across but to speak it you risk hurting your throat.

A few months after having arrived from the refugee camp in Guam, my voice broke. I thought it somehow had to do with my having to speak English and nothing to do with my going through puberty. Heck, I didn't know what puberty was. I was convinced that the harsh-sounding words had chafed the back of my throat and caused me to sound so funny that my family laughed and laughed and I, so chagrined by my own voice, stopped talking at home altogether.

It took me a while to figure things out, but by then I had already become an American teenager.

Vietnamese for me is primal. The word *chua*, for instance, which means sour, invokes a more sour taste to me than the English word sour. That is, I would salivate more if I heard *chua* instead of sour. But to deal with something like globalization, something abstract, Vietnamese is woefully inadequate.

I can read and write in Vietnamese and I can speak French but English is by far my favorite language. I think I've grown in love with it over the years. I am freer to express myself in English than in Vietnamese. The American "I" stands alone whereas the Vietnamese "I" is always a familial one. It is son, daughter, father, uncle, and so on and it is understood only in context of the communal whereas the American "I"...

Besides, there's more "money" and "honey" in English, and I knew this even before I spoke it. I am not a poet. If I were a poet, I'd write poetry in Vietnamese. But for now, for my money, and my honey, English is it.

Grandma's Tales

The day after Mama and Papa took off to Las Vegas, Grandma died. Nancy and I, we didn't know what to do, Vietnamese traditional funerals with incense sticks and chanting Buddhist monks not being our thing. We have a big freezer, Nancy said. Why don't we freeze her. Really. Why bother Mama and Papa. What's another day or two for Grandma now anyway?

Nancy's older than me, and since I didn't have any better idea, we iced her.

Grandma was 94 years, 8 months, and 6 days old when she died. She lived through three wars, two famines, and a full hard life. America, besides, was not all that good for her. She had been confined to the second floor of our big Victorian home, as her health was failing, and she did not speak English, only a little French, like *Oui monsieur, c'est evidemment un petit monstre,* and, *Non, Madame, vous n'etes pas du tout enceinte, je vous assure.* She was a head nurse in the maternity ward of the Hanoi hospital during the French colonial time. I used to love her stories about delivering all these strange two-headed babies and Siamese triplets connected at the hip whom she named Happy, Liberation, and Day.

Grandma's death came when she was eating spring rolls with me and Nancy. Nancy was wearing a nice black miniskirt and her lips were painted red, and Grandma said you look like a high-class whore. Nancy made a face and said she was preparing to go to one of her famous San Francisco artsy cocktail parties where waiters were better dressed than most upper-class Vietnamese men back home, and there were silver trays of duck paté and salmon mousse, and ice sculptures with wings and live musicians playing Vivaldi.

So get off my case, Grandma, because I'm no whore.

It was a compliment, Grandma said, winking at me, but I guess it's wasted on you, child. Then she laughed, as Nancy prepared to leave. Child, do the cha-cha-cha for me. I didn't get to do it when I was young, with my clubbed foot and the wars and everything else.

Sure, Grandma, Nancy said, and rolled her pretty eyes.

Then Grandma dropped her chopsticks on the hardwood floor—clack, clack, clatter, clack, clack—closed her eyes, and stopped breathing. Just like that.

So we iced her. She was small, the freezer was large. We wrapped her body in plastic wrap first, then sent a message to Circus-Circus, where Mama and Papa were staying.

Meanwhile Nancy had a party to go to, and I had to meet Eric for a movie.

I didn't care about the movie, but cared about Eric. He's got eyes so blue you can swim in them, and a warm laugh, and is really beautiful, a year older than me, a senior. Eric liked Grandma. Neither one knew the other's language, but there was this thing between them, mutual respect, like one cool old chick to one cool young dude. (Sometimes I would translate but not always 'cause my English is not all that good and my Vietnamese sucks.) What was so cool about Grandma was she was the only one who knew I'm bisexual. Even though she was Confucian bound and trained and a Buddhist and all, she was really cool about it.

One night, we were sitting in the living room watching a John Wayne movie together, *The Green Berets*, and Eric was there with me and Grandma. (Mama and Papa had just gone to bed and Nancy was at some weird black and white ball or something like that.) And Eric leaned over and kissed me on the lips and Grandma said, That's real nice, and I translated and we all laughed and John Wayne shot dead five guys. Just like that. But Grandma didn't mind, really. She's seen Americans like John Wayne shooting her people in the movies before. She always thought of him as a bad guy, uglier than a water buffalo's ass. And she'd seen us more passionate than a kiss on the lips and didn't mind. She used to tell us to be careful and not make any babies—obviously a joke—'cause she'd done delivering them. So you see, we liked Grandma a lot.

Anyway, after Nancy and I packed Grandma down into the twelve degree Fahrenheit, I went out to meet Eric, and later we came back to the house. We made out on the couch. After a while I said, Eric, I have to tell you something. Grandma's dead. You're kidding me, he whispered, with his beautiful smile. I kid you not, I said. She's dead, and Nancy and me, we iced her. Shit! he said. Why? 'Cause otherwise she would start to smell, duh, and we have to wait for my parents to perform a traditional Vietnamese funeral. We fell silent. Then Eric said, can I take a peek at Grandma? Sure, I said, sure you can, she was as much yours as she was mine, and we went to the freezer and looked in.

The weird thing was the freezer was on defrost and Grandma was nowhere in sight. There was a trail of water and plastic wrap leading from the freezer to her bedroom. We followed it. On the bed, all wet, sat Grandma, counting her Buddhist rosary and chanting her diamond sutra. What's weirder is that she looked real young. I mean around 54 now, not 94, the high cheeks, the rosy lips. When she saw us she smiled and said: "What do you say we all go to one of those famous cocktail parties that Nancy's gone to, the three of us?" I wasn't scared because she said it in English, I mean accentless, Californian English.

Wow, Grandma, Eric said, your English is excellent.

"I know," Grandma said, "that's just a side benefit of being reborn. But enough with compliments, we got to party."

Cool, said Eric. Cool, I said, though I was a little jealous 'cause I had to go through junior high and high school and all those damn ESL classes and everything to learn the same language while Grandma just got it down cold because she was reborn. Grandma put on this nice brocaded red blouse and black silk pants and sequined velvet shoes and fixed her hair real nice and we drove off downtown.

Boy, you should've seen Nancy's face when we arrived at her cocktail party. She nearly tripped over herself. She laid her face against the wing of an ice sculpture to calm herself. Then she walked straight up to us, haughty, and said, It's invitation only, how'd ya'll get in?

"Calm yourself, child," said Grandma, "I told them that I was a board member of the Cancer Society and flashed my jade bracelet and diamond ring and gave the man a forty dollar tip."

Nancy had the same reaction Eric and I had: Grandma, your English is flawless! Grandma was oblivious to compliments. She went straight to the punch bowl for some spirits. Since her clubbed foot was cured she had an elegant grace about her. Her hair floated like gray-black clouds behind her. Everyone stared, mesmerized.

Needless to say Grandma was the big hit of the party. She had so many interesting stories to tell. The feminists, it seemed, loved her the most. They crowded around her as she told them how she'd been married early and had eight children while being the matriarch of a middle-class family during the Viet Minh uprising. She told them about my grandfather, a brilliant man who was well versed in Molière and Shakespeare and who was an accomplished violinist but who drank himself to death because he was helpless against the colonial powers of the French. She told everyone how single-handedly she had raised her children after his death and they all became doctors and lawyers and pilots and famous composers. Then she started telling them how the twenty-four-year-old civil war divided her family up and brothers fought brothers over ideological notions that proved bloody pointless. Then she told them about our journey across the Pacific Ocean in a crowded fishing boat where thirst and starvation nearly did us all in until it was her idea to eat some of the dead and drink their blood so that the rest of us could survive to catch glimpses of this beautiful America and become Americans.

She started telling them, too, about the fate of Vietnamese women who had to marry and see their husbands and sons go to war and never come back. Then she recited poems and told fairy tales with sad endings, fairy tales she herself had learned as a child, the kind she used to tell me and my cousins when we were young. There was this princess, you see, who fell in love with a fisherman and he didn't know about her 'cause she only heard his beautiful voice singing from a distance, so when he drifted away downriver one day she died, her heart turning into this ruby with the image of his boat imprinted on it. (In Grandma's stories, the husbands and fishermen always come home, but they come home always too late and there was nothing they could do but mourn and grieve.)

Grandma's voice was sad and seductive and words came pouring out of her like rain and the whole place turned quiet and Nancy sobbed because she understood and Eric stood close to me and I cried a little, too. "I lost four of my children," Grandma said, "twelve of my grand-children, and countless relatives and friends to wars and famines and I lost everything I owned when I left my beautiful country behind. Mine is a story of suffering and sorrow, suffering and sorrow being the way of Vietnamese life. But now I have a second chance and I am not who I was, and yet I have all the memories, so wherever I go I will keep telling my stories and songs."

Applause broke out, then a rich-looking man with gray hair came up to Grandma and they talked quietly for a while. When they were done Grandma came to me and Nancy and Eric and said goodbye. She said she was not going to wait for my parents to come home for a traditional funeral. She had a lot of living still to do since Buddha had given her the gift to live twice in one life and this man, some famous novelist from Colombia, was going to take her places. He might even help her write her book. So she was going to the *mediteranee* to get a tan and to Venice to see the festivals and ride the gondolas and maybe afterward she'd go by Hanoi and see what they'd done to her childhood home and visit some long-forgotten ancestral graves and relatives and then who knows where she'd go. She'd send postcards though and don't you wait up. Then before we knew it Grandma was already out of the door with the famous novelist and the music started up again. Eric and I ran out after her but outside there was only this city under a velvety night sky, its highrises shining like glass cages, with little diamonds and gold coins kept locked inside them.

Mama and Papa came home two days later. They brought incense sticks and ox-hide drums and wooden fish and copper gongs and jas-mine wreaths and Oolong tea and paper offerings, all the things that we were supposed to have for a traditional funeral. A monk had even sent a fax of his chanting rate and schedule because he was real busy, and the relatives started pouring in.

It was hard to explain then what had happened, what we had always expected as the tragic ending of things, human frailty the point of mourning and grief. And wasn't epic loss what made us tell our stories? It was difficult for me to mourn now, though. Difficult 'cause while the incense smoke drifted all over the mansion and the crying and wailing resounded like cicadas humming on the tamarind tree in the summer back in Vietnam, Grandma wasn't around.

Bharati Mukherjee

"An Interview with Bharati Mukherjee,"
from Mosaic, Spring 1994

Mosaic: How and when did you decide to become a writer?

Mukherjee: I think I always knew since the age of three. I was very prejudiced in terms of reading and being able to [hand]write. I was always very good at games and not very good at math. I used to read and think my way through stories, at a very very young age. This was my escape from unhappy situations and my way of compensating for painful situations in a very large extended family of thirty or forty people.

Mosaic: Did you write these stories in English or Bengali?

Mukherjee: In Bengali—for the first eight years I was uniquely Bengali-speaking and I hardly ever heard English.

Mosaic: Is there anything about English in particular that appeals to you in terms of what the language offers—idioms, etceteras?

Mukherjee: What I think has become an advantage for me is making a foreign language into my own, or possessing a foreign language. I'm free from the cliché. I'm alert to the possibilities of the phrase, because for me it isn't a "closed off" language that I have to take for granted. It will always be for me real and foreign and therefore something that I have to make my own.

Mosaic: You identify yourself as an American writer...

Mukherjee: ...of Bengali origin.

Mosaic: An American writer of Bengali origin. Buy why American? You've lived in so many cities all across the world; why is it you've decided to assume that identity, and also why have you decided to bear so very strident a voice in it?

Mukherjee: For me it has been very empowering to have a national mythology that says restrictions in terms of class, gender, or poverty do not have to be permanent restrictions—that you can transform yourself and that your imagination and your daring count.

Mosaic: Is this opportunity for transformation what you've called "fluidly" American?

Mukherjee: Fluidity. I'm emphasizing the word "mythology." If you don't have that national mythology at all, as countries like the India I grew up in, or the European countries, or the Canada that I lived in, then there isn't even that potential for fluidity. In my fiction I'm thinking through the making of the American consciousness. For me the idea of America, "America" in quotation marks as opposed to "the U.S..," embodies the will to transform. It has its sinister side and it has its empowering [side]. So we must be alert to the sinister side.

Mosaic: In your work *The Middleman and Other Stories* you're dealing with a type of character, the Asian and Third World immigrant, that has pretty much been neglected in favor of the western European immigrants of canonized literature. You're dealing with immigrants from all across the world and you're dealing with immigrants in only this latter part of the century.

Mukherjee: What to me was one of the more striking and, in a way, painful recognitions of this country [was] in 1980 when I was taking part in a very heavy-duty conference on American culture. In 1980 they were thinking of American culture—which meant, as the keynote speech by George Steiner said, immigrant culture, imported culture—as exclusively European. I was waving my hand saying, Somehow you've really missed the point of what is going on, has been going on since the mid-60s; and especially the early 70s. Asians are coming in, Latin Americans are coming in, Caribbeans, non-Europeans are coming in large numbers, and they are making a difference in the culture. And that you are omitting any discussion, as if they simply don't exist, as if they are invisible, that you don't know or want to know that there has been this de-Europeanization of American culture. They were totally, totally off-center, or they refused to believe that there was a non-European factor of American culture. So how far have we moved? That's what makes me so impassioned a speaker, almost like a missionary. Getting the white people to see that we are not marginal, that we don't intend to remain marginal, that we want power-sharing.

Mosaic: Do you think that autobiographical writing by your students is the same as that which Amy Tan and Maxine Hong Kingston have been attacked for—that writing autobiographical works reinforces stereotypes?

Mukherjee: I think that's rubbish about stereotypes in the case of either. Well, I shouldn't say "rubbish," but I don't agree at all that those statements apply to the writing of Tan and Kingston. They are interested in doing and are inspired by material very different from mine. There are writers, like Tan and Kingston, who are inspired by the experience of little China in the Eurocentric sense. Whereas, because of the history of immigration of the South Asian community and because of my own personality, I'm interested in showing Americans an America they haven't seen before. The phrase that I have used in an essay is "making the familiar exotic, and the exotic familiar." I can show you Philadelphia in ways you haven't seen before because I am a writer with a unique sense of looking at things.

Mosaic: How would you characterize this aesthetic? Have you had any problems, commercially and critically, with just being accepted?

Mukherjee: I think that my battle has been much harder because I have refused to commodify ethnicity and because I have refused to write about the ghettoes—to be forced into writing about ghettoes. And also because I have refused to commodify things into uniform victim-status for all minorities. I've refused to commodify victimology. Publishers have always said "There isn't enough audience for material like yours." If you're writing about little India, then that's nicely exotic, but if you're writing about Iowa, as I do in *Jasmine*, or Florida, as I do in a story in *The Middleman and Other Stories*, that's too scary, that's too new. You're not doing the expected hyphenated American thing; you're not doing what's expected of Asian American writers.

EXCERPT FROM "A USABLE PAST: AN INTERVIEW WITH BHARATI MUKHERJEE,"
BY SHEFALI DESAI AND TONY BARNSTONE
IN *MĀNOA: A PACIFIC JOURNAL OF INTERNATIONAL WRITING*, 10:2, 1998

TB: A lot of Asian American writers, particularly your colleague at Berkeley Maxine Hong Kingston, as well as Amy Tan, Chitra Divakaruni, and others, have tried to find in folk tales, or the history of their ancestral country what Van Wyck Brooks called a "usable past." Particularly a usable past with woman warriors, strong women, which could somehow be distinguished from an unusable past of patriarchy—in the case of Kingston and Tan, of patriarchal Confucianism. Paradoxically, this unusable past is quite useful for providing conflict in their prose. What's your usable past? What aspects of your history can and can't you use in your fiction, and in your life?

BM: What an interesting, complicated question. I think that the reason that wonderful writers like Maxine Hong Kingston and Amy Tan use so much mythology, Chinese mythology, is that they are second-generation Americans. It's a kind of roots retrieval: "Who were my people?" Whereas I, being fresh off the jet, want to get away from a lot of the mythologies that were so genderist, that were created to reinforce patriarchy or the class system—not just caste system, but class system. When I grew up, I didn't have the bedtime tales of Hans Christian Andersen, but the Puranic tales, thousands of years B.C., and the Hindu epics. Which means that some of the stories, like that of Sita, the perfect wife who is self-sacrificing and self-effacing, are the ones that I want to attack, critique. Or I have rereadings of such legends in which I suddenly realize that the conventional interpretations were convenient to the male explicators, commentators. I would like to make up my own myths. As an immigrant I don't have models here in America.

Happiness

My father was dying of cancer, but he hung in long enough to select a groom for me out of Aunt Flower Garland's short list of three. The night before he passed away, he gave me his last advice and blessing. He said, "In the areas I can control, namely financial security and temperamental compatibility, I have hedged all bets. Happiness in marriage? That, even I can't guarantee."

He rejected the candidacy of a physics professor in Tulsa, Oklahoma, and a dentist in San Leandro, California, in favor of Arjun. The physics professor had a grandfather who had nearly won a Nobel prize in quantum theory, and the dentist's family owned a profitable pharmaceutical company, but Arjun had a Ph.D. in electrical engineering from Columbia University. Columbia was where my father would like to have studied, if his father, so the story went, hadn't died of a ruptured appendix at (even by the local standards) the premature age of twenty-six. My grandmother, two aunts, and father owed their second start in life to the generosity of a maternal uncle, who, being a relative from the maternal side, of course was under no obligation to take them in. This uncle, who had five daughters and three sons of his own, paid for the weddings of my Aunts Flower Garland and Leafy Vine, and, when my father turned seventeen, arranged an apprentice job for him with an engineer friend at a hydroelectric plant an overnight's train ride from the city.

"And as the Calcutta Chamber of Commerce knows," my father was fond of saying, and he said it always in English, "the rest is very much history, isn't it?"

In his anecdotes, he gave his youth Dickensian twists and darkenings, not all of which I believed, probably because by the time I was born he'd made one fortune in lumber up in Assam, and another down in Andhra in steel. In a previous incarnation, Horatio Alger had to have been Bengali.

My father and I were very close, closer than most fathers and daughters in our traditional neighborhood, Mother having died of an overnight fever when I was three. I can't visualize Mother since there are no photographs of her, no likeness for me to have had framed and hung on the wall next to my late grandfather's and grandmother's portraits above the altar of gods in the room of worship, but her presence or absence persists in my brain as a faint stain of melancholy.

A week before my father died, Arjun, whose full name is Arjun Kumar Roy Chowdhury, flew in from New York on a two-week vacation from his job—he was a vice-president in charge of operations research at an electronics company—interviewed the women on the Roy Chowdhury family's short list of bridal candidates that he thought he might survive a lifetime with on the basis of photo, bio, and relatives' preliminary impressions, and picked me. I need to believe that his family's short list was longer than my father's.

Given the long lines for immigrant visas at the U.S. consulate, Arjun was impatient to get the legal formality of marriage over with before he returned to New York at the end of his two-week leave, but we, Ghoses, insisted on letting a respectable time lapse between celebration of funeral and wedding. I don't call it *my* wedding, or Arjun's and my wedding, because the bride and groom played the least assertive roles during the lawyerly dowry negotiations, the by-fax-and-priority-mail transcontinental preparations, and the long, complicated, exhausting pre- and post-nuptial ceremonies. We fasted when we were told to, we bathed with turmeric paste in Ganges water as prescribed, we played the laid-down games auguring connubial contentment, and when, toward the end of all the chants by the Brahmin priest and the vows in Sanskrit by Arjun and my maternal great-uncle, the dramatic moment came for the veiled bride to lift her head and look into the groom's eyes, we both managed I'm-ready-for-whatever-adventure smiles.

Two days after the wedding, the day known as *bou-bhat*, which I later translated into English for Karin Stein, my neighbor in Upper Montclair, New Jersey, as *the day the bride moves to her husband's house and cooks rice perfect enough for him to eat, because if the rice is too crunchy or too sticky she'll be sent back in disgrace to her parents' house*, Arjun and I boarded an Air India 747, and, strangers safety-belted into side-by-side seats, headed for instant intimacy.

Within a month of making my home in America, I learned how wise my father, the Cheetah of the Calcutta Chamber of Commerce, had been to hedge those bets that he could. At social gatherings, like the Tagore Society evenings in the Bannerjees' split-level in Chappaqua, New York, or at the organizational meetings of the Bengali Heritage Preservation Association in the Dases' condo in Queens, I sniffed out heartache and heard deceit. I picked up words and phrases that I hadn't been taught by Aunts Flower Garland and Leafy Vine: Creedmore, Prozac, shelter for abused women, defenestration.

Comfortable living and decent conduct had been taken for granted by my family. I was grateful that the Ghoses hadn't been deceived by the Roy Chowdhurys. Arjun hadn't lied about his degrees, his salary, his stocks and bonds holdings. He owned the Tudor-style house in Montclair, and the black BMW we had been shown photos of. And he owned things I hadn't seen before: a refrigerator with an ice-water faucet set in its door, a convection oven, an outdoor gas barbecue grill.

The more personal habits and peeves revealed themselves enticingly to me. For instance, every night before coming to bed, he dropped two Alka-Seltzer tablets into a highball glass of water, said, "Plop, plop, fizz, fizz, bottoms up! Prosit!" and gulped the noisy drink down while pinching his nose. I got to look forward to chasing the antacid grains off his lips with my tongue. It made me feel uninhibited. Who cares about long-term happiness when the tongue is tracing, teasing, tormenting, in fulfillment of its own, distinct destiny?

Arjun and I made our voluntary accommodations. At the dinner table, I learned to taste the differences between chardonnay and sauvignon blanc, and pretended preferences for merlots and pinot noirs and contempt for all California cabernets. He cut back on pork and beef. I filled him in on Indian politics: he'd missed so much of which party leaders had defected and why, and which cabinet ministers had been arrested and on what charges among the usual frauds, graft, currency violations, embezzlements. He reciprocated by dictating which senators and Congress representatives I was to trust and explaining the glories and ghastlinesses of the American two-party system. Politics was bedtime story. It didn't matter that I didn't have a vote in this country, that

I hadn't voted in any election in any country. I still think of politics as love's foreplay.

Give and take; take and give: that was the flow of our intimacy. Arjun liked to make money, and he liked me to spend it. I did. I drove the BMW—bigger, shinier than in the photos I'd been shown—to the malls, and displayed what money could buy when, late in the New Jersey night, he came through the front door, carrying a briefcaseful of work he had yet to get through. It wasn't about being pliant. My father taught me, through example, that self-worth based on cash-worth is the shortest cut to tragedy.

"Class and conscience," my father said, "go together like a washer-man and his donkey. Class is the washerman, but he has to follow the path that his stubborn donkey takes, isn't it?"

My father's analogies were not for me to question. In his adolescent days as apprentice laborer, he'd composed a notebookful of morally uplifting couplets in Bengali, the point of all of which was, cultivate your conscience so that money and rank may not lead you astray.

I have followed his advice by never buying insurance. I wouldn't shed a tear if a burglar broke into the house while Arjun was in the Softron, Inc., offices in Manhattan and I at the cosmetics counter at Bendel's, and made off with a van-load of our belongings. But I have followed his advice for lascivious reasons. Penury neither alarms me nor goads me to covetous ambitiousness. Money, in my marriage to Arjun, was the consensual currency of intimacy. All around me in suburban New York and New Jersey, love was ending in sleeping pills, straitjackets, fatal automobile accidents. Not love, not loyalty, but steel-tipped intimacy, so sharp and thrilling that it has entered and exited before you have touched the wound, felt the pain: that intimacy was our strength. Forget the prenuptial haggling between the Roy Chowdhurys and the Ghoses. To each other we made no promises. We gave and took freely, greedily. We demonstrated large-hearted poor sense instead of self-inter-est. There should have been time for me to let my father know that before intimacy, happiness in marriage pales.

This is the way that our most special night happened. What does it matter which year, which season. It was a weeknight like any other weeknight in our American life. Arjun came through the front door, which the previous owner, whom Karin Stein remembered as "a moody Middle East type, don't ask me from where exactly, except that he was definitely not from Israel," had fitted with chimes that tinkled out a bar or two of what Karin identified as "It's a Most Beautiful Day"; he dropped his umbrella in its ceramic stand, hung up his all-weather coat in the hall closet; he thrust a cold, heavy bottle of champagne instead of the usual chardonnay against my bosom, grabbed me in a bear hug, and whispered, "Tonight we celebrate!" into the Austrian crystal necklace, which was what I had bought from a just-opened boutique earlier in the day.

"Celebrate what?" I assumed a bonus or promotion, or, for Arjun, more pleasing still would be a stock market coup. My role in our partnership was to draw the answers out of him.

"Who cares what?" He popped the cork right there in the hall, and with the champagne foaming down the sides of the bottle and leaving sticky droplets on the wood floor, dragged me in a bear hug to the kitchen.

A finicky housemaker would have blotted clean the champagne trail while Arjun was reaching for the fluted glasses I'd stuck way in the back of the highest cabinet shelf. They were still in the manufacturer's box. I'd bought them at a going-out-of-business sale in Paramus Mall. Arjun was a Glenfiddich drinker. Wine collecting was a hobby with him. He'd made a wine cellar out of what had been the last owner's woodworking shop. "Forget carpentry," Karin scoffed when she came over for our first wine-tasting party, "the guy was making bombs. Don't you hear any funny ticking noises when you're in the basement?"

A woman with good sense would have first turned off the gas flames under the pots of Basmati rice and goat vindaloo, then attended to whatever adventure destiny had lassoed.

"Let me guess," I laughed. "I've never seen you this happy, so it has to be something special."

Arjun pulled two champagne flutes out of their box, and held them under the kitchen faucet. I'd forgotten they were etched with a cloudy circlet of leaves and rimmed with a bright thin band of gold.

"So happy," Arjun retorted, "that I'm not complaining about having to rinse dishes."

"We aren't in Calcutta anymore." I tore off squares of paper towels and held them out to Arjun. Rolls of parch-tongued paper towels, packages of thick, crisp bond paper into which no insect bodies have been processed: those are the American marvels I prize.

"Try telling that to your Chappaqua friends. You think Prafulla Bose comes home at eight and does the dishes?"

He crumpled the dry paper squares and tossed them in the garbage. The track light aimed at the sink caught the bright slitheriness of water coating the inside of each flute.

"You've been nominated Most Valuable Functionary by your CEO."

"Don't even try," Arjun said. He poured the champagne carefully into a glass for me.

I had watched him pour wine before, but I hadn't noticed, really noticed, his wrists. I'd admired his fingers before, told him many times how movingly delicate I found them on a man who claimed to abhor painters and poets. The wrist that rotated with the bottle neck had the showy, arrogant sureness of wrists of the concert pianists I caught by chance on cable channels. "All right, you're a secret gambler, and you've just made a killing." I arced my body to kiss that confident wrist. So what that my head knocked the filled glass out of his surprised grasp.

"A gambler?"

I heard his shoes push aside broken glass. He was thinking of my feet, not his tile floor. I don't wear shoes or slippers at home. I didn't in Calcutta where our floors were of cool marble or stone mosaic, and I didn't in Upper Montclair with its oak, tile, lino, and wool-blend wall-to-wall.

"You don't mind drinking a toast to gambling?" He poured champagne into the second flute.

"Plop, plop, fizz, fizz!" I whispered. "Bottoms up!"

"Prosit!" he whispered back.

I took a gulp, he an assessor's sip. "How much, Arjun?" I was thinking how large a sum I would have to find creative ways for spending.

"Every asshole gambler should be so lucky to have you as a wife."

Then he whirled me into the living room with strides that resembled waltzers' on colorized, afternoon movies on TV, humming tunes I didn't know and at the same time wriggling out of his suit jacket, stiffening his spine and outstretched arms, tightening his buttocks.

It wasn't natural clumsiness that kept me stepping on his champagne-dampened shoes. Like most young women on my block, I took years of weekend classes in Tagore-style singing and dancing. Aunt Leafy Vine keeps my certificates in the vault compartment of her most secure cabinet, which by the way is made of steel manufactured in one of my father's factories. I am no more and no less physically graceful than the other Tri-State Bengali wives who have volunteered for bit parts in Tagore's drama *Red Oleander*, which the Tagore Society intends to stage next October.

That night I tripped, I kept tripping, stumbling, apologizing, because I couldn't feel the beat to his hummed tune. He rose on the balls of his feet: I thumped with my heels as though I was wearing dance bells on my ankles. He covered the available floor space with wide swoops in circles; I concentrated my energies on the slightest movements of finger joints and neck muscles. I had danced duets as Radha the Milkmaid to a girl-cousin's Krishna the God Biding His Time as Amorous Goatherd in family theatricals. But in those duets, Radha and Krishna never touched. Nobody led, nobody followed. There wasn't any need to. Power was shared by god and mortal. We improvised the depths of the lovers' passion, but never the way their love turned out. That was the trouble, I told myself. I had no way of telling when the humming and the prancing would come to their natural close. There were no scripted roles, no sage-revealed unalterable storyline, no faith that through dance I might discover the simple secret of cosmic chaos.

"It's no good," Arjun said.

He let go of me, suddenly, and I fell back into his favorite chair, a massive leather rocker, embarrassed at my own ungainliness, but thankful the ordeal was over while he hummed, whistled, twirled around the room solo.

"See how easy it is?"

I heard relief, not taunt, in Arjun's question. From the rocker, the posture and the footwork did seem easy. "I think my problem is I'm not hearing what you're hearing, I'm not *feeling* what you're feeling."

"What am I feeling?" he dipped his head back to ask his question, but by the time I answered, "You're feeling good, very good," he'd waltzed away to the farthest corner of the living room.

For another hour I watched, cowering at the unself-conscious celebration of...what was it that he was celebrating? What had he gambled on? How destructive could his winnings be? Was I a witness to bliss or lunacy?

When I went to bed that night, he was still dancing.

The next morning he left home at six-thirty as he always did to catch his commuter train. I haven't seen him since. I did find a note, an orange Post-It actually, stuck to the neck of the champagne bottle. It said: *There is another woman, but that's not the reason. Arranged marriages carry no risk. I know you'll react to my leaving, and to a gambler, certainty is boring. Ciao! Have a happy life.*

That was seven years ago. The changes in my life are mostly invisible. I still have the BMW and the house on North Fullerton Street. Karin Stein is still my friend, but she chucked her law practice for a bearded baker somewhere in the Northwest. She sends me postcards with grease stains. Last year I talked myself into starting law school. Night classes, not Harvard or Yale. All the same, it's exciting work, and I am a hardworking student. My father's failure to arrange a lasting marriage has alchemized into new strengths and excitements. Now, for instance, I stay awake nights arguing the legal rights of frozen sperm or defending UFO-borne alien scientists against charges of rape. Are UFO abductions and orifice penetrations punishable crimes in U.S. courts? For amendments to immigration bills, do "UFObacks" fall into the category of undocumenteds? Is Arjun physically as well as legally dead? In American English is self-esteem a synonym for happiness?

ANDREI CODRESCU

I have written two early autobiographies in English (the facts, like languages, kept changing). The piece herein is from the second of these, *In America's Shoes*, a book less concerned with language than with the physical fact of becoming Homo Americanus. My original three languages were, in order, German, Hungarian, and Romanian. At age seven I lost German (when my mother fired our Fräulein and I began attending Romanian school), at age twelve Hungarian (when I stopped seeing my grandmother very much), and at age twenty-five I nearly lost my Romanian (after being in the United States for six years). Happily, the dormant Romanian I had ceased all but dreaming in, came back to me full force in 1989 when I returned to Romania to write about the drama of those days. Now I have been re-adopted by my native land and my books are being translated in Romanian, an irony made more maddening (for my translators) by the fact that I am not happy with their renderings because, had I written my books in Romanian, I would have written them differently. But I did not. I write only in English now, with a smattering of interviews, essays, and occasional verselets in my old tongue. Do I miss it? No. But I do admire the plasticity and poetic power of Romanian writers (especially poets) who wield their language with a sophistication that is way beyond me now. I am an American writer with some twisted roots in other tongues: this has always seemed to me an occasion for joy, never a loss. My good luck was coming to the United States when I was twenty-one. Older writers experienced the loss of their native language as tragic. I didn't.

Born Again

I stood in the windowless womb of the Justice Department's Immigration and Naturalization Bureau, waiting to be born American. It was Baltimore, Maryland, February 13, 1981. The Nixon-Mitchell style of impenetrable anti-terrorist architecture resembled exactly the V.I. Stalin style of the 1950s in Eastern Europe.

I stood there, about to be born out of all that steel and cement, and thought myself to be standing in the lobby of the People's Culture Palace in Bucharest. If I hadn't died to my country, I might as well have been standing there, with a parcel of my newest books of poems under my arm. Instead, I carried my *Life & Times of an Involuntary Genius* under one arm, my leather jacket thrown casually over a shoulder. The knife wound in the leather, under the left breast, came from a knife that killed the last one to wear it, the biker who sold it to me had assured me.

The lobby was filled to the brim with hopeful new Americans, mostly Vietnamese, Chinese and Russians. Dressed in impeccable suits, accompanied by grandmothers holding back hordes of grandchildren dressed with similar meticulousness, they babbled excitedly about this, the greatest day of their lives. A stone policeman stood guard in the lobby behind a cage of metal detectors and X-ray machines that saw under dresses and retained exquisite pink aureolas and deliciously erect but tentative nipples. Another policeman, ten feet from him, surveyed the crowd from the height of his mirrored glasses inside a glass cage equipped with television monitors. In these monitors, the faces in the lobby shone like dimes at the bottom of a wishing well. In the walls, in comfortable caves carved in the flesh of the building, stood other policemen, hundreds of them, each holding a shiny scalpel in one hand and a Big Mac in the other. At the appointed time, they would stream from the walls, open up the chests of the applicants in the womb and replace their hearts with burgers.

"All official buildings, whether here or in the Soviet Union or in the Mongolian People's Republic, communicate by means of an elaborate system of tunnels of unfolding inner rooms with secret doors," I said to Alice, my wife, and to my two sons, Lucian and Tristan, and to my friend Rodger who was there, in a suit, to witness the birth.

"Furthermore, all the official buildings in the world with their attending officials, exist on a geographical plane completely separate from the one we presently dwell in, so it can be said without exaggeration, that we are in another world," I said.

A slight activity, a tremor of a leaf in a pond, began to course through the assorted foreigners. They began adjusting collars, smoothing down pants and skirts, stuffing rags into the smaller children's mouths. The sound came and went, like the pages of a passport being rapidly turned. The moment had arrived, or someone in charge of the moment had arrived. Suddenly, the clumps of people began arranging themselves in a line. The official magnet drawing this line was somewhere inside the uterus, but the doors were still closed.

"I am a student of lines," I said, "and in my opinion this is a milk line. I have stood, as a child, in bread and meat lines as well as milk lines, and this line has most definitely that sinuous and quiet despair of the milk line rather than the gritty and vicious heat of the meat line or the disorderly, gossipy and loud relaxation of the bread line."

A Russian emigrant, who was carefully eavesdropping, turned to us and smiled widely: "No more lines, eh? No more get up in cold and go buy bone that's gone."

My wife smiled back as if to say "What do you call this?" I loved her at this point, for her understanding, and wondered how she had suffered all my madness for these many years. There she was, blond and skinny, a witness to the official confirmation of an American she had created long before. The American I spoke was hers, and the little habits and gestures by which a native guides his ship in the world, festooned my canoe. Hers were all the tiny phrases like "Let's bust this popcorn joint!," and "That's the breaks!," phrases which marked me as an incongruous specimen to everyone who heard them pronounced in Transylvanian-accented earnestness. And by the same token, she understood the alien part in the sense in which it was most like the familiar part, so that a line was a line, in Russian or in American. There was no fooling her there, just as there was no mistaking a line for heaven.

A bell rang and the lobby grew quiet. The line had now grown rigid enough for a plumber's line to be dropped from the glass cage by the cop. As the silence deepened, I considered the lines of my childhood. I'd stood in hundreds of them. My mother sent me to stand in line for bread in the morning in order to listen to what the neighbors said. When I came back, her first question was, "What did you hear in the line?" and only after, "Did you get the bread?" We needed the news more than the bread, and I suspect that there was plenty of bread, but the government withheld it so as not to spend money on newsprint. The news you got in line was always fresh too, not stale like ink or TV, and it was almost always rounded up by the softness and glow of rumor which, alone, makes life interesting.

The doors of the Federal Courtroom swung open then, and slowly the head of the line was engorged by them. "This is it?" I whispered to Alice, and squeezed her dry, cool hand with one hand and that of my oldest progeny, Lucian, which was sweaty and hot, with the other. The baby, on my leather-jacketed shoulders, received two stern bumps, meaning be quiet or else!

This baby, named Tristan after my fellow compatriopoet Tristan Tzara, had been born two years before in Johns Hopkins Hospital, a birth I had been present for and saw in all its bloody glory. The fraction of a second when I'd first glimpsed his big eyes and determined, serious expression, I had known that this was a fighter and a hero. There'd been, in his manner of entering the world, a sense of serious purpose. Character, I'm sure, is present at birth, and nothing much changes after that. When I first saw my son I had the fleeting impulse to name him Dempsey, because he seemed to me a boxer as well as a scholar. Which didn't mean, at the moment of my own birth as an American, that I would put up with any shrieks or howls a two-year-old is wont to commit. So I bumped him a couple of times more for insurance.

Before I had a chance to wonder what happened to the people ahead of me in the line, I was at the head of it. That's the thing about lines: you can fold time along their seams. Just as I came to the head of it I noticed my friend Rodger, a third-generation American Jew, sweating and turning pale. Rodger had just published a volume of verse exploring his grandfather's emigrant experience. The book, called *The Missing Jew,* was a personal search for roots and a nostalgia for the hardier race that came on the boat. In my person, Rodger had a first-hand, living example of a root. I was his grandfather. I patted him on the back of his well-tailored suit. His grandfather, old Kamenetz from Kamenetz, Lithuania, had been a tailor by trade.

"It's all right, grandson," I said.

The person seated behind a table with a voluminous computer list, looked up sharply. "I'm sorry," I mumbled. It would have been complicated to explain. "It's all right, granddaughter," I said.

"Name?" There was an unnecessary pitch there, one I often noticed in Immigration agents in particular as well as in many middle class Americans. It is a pitch of utter rage and disgust at foreignness. Many Americans, and Immigration agents in particular, hate foreigners. They speak too loud, as if they are talking to children and since they quickly become aware of what they are doing, they try to soften the impact in mid-pitch, making a saccharine and totally unnecessary sound that reveals more than anything a profound self-hatred.

"Andrei Codrescu," I said, "a made-up name."

This time, the other one looked up because there were two of them behind that list. This one had on a better uniform and judging by the pointed meanness of her features, she was a bigger fish.

"When you become a citizen," she barked, "you can change your name to anything you want."

"A. Bolshevik," suggested Alice.

"La Lupe," suggested Rodger.

"The Model T," suggested Lucian, who has a passion for mechanics. The officers looked up and down the list for Andrei Codrescu. It is curious how names carve their own paths and how, at critical moments, they repeat their genesis. In the book I carried under my arm, an earlier autobiography, I had told the story of my becoming Andrei Codrescu. It is an amusing and true story though there are other versions, the realistic one chief among them, with the oneiric close behind. In any case, what it boils down to is that the Writers Workshop of the Regional Section of the Sibiu Writers Union (WWRSSWU) tried in vain to name me. They changed my Jewish name of Goldmutter to the Romanian name of Steiu which when written down still read like "Stein." In despair at not being able to turn me into a Romanian, several members of the workshop committed suicide. It was said later that their linguistic impotence broke the straw on the camel's back. At last, I named myself in a bar with a little help from my friends, at just about the time we listened on smuggled tapes to that Beatles' song. Codrescu, the name I named myself, means Sonofabitch From The Woods. It is also the name, with a different ending, of the greatest anti-semite, or one of the greatest of all times, Captain Codreanu, the head of the fascist Iron Guard. The drunken Legionnaires smashed all the windows of my grandmother's home in Alba Iulia and dragged her through the streets in her nightgown at night, singing by the light of torches this little ditty: "The World Knows What it Likes/We have a new Religion/We will kill all the Kikes/Long Live the Captain and the Legion!" I always felt that by taking on the name of that mystical dog I was adhering to that great tradition of Super-Crypto-Jews, men like Monsieur Antipyrrine, Jesus Christ and Des Esseintes, and women like Sarah Bernhardt and Magda Lupescu.

"Ah, here it is. Number One." The officer pointed a chipped rose nail at the top of the list.

I was flattered. I was Number One Immigrant of 1981. An honor indeed. I was aware of course that the high distinction was due to the fact that my case was the oldest one in the files of the local Immigration Bureau. I had applied five years before in San Francisco, reapplied three years later in Baltimore, was the subject of an extensive investigation and I was their least favorite foreigner, a decidedly uppity and lippy pseudo-commie who was nothing but trouble. Well, suffer ye dogs, you can't do shit about it, I said mentally to the sharp-angled fence with the dirty rose nails.

She made a little check by my name and let us into the womb.

The courtroom, designed for trying racketeers and hearing government cases against small corporations overthrowing banana republics, was bathed in state-of-the-art neon horror. An amphitheater, seating four hundred in modernist institutional buckets, positively reeked of electronic security devices. This room was a case, the best that could be made, against the Hitlerian upshot of Modern Art. Modern Art, with its fascistic underquilting, has made much of our world possible in all its ultra-rational and muffled horror. Looking carefully under my seat, I saw, written right below the small mike recording anus tempera-ture, the signatures of all the Bauhaus furniture designers, and a microchip containing the complete list of all the patrons of the Museum of Modern Art. But I had no time for such investigations. I looked up instead at the semicircular bench of his Exalted Honor, Judge Physician & Deliverer of New Americans, who wasn't there yet. His chair, made from the purest naugahyde and hardy DuPont Plastics, was a severe imi-tation throne. The wide, comfortable arms had, barely visible but clearly there, the imprints of the underside of the Judge's arms, from the elbows down, where they rested in judicial repose. Glinting from their rounded tips, the hollow barrels of two machine guns flashed cheerily. Above His Honor's absent head were the Exalted Portraits of The High Judges of the Land. The Supreme Court, wrapped in folds of stern fat, stared down on the nouveauish New Americans.

"All rise!" We all rose.

An emotion entirely alien to my fervently unpatriotic make-up burnt in my solar plexus. Yes, I was moved. And moved with me, wherever you looked, were all the foreigners. On some faces (older Chinese ones) I saw tears. An undeniable surge of mush was burying the room in molasses. After all these years! a little voice said inside me. After all these fucking years of trying to get a good passport that would enable you to finally leave America, here you are, at last, your dream about to come true! No more terror of cops asking for identification, no more short trips to Mexico and Canada with shaky papers, no more grind-ing of teeth over applications for jobs and grants marked "For U.S. Citizens Only," no more inability to explain discrepant names on incomprehensible documents, no more of that beaten old Italian docu-ment inscribed in Italian "good for entry only" (luckily, no one can read Italian), no more "white passport," that chintzy & grudging re-entry booklet and, most of all, no more fear that if you get arrested, they could put you in a rowboat outside the territorial waters of the United States with two days' worth of Spam. Best of all, I could now get arrested, just like the next guy. The dizzying possibilities of a world without constant official ruses broke upon me like my water bag. The water bag was broken. The Judge had come in.

The Judge looked like a blunt instrument, forged by the Army to break the water bags of fledgling foreigners. Above him, his supreme bosses gave piercing glances at the silky knees of several young Soviet wives dressed like Julie Christie in *Darling*. The old Chinese dabbed at their tears.

"You may be seated," the bailiff announced.

"You may be sure," said the Judge, "that I share your feelings on this important day. This country was founded by people just like you who came here and made a big bubbling pot that's still boiling."

At the word "boiling," my youngest let out a series of modulated sounds made by pressing an inflated cheek down with the palm. The air, forced through his pursed lips, sounded like farts or like a bubbling pot. In the profound silence, the soundtrack to the Judge's words was natural. He continued undaunted.

"There is everything in this pot: Asians, Latinos, Jews, Russians, Blacks. But this is a tough world we live in, a real witch of a world. With her ugly broom, this witch is stirring the pot, causing ferment and trouble among our blended but various chunkiness."

My chunky heir, emboldened by the success of his first experiment and impressed by the attention of the crowd, decided to try out some engine sounds. These, he had rehearsed many times on the living room rug, running his Tonka truck over the feet of guests.

"Bllffrrr! Bllllffffrrrr! Blllfffflllffffrrrrrrr!"

I pressed my thumbs hard into his fat leg: one more Tonka truck sound and I'll press the other one! Parents and children develop marvelous languages together, almost as good as the one the Judge was trying out. But this time, the Judge stopped speaking altogether and looked directly at us. What he saw couldn't have pleased him: in that sea of suits stood a leather-jacketed punk with a book under his arm and a baby on his shoulders. Maybe it was all a dream. He decided to ignore us.

There were other children in the room, to be sure, but there was something wrong with them. They looked rented from *The Village of the Damned*. They sat in perfect silence, with glazed eyes (that's it, of course! They'd been drugged!), their knees perfectly aligned, one next to another, not a smudge on their pink little faces, their hair in braids that had taken months to knot. (That's it! Their braids were knotted so tight, the slightest movement of the head caused unbearable pain!)

"Mixed in this stew of hard work, good will and faith in the American dream, there are a few bits of bone, a few sharp, dangerous, rotten, disbelieving bits of bone that would see our way of life choked, our values stomped out, our families discombobulated, our business and industry gone to rack, ruin and Japanese competition." The Judge's voice rose markedly upon the theme of the bones. He looked significantly in our direction.

Tristan-Dempsey, the Gentleman Boxer and Scholar, stuck his tongue out at him and made a "mffff, mfffff" type of snort by means of his nose. This was a feeble response and the Judge thought that he had won. But it was only a lull. Confidently, his Honor continued.

"To root out these bits of evil bone, we must exercise eternal vigilance. Even among you there are some whose faith and values have been subtly warped by the places you come from. Sure, keep your dances, keep your costumes, certainly keep your food... I myself have enjoyed a Polish sausage or two and I have been known to dive into a blintz now and then..."

At this, there was a stir in the room because nobody had brought their costumes and how could they have forgotten? A little food might have been in order. A few blinis with sour cream perhaps? Some pork buns? A few egg rolls? A steaming pot of borscht? A hot plaited bread under a towel? The steaming dishes of regret rose before the Judge, momentarily blocking him from view. The old ones remembered the days when you couldn't as much as face a Judge without a chicken in hand or a bushel of apples or a leg of lamb. How could they have forgotten? Higher and higher rose the national dishes of the near-

Americans boiling in the melting pot around the bits of evil bone. The Judge's voice could barely be heard from behind the wall of stuffed cabbage rolls, egg rolls and placinte.

For thirteen years I had been a stateless person, a man without a country, a creature from the twilight zone of legalistic definition, and now, just as I was about to become someone legitimate, a wall of food was rising between me and my goal. I used all my powers to dissolve that mirage of food. Sure enough, I succeeded. The Judge changed the subject.

"Some new Americans have trouble in the beginning adjusting to our way of life. They might grumble and complain and wish sometimes that they still lived in their old village where the policeman beat them... And sometimes, our new citizens, instead of working hard, become a burden to our social agencies..."

My son, Tristan, who hadn't yet been paid for in full—we paid $50 a month to the JHU Hospital and had been told that babies were being repossessed all the time for failure to meet payments—heard the ring of the bell for Round Two.

"Rodger," he said, loudly and distinctly.

Rodger, who appeared absorbed in various heroic strains of thought occasioned by memories that were not, properly speaking, his, looked startled.

"Yes, honey," he said, just as loud, forgetting for a moment where he was.

Three hundred pairs of foreign eyes, slanted, round, almond-shaped, blue, brown, violet and red turned on our group. His Honor addressed us directly. Speaking for all those eyes, he said:

"The eyes of the world are on our system of justice. It is a fair and just system but it is not, I repeat, it is definitely not to be mocked!" He looked up at the Justices above his head.

"From the mouths of babes, Your Honor..." I said.

Tristan, stimulated by the exchange, and heady with his first public success, now pointed a chubby finger at His Honor and said:

"Bad boy!"

Normally, it would have brought the house down. As it was, only mild guffaws—very low on the scale of mirth—escaped the compressed Near Americans. I could have now asked my wife or Rodger to take Tristan out of the room but a stubborn rage began inside me. What? Have my youngest miss his father's induction into a new nationalism? Not a chance. In the first row across from me, I spotted Mike Curdle, my Immigration Agent. That really brought back some memories.

"Let's see now," said Curdle upon our first encounter, "Write 'I wish to speak English' thirteen times on this piece of paper, please!"

"How about American, buster?" I thought, as I did what he asked.

"Who are the two senators from Maryland?" he continued.

I knew about Wild Bill Hagy but I couldn't remember Pollock Johnny just then. The exam continued like this while my sentiments kept up a contrapuntal beat. My wife is American, my children are American, I have been here thirteen years, five of which I've spent trying to obtain citizenship, and here I am, facing my file (which he hadn't yet opened) like a translation in a bilingual book, being asked silly questions. I was obviously at home, whether he knew it or not.

Excellent, excellent, his expression said. Now, there is only the little matter of your file here, we'll take a quick look, let's, shall we, and then you bring in your wife and another witness and sign here and everything will be hunky-dory and we'll go have lunch.

I studied Curdle. He had the mustache and the weight of a man about my age who looks about a hundred years older. I am startled still when I run into members of my generation who look older than their parents. It was obvious that a certain effort to stay alive stirred in the man but it was being sucked downward into the buttocks that occupied his office chair. He could have been a weather reporter on TV; in fact he looked like one, and that would have fulfilled the hopes of his youth which I could see plainly in his face. There was a girl in this youth of his, an arty and intelligent type who could have changed his life if only she hadn't run off with her lesbian lover to join a dyke marina. Before he opened my file, he said, "What is it like to be stateless?" A curious question, from someone who must have processed the stateless like smoked oysters. But he must have sensed my keen powers. I often run into people who, for no reason at all, ask me questions that they ought to know the answers to better than anyone else.

"It's like living out of wedlock," I said, "you have no security and few rights. The Relationship causes itself to be capitalized by constant thinking about it, and it's a lot more trouble than it's worth. I can't vote but I have to pay taxes. I can't own a gun but they want me for cannon fodder. The worst of it is, I can't get into trouble like everyone else. I'm sure you can appreciate my difficulty. I've been suppressing all my petty criminal instincts to the degree that now, as soon as they make me a citizen, I may well be capable of a major crime."

"Like what?"

"Like wiping my ass with that file you keep staring at," I said.

"For a while there," he said slowly, "having a file was a real sign of status in this country."

What do you know? The jelly fish had a rudimentary brain.

"Well, that may be for Americans... But for me it's just an anagram of life. I'm sure there is stuff in there even I couldn't believe, and I once bought a gold watch from a Neapolitan bum..."

And he began leafing through my past. He leafed and leafed and then he would come to an interesting part and look up at me. I stood stock still, watching my life being leafed through...who knows what was in there...whole episodes of blocked-out life...forgotten deeds...bygone conversations...whole autumn days with their peculiar sensations...telephone calls from rainy booths in big cities...the names and shapes of the phantoms I bedded...the poems that come to me in dreams and stubbornly refuse to reappear in the morning...all my money-making schemes intact, down to the brilliant clarity of their hypnagogic half-life...a Proustian wealth of detail. The seasons changed as he leafed through my file... They say your life passes before your eyes when you die. I say your life passes before your eyes when someone leafs through your file. Perhaps I had completely underestimated my new government: with superior recording techniques, it was possible that they had, indeed, saved more than I could ever hope for. "The Boswells of the bureaucracy," as Ed Sanders calls them, may have done OK this one time. This, after all, had been the moment I had been waiting for. On tedious rainy days in the country, I would make long, endless telephone calls to people who didn't understand half of what I said and nothing of what I implied, hoping that on the other side of the wall, a serious, humming little device was recording me for posterity. In my wildest dreams I beheld a room full of skinny, intelligent, young FBI stenographers of both sexes and with strong and frustrated sexual urges, taking down every word I said. I hoped they were intelligent enough not to mess up paragraphs but clumsy enough to make superb and illuminating mistakes. I would meet them later in life, perhaps after all this had cleared and I had garnered my share of Nobels and was thus beyond prison, and I would get drunk with them, maybe smoke an opiate and then we would all undress and I would fuck them magnificently, a fitting reward for such life-long devotion.

"Now," said Curdle, "what's this? 'An automatic weapon must be spotless at all times. The way to clean the trigger...'"

"Your Marine drill?" I enquired tentatively.

"And this..." he said, reading on, "'When the bomb is completely assembled, put at the bottom of basket and cover with strawberries. You are now ready to walk into the forest and meet the Big Bad Pig...'"

"That's someone who got their Red Riding Hood mixed up with the Three Little Pigs..."

"They are all from *Guerilla*, a radical newspaper from Detroit. You are listed on the mast as *Eastern European Editor*."

"All I ever published in there was a poem. Is my poem there?" I had actually lost the poem and would have affectionately looked at it.

"No. No poem. Just these quotations."

"You mean to tell me, Mr. Nurdle, that *my* file is filled with quotations from a newspaper where I once published a poem but there is no quotation from *my* work?"

"I'm afraid so..." mumbled Nurdle.

"Splendid. Then perhaps we ought to take the newspaper where the announcement of your graduation from the Nitwit Academy appeared and quote some of the wisdom of Richard Speck who, I am sure, was amply quoted in there at one time or another. Even in the darkest days of Stalin nobody thought of quoting somebody else's work, simply because it appeared in something by the same name...though I'm sure that it happened..."

"Well, we shouldn't let your past stand against you." Nurdle was embarrassed. He wanted to be conciliatory, but he'd said the wrong thing.

"My past doesn't stand for or against anything. It doesn't lie, it doesn't recline, it doesn't do a damn thing. It just *is*, dig?"

I wanted to have a look in there for myself. I had a sinking feeling that I was dead wrong: the "Boswells" didn't pay a dingle's worth of attention to their Dr. Johnsons. On the contrary, they arrived at their files by ignoring them entirely. I could have fainted, thinking about all that lost energy, all that talking to the walls and into telephones. The chilling thought ran through me that there might be *nothing* about me in there. I can take condemnation, disgust, shock and opprobrium but being ignored kills me. With a voice choked by truth, I asked, "Does it say in there that I write books?"

He leafed and leafed. "No," he said.

"Well, I do!" I shouted. "I wrote an autobiography in which I confessed to grievous sins, each of which would be sufficient to cause my deportation! Drugs! Homosexuality! Anarchism! Petty theft! Larceny! Defacing civic sculpture!"

Nurdle looked bored. "We will investigate your case, I promise you."

"Promise me only one thing. Promise me you'll read my book."

"I'm sure that there will be an agent in the field who will forward us the appropriate quotations."

"It's a book, man, don't you ever read books?"

Nurdle's investigation took three years. The agents in the field kept disappearing. One agent, dispatched especially to San Francisco by TWA, never came back. Traces of his appearance surfaced here and there. He is known, for instance, to have visited a number of my friends and asked them if my poetry was Anti-American. In Monte Rio, California, Hunce Voelcker explained to him that there was serious speculation in many circles that I might not be from Transylvania at all. Some said that I was born in Brooklyn and my accent is Berlitz fake. Harold Norse declared that I was the most American person he knew. "He smokes Marlboros, drinks bourbon and if he knew how to drive, he'd probably drive a Datsun, so help me Buddha, pass the Doritos!" After which the agent never filed his report and disappeared. Another agent, dispatched in all haste after the first one, decided to retire in San Francisco. None of them, to my knowledge, tried to read the book although I heard some farfetched speculation that upon contact with the tome, the agents lost their memories and started talking funny.

When it became clearly impossible to investigate me, Nurdle gave in to my insistent and bothersome phone calls. Besides, I'd begun dropping little hints in the newspaper. "Nurdle, nurdle on the floor," I would say, apropos of nothing in some of my articles, "Can you read your name on the door?" At last, he summoned me to his office and said, "If you swear to be a good boy, I'll press forward with your request for citizenship and grant it."

The Dracula half of my schizo-person would have liked to make a big hole in the man and eat the file. I feel the gritty taste of Xerox paper, wadded and shoved down the throat even as I type. In Russia, I know, writers eat their manuscripts regularly. They get together in secret and have veritable orgies of manuscript swallowing. It beats potatoes, day in and day out. Here, it would be a good idea to form several secret societies of File Eaters for the same purpose. We can consume the inaccurate versions of our lives and grow fat and strong on the rich refuse.

But the American half of my mezo-unit, the one that likes to talk cars and ask for extra grease with the cheeseburger, decided to go ahead with it and promise them anything. After all, by becoming an official American, this half of the mezo-unit would gain considerably on the Romanian Schizo-sketch (now fading quickly).

"I'll be a good boy," I said, "But..."

"But what?" the agent said sharply.

"But you have to promise to read my book..."

"Fine, fine," he agreed.

I know that he was being perfunctory and that the copy I sent him lies still unread in a locked drawer. But there will come a rainy, long afternoon when that girl from his past will come back to him in the shape of a hypno-mystical authority-figure complicated by an insane desire, untouched since her departure, and with a finger pointing straight between his eyes and another poised dreamily at the entrance of her honey boat with the-man-in-the-boat standing at attention, she will order him to begin reading my book.

I unglued my eyes from Mike Nurdle, conscious that the Judge's speech was all but over and the main course about to begin.

"I therefore congratulate you and ask you to stand with me to take the oath."

The compressed neo-Americans stood with a relief that could have come only from escaping those vicious metal chairs. The cracking of stretching bones was heard and a tiny voice said: "Mommy, peepee!" followed immediately by a hiss like that of a serpent, shushing the innocent. My own son, Tristan, who for some reason beyond my ken, had been quiet until now, came back to life.

"Mommy, peepee!" he took up the cry.

"Not now."

"Please raise your right hand."

A man with his right hand chopped off by the Comintern demanded timidly if he could use his left. The Judge granted the motion.

"Do you solemnly swear to pay allegiance..."

I could feel the anger building up in the two-year-old denied the toilet he had been only recently trained to use. He had been so amply rewarded and fawned over for going peepee and caca in the potty and now, only a few hours later, he is denied the reason of his undeniable triumph by a fat man with his hand in the air. It was more than he could take.

I too felt pressure building inside me, both from my bladder and from the fact that a few simple sentences later and a mass hum of approval, I would become an American citizen. I also felt, more strongly than at any point, that I was about to be expelled from the womb. My last autobiography began also *in utero* where I am made to contemplate the advisability of getting born. Mirror, mirror on the wall, I think I asked, ought I to be born at all? The womb, as I recall, contained a little vanity table with an oval mirror above it. My cigarettes were on the table. I was amazed at the simplicity of my mother's interior. Through the thick walls of my room came the muffled screams of the woman in the next cubicle, giving birth to a still-born infant. I didn't want to be still-born. I came out saying yes. In the rush of the exit I'd forgotten to take my identification card from the drawer of the little table. Even before oxygen burnt my memory I'd already forgotten who I was supposed to be. I have since had to invent myself a good number of times, content in the knowledge that I can be anybody.

Beginning a semblance of conscious life in the womb has its advantages too, later in life, when you are living in California, for instance, and the intra-uterine conditions are duplicated by the climate and the surf. Life is, in fact, a series of wombs from which you are successively or simultaneously ejected into brief thoughts—maxims, really—before being swallowed up again. The practice of thinking *in utero* is the most dangerous discipline of our times. I teach it. I find it necessary to teach because I think that soon we will all be living in Utopia, which comes from the Greek *Ou Topos* or No Place. The inhabitants of Nowhere, already in such profusion in the Zombified West, need this teaching more than life itself. The intermittent to nonexistent thinking life of *Homo Americanus* is like a failing watch-tower at night. We are going to be wrecked upon our own bodies.

"...to obey the laws..."

"TO OBEY THE LAWS..." thundered the room.

Suddenly, Tristan, taking advantage of that charged lull after the voice of the room, and just before the next line of the oath, noticed the Supreme Court Judges on the wall. Delighted, he shrieked and pointed his finger at them: "Doggy! Piggy! Monkey!"

"To cherish and to defend..."

"TO CHERISH AND TO DEFEND..."

"PORKY! DOGGY! MONKEY! PIGGY! KITTY!"

The louder we got, the louder he got. I think that Alice and Rodger were embarrassed. All the new Americans were. But Lucian and I were thrilled. We had understood. Not only had Tristan inserted the glorious text of his own knowledge into the fossilized rituals of the grownups, but he had also discovered and told us that an enumeration is an enumeration, no matter what the bullshit it enumerates is. A series of statements echoed by thousands was the same as a series of animals in a book or judges on a wall. In other words, he had successfully sabotaged the attack of empty morality. I think it was time we made him a colonel in the Transylvanian Liberation Front.

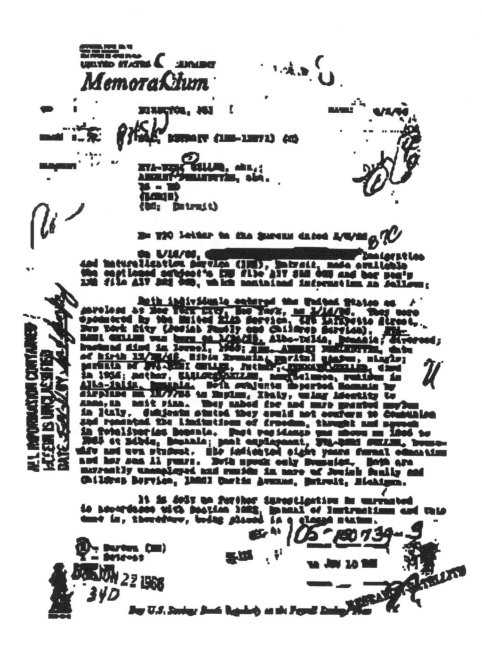

EDWIDGE DANTICAT

FROM "TRAVELING WORLDS WITH EDWIDGE DANTICAT"
BY RENEE H. SHEA
POETS & WRITERS MAGAZINE, JANUARY/FEBRUARY 1997

Danticat's gifted command of English would be extraordinary under any circumstances but it is even more stunning since she did not speak any English at all when she arrived in the United States at age twelve: "I had an uncle in Haiti who was always trying to learn English, so he would play those Berlitz-type records in the morning when he was shaving. That was the only time I really heard English. But I started learning right away when I came here. I immediately went to school: I came on a Friday and went to school on Monday. My parents were serious about education. I was in a bilingual class, but there were other classes where I just kind of went in and tried to figure out what was happening."

Danticat's parents spoke English, though "at home, we always spoke Creole. With my brother, we speak something of a mix, but we never really spoke French at home." She sees French Caribbean writers struggling with voice: "That's a question people face when they're writing a language that's not their first. I learned a great deal from reading Jacques Roumain because he captured so much of Creole in French. That's what I try to do in English, so that our voices can still come across, so that people can recognize a different voice even if I'm translating myself when I write. I often had to struggle with French because when I spoke Creole at school, the teacher would act like she didn't hear me. If I started a sentence in Creole, she would say, 'No, speak French.' It was like Creole was something you could not do in offices." Although Danticat does not write in Haitian Creole, she recognizes the importance of those who are choosing to do so: "It's something Haiti is struggling with now because some want to bring Creole into the schools, and others object; they say you have to learn French for a reason—business success. They say that people who have means and money will always teach their children French anyway, so the poor children in the government schools where the requirement is to teach Creole are at a disadvantage. Some see this as another way to keep the society unequal."

The English language comes in for its share of mockery and humor, especially in *Breath, Eyes, Memory*, where the "colorful" Haitian language in the marketplace makes arguing "a sport": "People rarely hit each other. They don't need to. They wound just as brutally by cursing your mother, calling you a sexual misfit, or accusing you of being from the hills. If you couldn't match them with even stronger accusations, then you would concede the argument by keeping your mouth shut." In contrast, Sophie claims that English sounds "like rocks falling in a stream," and Grandmother Ife scoffs when Martine and Sophie talk to one another in English: "Oh that cling-clang talk....It sounds like glass breaking."

The Book of the Dead

My father is gone. I am slouched in a cast-aluminum chair across from two men, one the manager of the hotel where we're staying and the other a policeman. They are waiting for me to explain what has become of him, my father.

The manager—"Mr. Flavio Salinas," the plaque on his office door reads—has the most striking pair of chartreuse eyes I have ever seen on a man with an island-Spanish lilt to his voice.

The officer is a baby-faced, short white Floridian with a pot belly.

"Where are you and your daddy from, Ms. Bienaimé?" he asks.

I answer "Haiti," even though I was born and raised in East Flatbush, Brooklyn, and have never visited my parents birthplace. I do this because it is one more thing I have longed to have in common with my parents.

The officer plows forward. "You down here in Lakeland from Haiti?"

"We live in New York. We were on our way to Tampa."

I find Manager Salinas's office gaudy. The walls are covered with orange-and-green wallpaper, briefly interrupted by a giant gold-leaf-bordered print of a Victorian cottage that somehow resembles the building we're in. Patting his light-green tie, he whispers reassuringly, "Officer Bo and I will do the best we can to help you find your father."

We start out with a brief description: "Sixty-four, five feet eight inches, two hundred and twenty pounds, moon-faced, with thinning salt-and-pepper hair. Velvet-brown eyes—"

"Velvet brown?" says Officer Bo.

"Deep brown—same color as his complexion."

My father has had partial frontal dentures for ten years, since he fell off his and my mother's bed when his prison nightmares began. I mention that, too. Just the dentures, not the nightmares. I also bring up the claw-shaped marks that run from his left ear down along his cheek to the corner of his mouth—the only visible reminder of the year he spent at Fort Dimanche, the Port-au-Prince prison ironically named after the Lord's Day.

"Does your daddy have any kind of mental illness, senility?" asks Officer Bo.

"No."

"Do you have any pictures of your daddy?"

I feel like less of a daughter because I'm not carrying a photograph in my wallet. I had hoped to take some pictures of him on our trip. At one of the rest stops I bought a disposable camera and pointed it at my father. No, no, he had protested, covering his face with both hands like a little boy protecting his cheeks from a slap. He did not want any more pictures taken of him for the rest of his life. He was feeling too ugly.

"That's too bad," says Officer Bo. "Does he speak English, your daddy? He can ask for directions, et cetera?"

"Yes."

"Is there anything that might make your father run away from you—particularly here in Lakeland?" Manager Salinas interjects. "Did you two have a fight?"

I had never tried to tell my father's story in words before now, but my first sculpture of him was the reason for our trip: a two-foot-high mahogany figure of my father, naked, crouching on the floor, his back arched like the curve of a crescent moon, his downcast eyes fixed on his short stubby fingers and the wide palms of his hands. It was hardly revolutionary; minimalist at best, but it was my favorite of all my attempted representations of him. It was the way I had imagined him in prison.

The last time I had seen my father? The previous night, before falling asleep. When we pulled into the pebbled driveway, densely lined with palm and banana trees, it was almost midnight. All the restaurants in the area were closed. There was nothing to do but shower and go to bed.

"It is like a paradise here," my father said when he saw the room. It had the same orange-and-green wallpaper as Salinas's office, and the plush green carpet matched the walls. "Look, Annie," he said, "it is like grass under our feet." He was always searching for a glimpse of paradise, my father.

He picked the bed closest to the bathroom, removed the top of his gray jogging suit, and unpacked his toiletries. Soon after, I heard him humming, as he always did, in the shower.

After he got into bed, I took a bath, pulled my hair back in a ponytail, and checked on the sculpture—just felt it a little bit through the bubble padding and carton wrapping to make sure it wasn't broken. Then I slipped under the covers, closed my eyes, and tried to sleep.

I pictured the client to whom I was delivering the sculpture: Gabrielle Fonteneau, a young woman about my age, an actress on a nationally syndicated television series. My friend Jonas, the principal at the East Flatbush elementary school where I teach drawing to fifth graders, had shown her a picture of my "Father" sculpture, and, the way Jonas told it, Gabrielle Fonteneau had fallen in love with it and wished to offer it as a gift to her father on his birthday.

Since this was my first big sale, I wanted to make sure that the piece got there safely. Besides, I needed a weekend away, and both my mother and I figured that my father, who watched a lot of television, both in his barbershop and at home, would enjoy meeting Gabrielle, too. But when I woke up the next morning my father was gone.

I showered, put on my driving jeans and a T-shirt, and waited. I watched a half hour of midmorning local news, smoked three mentholated cigarettes even though we were in a nonsmoking room, and waited some more. By noon, four hours had gone by. And it was only then that I noticed that the car was still there but the sculpture was gone.

I decided to start looking for my father: in the east garden, the west garden, the dining room, the exercise room, and in the few guest rooms cracked open while the maid changed the sheets; in the little convenience store at the Amoco gas station nearby; even in the Salvation Army thrift shop that from a distance seemed to blend into the interstate. All that waiting and looking actually took six hours, and I felt guilty for having held back so long before going to the front desk to ask, "Have you seen my father?"

I feel Officer Bo's fingers gently stroking my wrist. Up close he smells like fried eggs and gasoline, like breakfast at the Amoco. "I'll put the word out with the other boys," he says. "Salinas here will be in his office. Why don't you go back to your room in case he shows up there?"

I return to the room and lie in the unmade bed, jumping up when I hear the click from the electronic key in the door. It's only the housekeeper. I turn down the late-afternoon cleaning and call my mother at the beauty salon where she perms, presses, and braids hair, next door to my father's barbershop. But she isn't there. So I call my parents' house and leave the hotel number on their machine. "Please call me as soon as you can, Manman. It's about Papi."

Once, when I was twelve, I overheard my mother telling a young woman who was about to get married how she and my father had first met on the sidewalk in front of Fort Dimanche the evening that my father was released from jail. (At a dance, my father had fought with a soldier out of uniform who had him arrested and thrown in prison for a year.) That night, my mother was returning home from a sewing class when he stumbled out of the prison gates and collapsed into her arms, his face still bleeding from his last beating. They married and left for New York a year later. "We were like two seeds planted in a rock," my mother had told the young woman, "but somehow when our daughter, Annie, came we took root."

My mother soon calls me back, her voice staccato with worry.

"Where is Papi?"

"I lost him."

"How you lost him?"

"He got up before I did and disappeared."

"How long he been gone?"

"Eight hours," I say, almost not believing myself that it's been that long.

My mother is clicking her tongue and humming. I can see her sitting at the kitchen table, her eyes closed, her fingers sliding up and down her flesh-colored stockinged legs.

"You call police?"

"Yes."

"What they say?"

"To wait, that he'll come back."

My mother is thumping her fingers against the phone's mouthpiece, which is giving me a slight ache in my right ear.

"Tell me where you are, she says. "Two more hours and he's not there, call me, I come."

I dial Gabrielle Fonteneau's cellular-phone number. When she answers, her voice sounds just as it does on television, but more silken and seductive without the sitcom laugh track.

"To think," my father once said while watching her show, "Haitian-born actresses on American television."

"And one of them wants to buy my stuff," I'd added.

When she speaks, Gabrielle Fonteneau sounds as if she's in a place with cicadas, waterfalls, palm trees, and citronella candles to keep the mosquitoes away. I realize that I, too, am in such a place, but I can't appreciate it.

"So nice of you to come all this way to deliver the sculpture," she says. "Jonas tell you why I like it so much? My papa was a journalist in Port-au-Prince. In 1975, he wrote a story criticizing the dictatorship, and he was arrested and put in jail."

"Fort Dimanche?"

"No, another one," she says. "Caserne. Papa kept track of days there by scraping lines with his fingernails on the walls of his cell. One of the guards didn't like this, so he pulled out all his fingernails with pliers."

I think of the photo spread I saw in the Haitian Times of Gabrielle Fonteneau and her parents in their living room in Tampa. Her father was described as a lawyer, his daughter's manager; her mother a court stenographer. There was no hint in that photograph of what had once happened to the father. Perhaps people don't see anything in my father's face, either, in spite of his scars.

"We celebrate his birthday on the day he was released from prison," she says. "It's the hands I love so much in your sculpture. They're so strong."

I am drifting away from Gabrielle Fonteneau when I hear her say, "So when will you get here? You have instructions from Jonas, right? Maybe we can make you lunch. My mother makes great *lanbi*."

I'll be there at twelve tomorrow," I say. "My father is with me. We are making a little weekend vacation of this."

My father loves museums. When he isn't working in his barbershop, he's often at the Brooklyn Museum. The ancient Egyptian rooms are his favorites.

"The Egyptians, they was like us," he likes to say. The Egyptians worshipped their gods in many forms and were often ruled by foreigners. The pharaohs were like the dictators he had fled. But what he admires most about the Egyptians is the way they mourned.

"Yes, they grieve," he'll say. He marvels at the mummification that went on for weeks, resulting in bodies that survived thousands of years.

My whole adult life, I have struggled to find the proper manner of sculpting my father, a man who learned about art by standing with me most of the Saturday mornings of my childhood, mesmerized by the golden masks, the shawabtis, and Osiris, ruler of the underworld.

When my father finally appears in the hotel-room doorway, I am awed by him. Smiling, he looks like a much younger man, further bronzed after a long day at the beach.

"Annie, let your father talk to you." He walks over to my bed, bends down to unlace his sneakers. "*On ti koze,* a little chat."

"Where were you? Where is the sculpture, Papi?" I feel my eyes twitching, a nervous reaction I inherited from my mother.

"That's why we need to chat," he says. "I have objections with your statue."

He pulls off his sneakers and rubs his feet with both hands.

"I don't want you to sell that statue," he says. Then he picks up the phone and calls my mother.

"I know she called you," he says to her in Creole. "Her head is so hot. She panics so easily. I was just out walking, thinking."

I hear my mother lovingly scolding him and telling him not to leave me again. When he hangs up the phone, he picks up his sneakers and puts them back on.

"Where is the sculpture?" My eyes are twitching so hard now that I can barely see.

"Let us go," he says. "I will take you to it."

As my father maneuvers the car out of the parking lot, I tell myself he might be ill, mentally ill, even though I have never detected anything wrong beyond his prison nightmares. I am trying to piece it together, this sudden yet familiar picture of a parent's vulnerability. When I was ten years old and my father had the chicken pox, I overheard him say to a friend on the phone, "The doctor tells me that at my age chicken pox can kill a man." This was the first time I realized that my father could die. I looked up the word "kill" in every dictionary and encyclopedia at school, trying to comprehend what it meant, that my father could be eradicated from my life.

My father stops the car on the side of the highway near a manmade lake, one of those artificial creations of the modern tropical city, with curved stone benches surrounding stagnant water. There is little light to see by except a half-moon. He heads toward one of the benches, and I sit down next to him, letting my hands dangle between my legs.

"Is this where the sculpture is?" I ask.

"In the water," he says.

"O.K.," I say. "But please know this about yourself. You are an especially harsh critic."

My father tries to smother a smile.

"Why?" I ask.

He scratches his chin. Anger is a wasted emotion, I've always thought. My parents got angry at unfair politics in New York or Port-au-Prince, but they never got angry at my grades—at all the B's I got in everything but art classes—or at my not eating vegetables or occasionally vomiting my daily spoonful of cod-liver oil. Ordinary anger, I thought, was a weakness. But now I am angry I want to hit my father, beat the craziness out of his head.

"Annie," he says. "When I first saw your statue, I wanted to be buried with it, to take it with me into the other world."

"Like the ancient Egyptians," I say

He smiles, grateful, I think, that I still recall his passions.

"Annie," he asks, "do you remember when I read to you from *The Book of the Dead?*"

"Are you dying?" I say to my father. "Because I can only forgive you for this if you are. You can't take this back."

He is silent for a moment too long.

I think I hear crickets, though I cannot imagine where they might be. There is the highway, the cars racing by, the half-moon, the lake dug up from the depths of the ground, the allée of royal palms beyond. And there is me and my father.

"You remember the judgment of the dead," my father says, "when the heart of a person is put on a scale. If it is heavy, then this person cannot enter the other world."

It is a testament to my upbringing that I am not yelling at him.

"I don't deserve a statue," he says, even while looking like one: the Madonna of Humility, for example, contemplating her losses in the dust.

"Annie, your father was the hunter," he says. "He was not the prey."

"What are you saying?" I ask.

"We have a proverb," he says. "'One day for the hunter, one day for the prey.' Your father was the hunter. He was not the prey." Each word is hard-won as it leaves my father's mouth, balanced like those hearts on the Egyptian scale.

"Annie, when I saw your mother the first time, I was not just out of prison. I was a guard in the prison. One of the prisoners I was questioning had scratched me with a piece of tin. I went out to the street in a rage, blood all over my face. I was about to go back and do something bad, very bad. But instead comes your mother. I smash into her, and she asks me what I am doing there. I told her I was just let go from prison and she held my face and cried in my hair."

"And the nightmares, what are they?"

"Of what I, your father, did to others."

"Does Manman know?"

"I told her, Annie, before we married."

I am the one who drives back to the hotel. In the car, he says, "Annie, I am still your father, still your mother's husband. I would not do these things now."

When we get back to the hotel room, I leave a message for Officer Bo, and another for Manager Salinas, telling them that I have found my father. He has slipped into the bathroom, and now he runs the shower at full force. When it seems that he is never coming out, I call my mother at home in Brooklyn.

"How do you love him?" I whisper into the phone.

My mother is tapping her fingers against the mouthpiece.

"I don't know, Annie," she whispers back, as though there is a chance that she might also be overheard by him. "I feel only that you and me, we saved him. When I met him, it made him stop hurting the people. This is how I see it. He was a seed thrown into a rock, and you and me, Annie, we helped push a flower out of a rock."

When I get up the next morning, my father is already dressed. He is sitting on the edge of his bed with his back to me, his head bowed, his face buried in his hands. If I were sculpting him, I would make him a praying mantis, crouching motionless, seeming to pray while waiting to strike.

With his back still turned, my father says, "Will you call those people and tell them you have it no more, the statue?"

"We were invited to lunch there. I believe we should go."

He raises his shoulders and shrugs. It is up to me.

The drive to Gabrielle Fonteneau's house seems longer than the twenty-four hours it took to drive from New York: the ocean, the palms along the road, the highway so imposingly neat. My father fills in the silence in the car by saying, "So now you know, Annie, why your mother and me, we have never returned home."

The Fonteneaus' house is made of bricks of white coral, on a cul-de-sac with a row of banyans separating the two sides of the street.

Silently, we get out of the car and follow a concrete path to the front door. Before we can knock, an older woman walks out. Like Gabrielle, she has stunning midnight-black eyes and skin the color of sorrel, with spiraling curls brushing the sides of her face. When Gabrielle's father joins her, I realize where Gabrielle Fonteneau gets her height. He is more than six feet tall.

Mr. Fonteneau extends his hands, first to my father and then to me. They're large, twice the size of my father's. The fingernails have grown back, thick, densely dark, as though the past had nestled itself there in black ink. We move slowly through the living room, which has a cathedral ceiling and walls covered with Haitian paintings—Obin, Hyppolite, Tiga, Duval-Carrié. Out on the back terrace, which towers over a nursery of orchids and red dracaenas, a table is set for lunch.

Mr. Fonteneau asks my father where his family is from in Haiti, and my father lies. In the past, I thought he always said a different province because he had lived in all those places, but I realize now that he says this to keep anyone from tracing him, even though twenty-six years and eighty more pounds shield him from the threat of immediate recognition.

When Gabrielle Fonteneau makes her entrance, in an off-the-shoulder ruby dress, my father and I stand up.

"Gabrielle," she says, when she shakes hands with my father, who blurts out spontaneously, "You are one of the flowers of Haiti."

Gabrielle Fonteneau tilts her head coyly.

"We eat now," Mrs. Fonteneau announces, leading me and my father to a bathroom to wash up before the meal. Standing before a pink seashell-shaped sink, my father and I dip our hands under the faucet flow.

"Annie," my father says, "we always thought, your mother and me, that children could raise their parents higher. Look at what this girl has done for her parents."

During the meal of conch, plantains, and mushroom rice, Mr. Fonteneau tries to draw my father into conversation. He asks when my father was last in Haiti.

"Twenty-six years," my father replies.

"No going back for you?" asks Mrs. Fonteneau.

"I have not had the opportunity," my father says.

"We go back every year to a beautiful place overlooking the ocean in the mountains in Jacmel," says Mrs. Fonteneau.

"Have you ever been to Jacmel?" Gabrielle Fonteneau asks me.

I shake my head no.

"We are fortunate," Mrs. Fonteneau says, "that we have another place to go where we can say our rain is sweeter, our dust is lighter, our beach is prettier."

"So now we are tasting rain and weighing dust," Mr. Fonteneau says, and laughs.

"There is nothing like drinking the sweet juice from a green coconut you fetched yourself from your own tree, or sinking your hand in sand from the beach in your own country," Mrs. Fonteneau says.

"When did you ever climb a coconut tree?" Mr. Fonteneau says, teasing his wife.

I am imagining what my father's nightmares might be. Maybe he dreams of dipping his hands in the sand on a beach in his own country and finds that what he comes up with is a fist full of blood.

After lunch, my father asks if he can have a closer look at the Fonteneaus' back-yard garden. While he's taking the tour, I confess to Gabrielle Fonteneau that I don't have the sculpture.

"My father threw it away," I say.

Gabrielle Fonteneau frowns.

"I don't know," she says. "Was there even a sculpture at all? I trust

Jonas, but maybe you fooled him, too. Is this some scam, to get into our home?"

"There was a sculpture," I say. "Jonas will tell you that. My father just didn't like it, so he threw it away."

She raises her perfectly arched eyebrows, perhaps out of concern for my father's sanity or my own.

"I'm really disappointed," she says. "I wanted it for a reason. My father goes home when he looks at a piece of art. He goes home deep inside himself. For a long time, he used to hide his fingers from people. It's like he was making a fist all the time. I wanted to give him this thing so that he knows we understand what happened to him."

"I am truly sorry," I say.

Over her shoulders, I see her parents guiding my father through rows of lemongrass. I want to promise her that I will make her another sculpture, one especially modelled on her father. But I don't know when I will be able to work on anything again. I have lost my subject, the father I loved as well as pitied.

In the garden, I watch my father snap a white orchid from its stem and hold it out toward Mrs. Fonteneau, who accepts it with a nod of thanks.

"I don't understand," Gabrielle Fonteneau says. "You did all this for nothing." I wave to my father to signal that we should perhaps leave now, and he comes toward me, the Fonteneaus trailing slowly behind him.

With each step he rubs the scars on the side of his face.

Perhaps the last person my father harmed had dreamed this moment into my father's future—his daughter seeing those marks, like chunks of warm plaster still clinging to a cast, and questioning him about them, giving him a chance to either lie or tell the truth. After all, we have the proverb, as my father would say: "Those who give the blows may try to forget, but those who carry the scars must remember."

HA JIN

English is a very expressive language. It's quite common among Chinese immigrants that when they begin to write in English, they feel there is more to say and sometimes even dull subject matter becomes interesting. This means writing in this tongue can be a liberating experience for them. However, I adopted English mainly out of necessity, driven by the instinct for survival. Before the Tiananmen Massacre I had planned to return to China after completing my dissertation, hoping to become a writer in Chinese, in which I had published very little.

The massacre shattered my plan and made me decide to immigrate and give up my mother tongue. To write poetry and fiction in English, I had to relearn the language, since I had studied mainly academic English before. It was difficult, and sometimes a word or a phrase would take me a few weeks to get right. I had begun to learn English at the age of twenty-one, so I wasn't sure whether I could write in English. But I had no choice. All my degrees are in English; try as I did, I couldn't find any job related to Chinese. Even Chinese restaurants wouldn't hire me as a waiter. As a result, I worked in American restaurants when I was a graduate student. So English was my means of survival.

In addition to the difficulty in using the language, there was another overwhelming problem consequent on my abandoning Chinese, namely that my goal as a writer had to change. Owing to the Communist rule, Chinese literature in the mainland was quite bleak from 1950s to 1980s. This means there was a lot of space and opportunities for young writers. In poetry, for instance, even the language proper should be overhauled in order to establish a new tradition. That kind of ambition had to be laid aside after I adopted English. In English, we writers whose mother tongues are not English face a different kind of tradition and task. In prose there are Conrad and Nabokov, two giants we have to come to terms with one way or another. Should we follow the paths they opened? Or should we seek new space unexplored by them? For a writer, the sense of space is vital, because the space you have positioned yourself in determines what kind of writer you will become, provided you have the talent and luck to accomplish what you have envisioned. Though I am no longer troubled by this problem, it did bother me for a long time. To put it in a simpler way, I had no idea where to go and how far I could go in English. Without proper bearings, the writing act is meaningless.

Having written in English for more than a decade, I have figured out some basic issues. I believe that Conrad and Nabokov became masters of English prose mainly because of their styles. They invented new ways of writing prose; as a result, without their works English letters would feel incomplete. Style and sensibilities are much more vital than subject matter. They are the energy a writer from an alien tongue should strive to bring into English. Of course, in practice few of us can be certain whether we are fortunate enough and adequately equipped for such a goal.

I have grown less worried about ambition or vision. For me, a writer's identity cannot be claimed and can only be created by their writings. Therefore it's more meaningful to write devotedly and give whatever I have to a book. Eventually my work will give me an identity. As for my mother tongue, I don't think I will return to it, because I am a solitary. In English there is more solitude.

Saboteur

Mr. Chiu and his bride were having lunch in the square before Muji Train Station. On the table between them were two bottles of soda spewing out brown foam, and two paper boxes of rice and sautéed cucumber and pork. "Let's eat," he said to her, and broke the connected ends of the chopsticks. He picked up a slice of streaky pork and put it into his mouth. As he was chewing, a few crinkles appeared on his thin jaw.

To his right, at another table, two railroad policemen were drinking tea and laughing; it seemed that the stout, middle-aged man was telling a joke to his young comrade, who was tall and of athletic build. Now and again they would steal a glance at Mr. Chiu's table.

The air smelled of rotten melon. A few flies kept buzzing above the couple's lunch. Hundreds of people were rushing around to get on the platform or to catch buses to downtown. Food and fruit vendors were crying for customers in lazy voices. About a dozen young women, representing the local hotels, held up placards that displayed the daily prices and words as large as a palm, like *Free Meals, Air Conditioning,* and *On the River.* In the center of the square stood a concrete statue of Chairman Mao, at whose feet peasants were napping with their backs on the warm granite and with their faces toward the sunny sky. A flock of pigeons perched on the chairman's raised hand and forearm.

The rice and cucumber tasted good and Mr. Chiu was eating unhurriedly. His sallow face showed exhaustion. He was glad that the honeymoon was finally over and that he and his bride were heading for Harbin. During the two weeks' vacation, he had been worried about his liver because three months ago he had suffered from acute hepatitis; he was afraid he might have a relapse. But there had been no severe symptom, despite his liver being still big and tender. On the whole he was pleased with his health, which could even endure the strain of a honeymoon; indeed, he was on the course of recovery. He looked at his bride, who took off her wire glasses, kneading the root of her nose with her fingertips. Beads of sweat coated her pale cheeks.

"Are you all right, sweetheart?" he asked.

"I have a headache. I didn't sleep well last night."

"Take an aspirin, will you?"

"It's not that serious. Tomorrow is Sunday and I can sleep longer. Don't worry."

As they were talking, the stout policeman at the next table stood up and threw a bowl of tea in their direction. Both Mr. Chiu's and his bride's sandals were wet instantly.

"Hooligan!" she said in a low voice.

Mr. Chiu got to his feet and said out loud, "Comrade policeman, why did you do this?" He stretched out his right foot to show the wet sandal.

"Do what?" the stout man asked huskily, glaring at Mr. Chiu while the young fellow was whistling.

"See, you dumped water on our feet."

"You're lying. You wet your shoes yourself."

"Comrade policeman, your duty is to keep order, but you purposely tortured us common citizens. Why violate the law you are supposed to enforce?" As Mr. Chiu was speaking, dozens of people began gathering around.

With a wave of his hand, the man said to the young fellow, "Let's get hold of him!"

They grabbed Mr. Chiu and clamped handcuffs around his wrists. He cried, "You can't do this to me. This is utterly unreasonable."

"Shut up!" The man pulled out his pistol. "You can use your tongue at our headquarters."

The young fellow added, "You're a saboteur, you know? You're disrupting public order."

The bride was too terrified to say anything coherent. She was a recent college graduate, had majored in fine arts, and had never seen the police make an arrest. All she could say now was "Oh please, please!"

The policemen were pulling Mr. Chiu, but he refused to go with them, holding the corner of the table and shouting, "We have a train to catch. We already bought the tickets."

The stout man punched him in the chest. "Shut up. Let your ticket expire." With the pistol butt he chopped Mr. Chiu's hands, which at once released the table. Together the two men dragged him away to the police station.

Realizing he had to go with them, Mr. Chiu turned his head and shouted to his bride, "Don't wait for me here. Take the train. If I'm not back by tomorrow morning, send someone over to get me out."

She nodded, covering her sobbing mouth with her palm.

After removing his shoelaces, they locked Mr. Chiu into a cell in the back of the Railroad Police Station. The single window in the room was blocked by six steel bars; it faced a spacious yard in which stood a few pines. Beyond the trees two swings hung from an iron frame, swaying gently in the breeze. Somewhere in the building a cleaver was chopping rhythmically. There must be a kitchen upstairs, Mr. Chiu thought.

He was too exhausted to worry about what they would do to him, so he lay down on the narrow bed with his eyes shut. He wasn't afraid. The Cultural Revolution was over already, and recently the Party had been propagating the idea that all citizens were equal before the law. The police ought to be a law-abiding model for common people. As long as he remained cool-headed and reasoned with them, they might not harm him.

Late in the afternoon he was taken to the Interrogation Bureau on the second floor. On his way there, in the stairwell, he ran into the middle-aged policeman who had manhandled him. The man grinned, rolling his bulgy eyes and pointing his fingers at him like firing a pistol. Egg of a tortoise!, Mr. Chiu cursed mentally.

The moment he sat down in the office, he burped, his palm shielding his mouth. In front of him, across a long desk, sat the chief of the bureau and a donkey-faced man. On the glass desktop was a folder containing information on his case. He felt it bizarre that in just a matter of hours they had accumulated a small pile of writing about him. On second thought, he began to wonder whether they had kept a file on him all the time. How could this have happened? He lived and worked in Harbin, more than three hundred miles away, and this was his first time in Muji City.

The chief of the bureau was a thin, bald man who looked serene and intelligent. His slim hands handled the written pages in the folder like those of a lecturing scholar. To Mr. Chiu's left sat a young scribe, with a clipboard on his knee and a black fountain pen in his hand.

"Your name?" the chief asked, apparently reading out the question from a form.

"Chiu Maguang."

"Age?"

"Thirty-four."

"Profession?"

"Lecturer."

"Work unit?"

"Harbin University."

"Political status?"

"Communist Party member."

The chief put down the paper and began to speak. "Your crime is sabotage, although it hasn't induced serious consequences yet. Because you are a Party member, you should be punished more. You have failed to be a model for the masses and you—"

"Excuse me, sir," Mr. Chiu cut him off.

"What?"

"I didn't do anything. Your men are the saboteurs of our social order. They threw hot tea on my feet and my wife's feet. Logically speaking, you should criticize them, if not punish them."

"That statement is groundless. You have no witness. How could I believe you?" the chief said matter-of-factly.

"This is my evidence." He raised his right hand. "Your man hit my fingers with a pistol."

"That can't prove how your feet got wet. Besides, you could hurt your fingers by yourself."

"But I told the truth!" Anger flared up in Mr. Chiu. "Your police station owes me an apology. My train ticket has expired, my new leather sandals are ruined, and I am late for a conference in the provincial capital. You must compensate me for the damage and losses. Don't mistake me for a common citizen who would tremble when you sneeze. I'm a scholar, a philosopher, and an expert in dialectical materialism. If necessary, we will argue about this in the Northeastern Daily, or we will go to the highest People's Court in Beijing. Tell me, what's your name?" He got carried away by his harangue, which was by no means trivial and had worked to his advantage on numerous occasions.

"Stop bluffing us," the donkey-faced man broke in. "We have seen a lot of your kind. We can easily prove you are guilty. Here are some of the statements given by the eyewitnesses." He pushed a few sheets of paper toward Mr. Chiu.

Mr. Chiu was dazed to see the different handwritings, which all stated that he had shouted in the square to attract attention and refused to obey the police. One of the witnesses had identified herself as a purchasing agent from a shipyard in Shanghai. Something stirred in Mr. Chiu's stomach, a pain rising to his ribs. He gave out a faint moan.

"Now, you have to admit you are guilty," the chief said. "Although it's a serious crime, we won't punish you severely, provided you write out a self-criticism and promise that you won't disrupt public order again. In other words, whether you will be released will depend on your attitude toward this crime."

"You're daydreaming," Mr. Chiu cried. "I won't write a word, because I'm innocent. I demand that you provide me with a letter of apology so I can explain to my university why I'm late."

Both the interrogators smiled with contempt. "Well, we've never done that," said the chief, taking a puff of his cigarette.

"Then make this a precedent."

"It's unnecessary. We are pretty certain that you will comply with our wishes." The chief blew a column of smoke at Mr. Chiu's face.

At the tilt of the chief's head, two guards stepped forward and grabbed the criminal by the arms. Mr. Chiu meanwhile went on saying, "I shall report you to the provincial administration. You'll have to pay for this! You are worse than the Japanese military police."

They dragged him out of the room.

After dinner, which consisted of a bowl of millet porridge, a corn bun, and a piece of pickled turnip, Mr. Chiu began to have a fever, shaking with a chill and sweating profusely. He knew that the fire of anger had got into his liver and that he was probably having a relapse. No medicine was available, because his briefcase had been left with his bride. At home it would have been time for him to sit in front of their color TV, drinking jasmine tea and watching the evening news. It was so lonesome in here. The orange bulb above the single bed was the only source of light, which enabled the guards to keep him under surveillance at night. A moment ago he had asked them for a newspaper or a magazine to read, but they had turned him down.

Through the small opening on the door, noises came in. It seemed that the police on duty were playing poker or chess in a nearby office; shouts and laughter could be heard now and then. Meanwhile, an accordion kept coughing from a remote corner of the building. Looking at the ballpoint and the letter paper left for him by the guards when they took him back from the Interrogation Bureau, Mr. Chiu remembered the old saying, "When a scholar runs into soldiers, the more he argues, the muddier his point becomes." How ridiculous this whole thing was. He ruffled his thick hair with his fingers.

He felt miserable, massaging his stomach continually. To tell the truth, he was more upset than frightened, because he would have to catch up with his work once he was back home—a paper that was to meet the publishing deadline next week, and two dozen books he ought to read for the courses he was going to teach in the fall.

A human shadow flitted across the opening. Mr. Chiu rushed to the door and shouted through the hole, "Comrade guard, comrade guard!"

"What do you want?" a voice rasped.

"I want you to inform your leaders that I'm very sick. I have heart disease and hepatitis. I may die here if you keep me like this without medication."

"No leader is on duty on the weekend. You have to wait till Monday."

"What? You mean I'll stay in here tomorrow?"

"Yes."

"Your station will be held responsible if anything happens to me."

"We know that. Take it easy, you won't die."

It seemed illogical that Mr. Chiu slept quite well that night, though the light above his head had been on all the time and the straw mattress was hard and infested with fleas. He was afraid of ticks, mosquitoes, cockroaches—any kind of insect but fleas and bedbugs. Once in the countryside, where his school's faculty and staff had helped the peasants harvest crops for a week, his colleagues had joked about his flesh, which they said must have tasted nonhuman to fleas. Except for him, they were all afflicted with hundreds of bites.

More amazing now, he felt he didn't miss his bride a lot. He even enjoyed sleeping alone, perhaps because the honeymoon had tired him out and he needed more rest.

The back yard was quiet on Sunday morning. Pale sunlight streamed through the pine branches. A few sparrows were jumping on the ground, catching caterpillars and ladybugs. Holding the steel bars, Mr. Chiu inhaled the morning air, which smelled meaty. There must be a restaurant or a delicatessen nearby. He reminded himself that he should take this detention with ease. A sentence that Chairman Mao had written to a hospitalized friend rose in his mind: "Since you are already in here, you may as well stay and make the best of it.

His desire for peace of mind originated from his fear that his hepatitis might get worse. He tried to remain unperturbed. However, he was sure that his liver was swelling up, since the fever still persisted. For a whole day he lay in bed, thinking about his paper on the nature of contradictions. Time and again he was overwhelmed by anger, cursing aloud, "A bunch of thugs!" He swore that once he was out, he would write an article about this experience. He had better find out some of the policemen's names.

It turned out to be a restful day for the most part; he was certain that his university would send somebody to his rescue. All he should do now was remain calm and wait patiently. Sooner or later the police would have to release him, although they had no idea that he might refuse to leave unless they wrote him an apology. Damn those hoodlums, they had ordered more than they could eat!

When he woke up on Monday morning, it was already light. Somewhere a man was moaning; the sound came from the back yard. After a long yawn, and kicking off the tattered blanket, Mr. Chiu climbed out of bed and went to the window. In the middle of the yard, a young man was fastened to a pine, his wrists handcuffed from behind around the trunk. He was wriggling and swearing loudly, but there was no sign of anyone else in the yard. He looked familiar to Mr. Chiu.

Mr. Chiu squinted his eyes to see who it was. To his astonishment, he recognized the man, who was Fenjin, a recent graduate from the Law Department at Harbin University. Two years ago Mr. Chiu had taught a course in Marxist materialism in which Fenjin had been enrolled. Now, how on earth had this young devil landed here?

Then it dawned on him that Fenjin must have been sent over by his bride. What a stupid woman! What a bookworm, who knew only how to read foreign novels. He had expected that she would talk to the school's security section, which would for sure send a cadre here. Fenjin held no official position; he merely worked in a private law firm that had just two lawyers; in fact, they had little business except for some detective work for men and women who suspected their spouses of having extramarital affairs. Mr. Chiu was overcome with a wave of nausea.

Should he call out to let his student know he was nearby? He decided not to, because he didn't know what had happened. Fenjin must have quarreled with the police to incur such a punishment. Yet this would not have occurred if Fenjin hadn't come to his rescue. So no matter what, Mr. Chiu had to do some thing. But what could he do?

It was going to be a scorcher. He could see purple steam shimmering and rising from the ground among the pines. Poor devil, he thought, as he raised a bowl of corn glue to his mouth, sipped, and took a bite of a piece of salted celery.

When a guard came to collect the bowl and the chopsticks, Mr. Chiu asked him what had happened to the man in the back yard. "He called our boss 'bandit,'" the guard said. "He claimed he was a lawyer or something. An arrogant son of a rabbit."

Now it was obvious that Mr. Chiu had to do something to help his rescuer. Before he could figure out a way, a scream broke out in the back yard. He rushed to the window and saw a tall policeman standing before Fenjin, an iron bucket on the ground. It was the same young fellow who had arrested Mr. Chiu in the square two days before. The man pinched Fenjin's nose, then raised his hand, which stayed in the air for a few seconds, then slapped the lawyer across the face. As Fenjin was groaning, the man lifted up the bucket and poured water on his head.

"This will keep you from getting sunstroke, boy. I'll give you some more every hour," the man said loudly.

Fenjin kept his eyes shut, yet his wry face showed that he was struggling to hold back from cursing the policeman or that he was probably sobbing in silence. He sneezed, then raised his face and shouted, "Let me go take a piss."

"Oh yeah?" the man bawled. "Pee in your pants."

Still Mr. Chiu didn't make any noise, holding the steel bars with both hands, his fingers white. The policeman turned and glanced at the cell's window; his pistol, partly holstered, glittered in the sun. With a snort he spat his cigarette butt to the ground and stamped it into the dust.

Then the cell door opened and the guards motioned Mr. Chiu to come out. Again they took him upstairs to the Interrogation Bureau.

The same men were in the office, though this time the scribe was sitting there empty-handed. At the sight of Mr. Chiu the chief said, "Ah, here you are. Please be seated."

After Mr. Chiu sat down, the chief waved a white silk fan and said to him, "You may have seen your lawyer. He's a young man without manners, so our director had him taught a crash lesson in the back yard."

"It's illegal to do that. Aren't you afraid to appear in a newspaper?"

"No, we are not, not even on TV. What else can you do? We are not afraid of any story you make up. We call it fiction. What we do care is that you cooperate with us; that's to say, you must admit your crime."

"What if I refuse to cooperate?"

"Then your lawyer will continue his education in the sunshine."

A swoon swayed Mr. Chiu, and he held the arms of the chair to steady himself. A numb pain stung him in the upper stomach and nauseated him, and his head was throbbing. He was sure that the hepatitis was finally attacking him. Anger was flaming up in his chest. His throat was tight and clogged.

The chief resumed, "As a matter of fact, you don't have to write out your self-criticism. We had your crime described clearly here. What we need is just your signature."

Holding back his rage, Mr. Chiu said, "Let me look at that."

With a smirk the donkey-faced man handed him a sheet, which carried these words: "I hereby admit that on July 13 I disrupted public order at Muji Train Station, and that I refused to listen to reason when the railroad police issued their warning. Thus I myself am responsible for my arrest. After two days' detention, I have realized the reactionary nature of my crime. From now on, I shall continue to educate myself with all my effort and shall never commit this kind of crime again."

A voice started screaming in Mr. Chiu's head, "Lie, lie!" But he shook his head and forced the voice away. He asked the chief, "If I sign this, will you release both my lawyer and me?"

"Of course, we'll do that." The chief was drumming his fingers on the blue folder—their file on him.

Mr. Chiu signed his name and put his thumbprint under his signature.

"Now you are free to go," the chief said with a smile, and handed him a piece of paper to wipe his thumb with.

Mr. Chiu was so sick that he didn't stand up from the chair at the first try. Then he doubled his effort and rose to his feet. He staggered out of the building to meet his lawyer in the back yard. In his chest he felt as though there were a bomb. If he were able to, he would have razed the entire police station and eliminated all their families. Though he knew he could do nothing like that, he made up his mind to do something.

"Sorry about this torture, Fenjin," Mr. Chiu said when they met.

"It doesn't matter. They are savages." The lawyer brushed a patch of dirt off his jacket with his trembling fingers. Water was still dribbling from the bottoms of his trouser legs.

"Let's go now," the teacher said.

The moment they came out of the police station, Mr. Chiu caught sight of a tea stand. He grabbed Fenjin's arm and walked over to the old woman at the table. "Two bowls of black tea," he said, and handed her a one-yuan note.

After the first bowl, they each had another one. Then they set out for the train station. But before they walked fifty yards, Mr. Chiu insisted on eating a bowl of tree-ear soup at a food stand. Fenjin agreed. He told his teacher, "Don't treat me like a guest."

"No, I want to eat something myself."

As if dying of hunger, Mr. Chiu dragged his lawyer from restaurant to restaurant near the police station, but at each place he ordered no more than two bowls of food. Fenjin wondered why his teacher wouldn't stay at one place and eat his fill.

Mr. Chiu bought noodles, wonton, eight-grain porridge, and chicken soup, respectively, at four restaurants. While eating, he kept saying through his teeth, "If only I could kill all the bastards!" At the last place he merely took a few sips of the soup without tasting the chicken cubes and mushrooms.

Fenjin was baffled by his teacher, who looked ferocious and muttered to himself mysteriously, and whose jaundiced face was covered with dark puckers. For the first time Fenjin thought of Mr. Chiu as an ugly man.

Within a month, over eight hundred people contracted acute hepatitis in Muji. Six died of the disease, including two children. Nobody knew how the epidemic had started.

STELLA POPE DUARTE

Formal English instruction began for me in grade school. This was at a time when ESL/BLE programs were non-existent. The old adage of "sink or swim" was in effect, and I observed that only a handful of students truly learned to swim, that is to succeed in American culture, while many others sank to the bottom of the economic ladder. The educational system was dictating English to us and shaming us for speaking Spanish, our native language. In fact, at my school, we were given demerits, and even sent home if we were caught speaking Spanish. This posed a huge problem, as my parents, although born and raised in the United States, were native Spanish speakers, and were limited in their ability to speak English. They felt alienated from the school culture, which, in opposing their language, made it impossible for them to communicate their views openly and without fear. I still recall my mother with tears in her eyes, begging me not to teach my children Spanish, as they would suffer ill treatment at school. This has caused great sorrow in me, for in obeying her request, my children lost the beauty of Spanish, which beat in my mother's heart. All the stories she knew in her native language were never told to her grandchildren. Not being able to communicate freely with my mother, my children were robbed of the deepest part of who she was, the inmost part of her where her words gave way to thoughts, ideas, and longings of the soul.

In *Fragile Night*, my first collection of short stories, I often use a mix of English and Spanish, sometimes described in the Southwest as Spanglish. My characters emerge from my experiences as a Chicana/Latina woman, then begin to take form as they embark on adventures of the heart and soul, often clashing with mainstream, Anglo-American culture. It is important to note that my characters always arise from images secured from my culture, and share their world with others from their own distinct, cultural perspective. I am anticipating the translation of *Fragile Night* in subsequent releases, first in Spanish, then in other languages as well.

I have written mainly educational material in Spanish, but have not carried the formal use of Spanish into other writing projects. English remains the stronger language for me, as it is the one that dominated my education. I have grown to love literature in English; however, invariably I turn to multicultural authors who are most aligned with my views of the world. In my presentations and readings I use a bilingual format, thus enriching my work with words and dialogue that draw people of all cultures to a better understanding of myself as a woman who seeks to lift up the human experience by way of language.

I was pleasantly surprised last year, as I studied Vietnamese, to learn that the Vietnamese alphabet is Latin-based. When I visited Saigon, Vietnam later that year to complete research for my first novel, it was a wonder how many words and sounds were familiar to me because I spoke Spanish. It is my opinion that my experiences as a native Spanish speaker have opened the way for me to accept other languages, and have freed me to live in harmony and joy with people from every walk of life.

Homage

There was a time last year when I stared at my checkbook and noticed I was overdrawn by eighty dollars. Imagine, overdrawn by eighty dollars after all the penny pinching I do. I wondered how much the penalties would be. The struggle for money took up a good part of my thinking and caused most of my headaches.

Walking to work every morning only served to remind me of my impoverished condition. Rushing between parked cars at the state capitol building, I made my way to my job, filing manuscripts that detailed the crimes of society's rejects in the basement of the Attorney General's office.

Most mornings I saw at least two Mercedes, one Lexus and what looked like a Porsche, which might have been another foreign car, for all I knew. There was a part of me that wanted to run my fingernail file across the shiny, slick surface of the yellow Mercedes parked at the entrance to the building. I looked around the parking lot to assure myself that no one was around and actually reached for my nail file, only to stop my hand in midair. They've got insurance, I thought, a few scratches won't matter. My damage would be minimal and at most they'd upgrade their car's security system. As it is, cars talk if you dare touch them. Their horns blare and whine like ambulances. They threaten would-be criminals with statements like, "Stand ten paces away from the vehicle," and record theft attempts in microscopic cameras loaded in their tail lights. All this while they sit motionless between painted lines in the parking lot. The twenty-first century is truly amazing!

"The rich get richer," said Amy, as we both reached for the same chocolate donut at break time.

"Who bought the donuts?" I asked.

"Who knows, probably some fat cat, with money to spare."

I thought of the Hostess cupcake I had paid seventy-nine cents for at the Circle K.

"Highway robbery the way prices are hiked up these days," I said. "What are these people thinking? Have they no mercy on the downtrodden?"

"Downtrodden?" asked Amy, gulping down her Pepsi. "Where did you get that word?"

"I looked it up in a the-sau-rus," I said, pronouncing the word carefully. I knew Amy had flunked reading in school. Her work at the Attorney General's office consisted of stuffing envelopes with summonses for upcoming hearings.

"Poor devils," Amy said as we sat together at a long metal table after our break. She was looking at an especially thick mailing, and weighing it up and down in her pudgy hands. "Wonder how much this will cost them?" she asked.

"More than they make," I answered. "They'll probably have to hock everything they have to pay attorney's fees and put their kids in an orphanage. I hope they have rich relatives."

"Or a ticket out of the country," added Amy. She was obviously smarter than I thought.

Amy and I always worked surrounded by inanimate objects. Looming over us were shelves of files that reached up to the ceiling. Row upon row of look-alike manila folders stood side by side, some leaning right, some leaning left. Murderers, rapists, potheads, pimps, drunk drivers, a whole array of scumbags shared the shelves, each with a story to tell. Of course, no one was guilty. Everything was circumstance, a frame-up. Someone was mistaken. Somebody was scared into confessing to a lie. The mafia had sent a dead fish to a juror, who then voted for acquittal. A hysterical bystander waved her finger in the air and it landed on the face of a totally innocent citizen, whose case was now three years old and still in court waiting for appeals. By the time the criminal gained due process, the victim had died of natural causes and the key witness had succumbed to Alzheimer's, making his testimony invalid in a court of law.

The Great American Dream was something I put in my back pocket everytime I looked up at the stacks of papers waiting for Amy and me to file. Almost every page was stamped CONFIDENTIAL. I ran my fingers over the word, as I read detailed information of crimes that beat the best action on TV.

Suspect was apprehended on 5th and Central and proceeded to climb a light pole to make his escape. Now, how smart was that? *Suspect stated that she did not know the gun was loaded when she fired a full round of shots at the victim.* I found out by reading into the case that the "victim" was none other than her ex-husband, who had fifty counts of domestic violence filed on him. When I saw pictures of his bloodied body, I felt little compassion, since I figured he had it coming.

"Amy, ever think that we're getting immune to right and wrong?" I asked.

"Immune?"

"You know, like we don't give a shit one way or another."

"We don't have much choice working in a place like this," she responded. Another point for Amy, I thought. I looked carefully at her and wondered if she had been zapped by electricity from a cracked cord the night before. Her hair still looked straight, so whatever had zapped her had caused minimal damage.

"I had my eyebrows done," she said, taking off her thick glasses to show me the curving arches of her eyebrows, minus stray hairs. Eyebrows were Amy's thing and she had them professionally waxed and trimmed twice a month. It was a pity I couldn't see her brows behind her glasses. The lenses acted like a reverse pyramid, causing her eyes to look shrunken. I felt I was looking from the base of a pyramid to its point, far away in the distance.

"Nice job," I said. To myself I asked the question: Why would a woman who was 150 pounds overweight bother to have her eyebrows done? One more conjecture: Who cares? We worked as slaves for a buzzing, corporate mongrel of dead-beat clients and wiser-than-thou, preppy-babes who walked through the jungle of paper wads and unre-turned phone messages like a herd of elephants eating their way across the landscape. The dead-beats felt dwarfed by the pompous splendor of diamond rings, Rolex watches, duplicates of degrees summa cum laude hanging on the walls, and exacting, manicured nails.

Now there was something I could identity with. Fingernails. Fingernails intrigued me. Amy had her eyebrows, I had my fingernails. I scrounged up money every week, by adding water to the dishwashing liquid so I wouldn't have to buy a new bottle, lining the garbage can with newspaper so I wouldn't have to buy garbage bags, and throwing all the clothes into the washer at the same time to avoid wasting laun-dry soap. It all worked together somehow. The kids only got mad when something red turned everything pink and they had to suffer for a week with pink T-shirts while the color faded. It was worth it when I saw my French-made acrylic nails, polished to perfection, poised over the word CONFIDENTIAL. They looked like they belonged to someone else, one of the preppy-babes, for instance. I felt justified in doing my nails because I, at least, could see them, and Amy had no way of looking at her eye-brows, except through the eyes of others.

Taking a deep breath before rising to start filing, I heard the swoosh of the elevator.

"Someone's coming to our dungeon," I said. Amy smiled. I liked to make her smile because the rolls of fat around her throat all moved col-lectively, like a kaleidoscope of human flesh.

"It's Mr. Jenkins," Amy said, importantly.

"So what," I said.

Amy put her index finger up to her lips. "Shhh..."

"Hello ladies—are you down there?"

His voice reached us before we saw him. "Where else would we be?" I answered.

"Sandra, quit. You'll get us in trouble," Amy said.

"My, my," said Jenkins as he walked into our cage. "I had no idea you had this much to do."

"Mr. Jenkins, if you only knew," I said. His crew cut bristled a bit as I said the words.

"Uh, Ms. Gomez, isn't it?"

"I've been called better," I said, extending my hand to shake his. I made sure my nails tapped his palm lightly. "It's my ex's name."

"You *do* speak Spanish, don't you Ms. Gomez?" he asked.

"I've got a handle on the language," I said. Amy's eyes opened wider, and I actually saw some of the smooth flesh right below her eyebrows.

"Could I impose on you a bit, Ms. Gomez?" he asked, looking a little startled. He gazed at me from between the stacks of papers piled at each end of the table.

"Name your game," I said. Amy stifled a gasp.

Jenkins looked into my eyes, then away. "Well, it's actually a matter of translating. I've got a couple of clients in my office who only speak Spanish. I wonder if you would do the honors?"

"Honors?"

"Uh, I mean, would you come in and translate?"

"What happened to Mr. Ramirez?" I asked. "I thought he did all your translating."

"Actually, he was apprehended for drunk driving last night, and well—as you know, the laws are pretty strict about things like that.

"In other words, he's in the can," I said.

"To put it bluntly, Ms. Gomez, yes."

"Then I *will* do the honors," I said. "I'm good about helping my people that way."

As we walked to the elevator, I whispered to Amy, "Stop shaking, he's only probate." I winked at her and she slid her glasses back up her nose.

"Probate?" she asked. I knew the old Amy was still alive.

I felt Jenkins giving me the up-and-down when we were in the elevator. Scum, I thought, probably uses his job to pick up women.

"I don't believe we've ever met before," he said.

"Belief, Mr. Jenkins, is more an attitude than a fact, if I may be so bold."

"Very reflective of you." Jenkins looked at me like I had wet varnish all over my clothes.

I kicked off one of my shoes as we made our way to the twelfth floor.

"I hate these shoes," I said. "I don't know why I wear heels. My feet are deformed, Mr. Jenkins. Bunions, you know. My mother never had enough money to send me to a podiatrist."

"She must have sent you somewhere. Your vocabulary's wonderful!"

"I'm a self-starter, Mr. Jenkins. I had to be. In a family of ten kids, it's dog-eat-dog to get to the dinner table. You move fast or you end up with crumbs, or somebody's leftovers. The weak don't survive in a world like that."

"I should say not. You should be proud that you made it out of there."

"Not proud, Mr. Jenkins, appreciative that I knew when my mother served dinner."

Jenkins laughed out loud, his shoulders shaking vigorously. "You are truly refreshing, Ms. Gomez."

"In a world like this, it doesn't take much," I said.

We walked leisurely into Jenkins' office, which was plastered wall to wall with photos of him playing golf, skiing, riding a horse, and standing next to a clown in a scene that looked like it had been clipped from *The Wizard of Oz*. The office was permeated with the smell of hardwood mixed with the dank odor of overstuffed furniture. I knew Jenkins had brought in his own decor to impress the seamy side of society. Furniture the state had issued was what Amy and I sat on downstairs in the basement.

In one of the plush, leather chairs sat a middle-aged woman. Her graying hair was swept back into a neat bun, and enormous gold loops hung at her ears. She was neatly dressed in a black pantsuit and a pair of sandals. Opposite her sat a man with brown, curly hair, a western shirt, Levi's, and boots. All that's missing is the cowboy hat, I thought, then noticed the hat tucked under the chair. A Mexican Tex Ritter. He gave me the up-and-down, like Jenkins.

Jenkins introduced us all around. I shook hands with Señora Rivas, and her brother Efrain Gutierrez.

"Sit here, Ms. Gomez," said Jenkins leading me to a straight-backed chair. My rotten luck. The only time I had gone into one of the attorney's offices and I had to sit on a chair that had no give. I arranged my hands on my plaid skirt and noticed how the lavender polish contrasted boldly with the greens and browns of the fabric.

"Now, where shall we begin?" asked Jenkins.

"The beginning would be a good start," I said. Jenkins leaned back in his chair, smiling broadly.

"OK, this is the deal. Their mother owned the property currently in probate, which sits in what is called Las Coo-atro Milpas."

"Las Cuatro Milpas," I corrected. "The four cornfields."

"Anyway, their parents bought the land on, or around, 1930. Father died several years ago, mother died last year. There is no will to designate a legal owner and there are three thousand dollars of back taxes owing on the property."

I translated the grim facts to Señora Rivas. She gasped in surprise. She glared at her brother, asking him what happened to the money she had sent to pay the taxes. His eyes shifted nervously and he reached for his hat under the chair. He held it in his lap, fingering the rim. Her voice rose several pitches before he looked at her and simply told her he had needed it. War would have broken out, except Jenkins was there to quell the impending disaster. If I had had it my way, I would have voted for letting Señora Rivas go for her brother's throat.

"Ask them about a will," he said.

"*Un testamento? Hay un testamento?*" I asked.

At this, Señora Rivas produced a crinkled piece of paper folded into several squares. She handed it to me and I noticed that it was the remains of an ancient paper bag. I held up the parchment to the light and finally made out the faint outline of words written in an elegant scrawl. The message designated Anna Maria Gutierrez as the legal owner of the property. She pointed to herself as the same person named in the document.

"I can't accept this," said Jenkins in frustration. "What kind of a fool do they take me for?"

"It's signed by her mother," I said.

"How do you know?"

"*Esta es la firma de su mamá?*" I asked Señora Rivas. She attested that it was, and pointed out the signature of the local priest who had witnessed the event.

"A priest signed as a witness," I said. "What more do you need? Would a priest lie?"

"I'm not in a position to prove things true or false at this point, Ms. Gomez. I'm simply trying to get at the facts. I don't think this paper will be admissible in court."

"Why?" I asked angrily. "Because it's not written on a word processor? They were poor. That's all they had to write on. It's a legal document."

"Nobody'll buy that," Jenkins said. "Besides, they owe back taxes and I doubt they can come up with the amount."

"Are you telling me they're gonna lose their property for three thousand dollars?" I sensed my heart beginning to thump. "You haven't even asked them if they can come up with the money."

"Obviously they can't," he said flatly.

"How dare you make assumptions you can't prove!" I accused loudly. "What's so precious about a measly piece of land in a barrio, anyway? There's gotta be a gimmick."

"The state wants the land to build the new baseball stadium," Jenkins said. "Their property will be condemned and turned over to state officials."

"I knew it!" I said. "I knew this was bourgeois stuff!"

Tension in the room was high. By this time, I had forgotten all about my nails and was ready to crack the phone receiver on Jenkins's head, thus ending my days as a translator.

"There's loopholes for *everything*," I said, punctuating the last word. "Loopholes as big as hula hoops. You know it as well as I do." Jenkins looked solemnly at the document before him, as if he were studying an Egyptian scroll. After squinting and frowning for a few seconds, his eyes lit up like he had just discovered the tomb of King Tut's twin brother.

"You know, Ms. Gomez, because you're so gutsy, I'm gonna help them," he said brightly.

"Don't pay homage to my guts, Mr. Jenkins."

"There is absolutely no understanding you, Ms. Gomez!" Jenkins said in exasperation. "What is it you want?"

"Why don't you try paying homage to honesty, integrity, and sleeping at night with a clear conscience," I said. "Traditional things?"

"Are you telling me that I've bought into the system?"

"Get a clue, Mr. Jenkins, you're on the other side of the desk, I'm not."

"I haven't bought into the whole thing, I can guarantee you that!"

"Prove it," I challenged.

"Tell them I'll help them."

I related the news to Señora Rivas and her sidekick. They were elated. Señora Rivas got up from her chair and swung around the desk to hug Jenkins and kiss the top of his crewcut. Her brother shook his hand and blew me a kiss.

"See, without your act of benevolence you would have missed this display of gratitude," I said.

"*Dile que no le va poder*," said Señora Rivas.

"The lady says you won't regret this," I translated. "That means get ready for tamales every Friday. You *do* like tamales, don't you?"

"I've lived in the Southwest all my life, of course I do."

"Then you've got it made in the shade," I said.

Jenkins smiled again and stood up as happy as Señora Rivas and her brother.

"Doing anything after work, Ms. Gomez?" he asked, as his clients walked out of the office.

I knew he was scum when I first laid eyes on him. Picks up women every chance he gets. Wait 'til I tell Amy.

"Not much," I said. "What about yourself?"

MIKHAIL IOSSEL

I started writing in English, some thirteen years ago, because (in no particular order):

A:...it was there, Everest-high (or rather, here)—just where I was (and still am); surrounding me on all sides...while the world of unbroken Russian all of a sudden had become much too geographically remote (not to mention, politically forbidding and emotionally overcharged) for a regular commute. (I probably would not be living in upstate New York—beautiful Schenectady, the Venice of the Capital region!—if the college where I teach had been located in Minnesota or Mississippi, for instance. Right?...Although this may not be too good an example, I'm afraid. Oh well...)

B:...when in Rome, write (if write you must; if you fancy yourself a writer) in the language that the Romans at least can understand. Which is to say, write in English. The Romans, en masse, tend not to know any (or many) foreign languages. (What? What? What'd I say? I'm not knocking my fellow Romans, I'm just making a factually correct observation!) They tend not to read too much of so-called "serious" (read: generally, lacking a gripping plot) fiction (or non-fiction), either—so it's a pretty safe bet that the great majority of them will give as wide a berth as possible to some unpronounceably named, dinky little Eastern-European émigré's gut-wrenching semi-autobiographical tale of (and—a fairly credible assumption here) suffering, courage and redemption. But even one reader, from amongst the book-reading Romans' ever-dwindling number, is better than none—and none is exactly the number you're going to get, my friend, if you continue to persist in your masochistic attachment to your native language in this literature-crazed land, America.

C:...I felt that, to paraphrase Samuel Beckett's apocryphal response to the same question (and the same situation, roughly—only his switch was from English to French, instead of from Russian to English...duh!; and he was forty-six years old, and not thirty-one; and he already was Beckett, while I was still and already...Ah! Better not go there—too painful), I knew too many words in Russian. Too many—for my own psychological comfort, as they say in this country. Too many words—too many word choices. (Too many synonyms! Too many verbal chiaroscuros!) Too many word choices —too much wasted time. Too much wasted time—well, too much wasted time. Too much needless existential agony, wallowing in self-pity, "remembering and not-forgetting" kind of stuff, heartache and sleeplessness, sheer hopelessness, inexplicable mortal fear of open spaces, and what have you. All that stupid nonsense. The last thing a nostalgia-besotted, half-mad-with-grief émigré writer needs is dealing with his life, the sum total of his losses to date, in a language which, instead of distancing him from his past (his beautiful, typically idyllic Soviet past...as soft and rosy-toned as a feminine-hygiene product TV-commercial) and bringing this damned past to some kind of proverbial closure (whatever ugly form this latter might assume), keeps further stirring it up, rehashing it...simply by dint of being an integral part of his past and constantly reminding you of it! If you're trying to get over an unfaithful lover, it makes no sense to keep her photo in your wallet! And you don't want to work (as it were) with, or in, a language that encourages your real or imagined suffering, instead of objectifying and estranging it, making it seem foreign; you need a Plexiglas wall of a foreign language for that. A foreign language you don't know well enough to allow yourself to lose sight of the story you're purporting to tell, by letting it wander aimlessly, for pages on end, in a narrow maze of complex sentences. (But a foreign language you know well enough to be able to use it for your story-telling purposes, of course. Unlike Beckett, I could not have started writing in French, for instance. I just don't know French! Ditto— German, Spanish, Greek, Estonian, and every other language on the planet. So be it. I accept the breathtaking scope of my writerly limitations. I'm cool with it, as they say. You have to make do with what you've got, in terms of your vocabulary and your intuitive feel for the foreign idiom. And no, you cannot always get what you want, when you're finished with a story in a foreign language—but sometimes, fortunately, you wouldn't know it...because you don't know the language well enough always to be able to tell the difference between a triumph and a failure.)

D:...because, too...well, no; I cannot think of the D "because" right now. (But I know there was a D, as well as an E, F, G, H, I...There were many, many—oh, many!— weighty rationales behind my decision to start writing in English, back some thirteen years ago. Sure there were. I'm pretty sure of that.)

Every Hunter Wants to Know

In 1968, when I was thirteen and unhappy, I wrote a story that could have won the prestigious inter-high school literary contest, "Leningrad Teenage Creative Spring." It was called "Kavgolovo" and was about a six year old's first journey into the woods on a mushroom hunt. Our literature teacher had always insisted that writing should be based on personal experience rather than on the power of imagination, and she judged and graded us in accordance with what she perceived as the honesty of our recollections. "Kavgolovo" was an autobiographical story. The reason it didn't win that contest was that shortly before the deadline I changed my mind and submitted another story, "A Fiery Engine," instead. It dealt with a six year old's growing up in Leningrad, his dreamlike childhood memories, his quiet, precocious fascination with the world of words (books!), and an episode of his getting lost—and nearly killed—while marching down Leningrad's main street chanting "We're Number One!" and "We've Made It!" in an exultant crowd celebrating Yuri Gagarin's space flight. Yuri Gagarin was the first man ever to orbit the Earth.

I remember staring at the two stories sitting on the table in front of me. I felt good. By going almost as far back as I could, I seemed to have begun to grapple with the infinite number of my vastly unaccounted for early childhood memories. I also remember being in doubt. "A Fiery Engine" was less autobiographical than "Kavgolovo," but I hoped that our literature teacher would find it more authentic. She knew my family: we were Jewish. Jewish people in Russia usually stay away from the woods.

There are exceptions, of course. One of my grandmothers had always been different. Both she and her older brother, a prominent theoretician in the cellulose industry who drowned swimming in a small northern river in 1968, had always felt out of place in the city. Strong, broadshouldered, rugged, they were inveterate mushroom gatherers. Neither of them spent much time reading like the rest of our family. Just about the only book I remember my grandmother reading in Kavgolovo (a village near Leningrad) was *The Mushroom Gatherer's Guide*. Published in 1940, it was full of color pictures. I remember looking at them, wondering if a real mushroom looked even half as good. That was a long time ago, in 1961.

The words "mushroom gatherer" (*gribnik*) and "guide, fellow traveller" (*sputnik*) were pitted against one another to form the title in deep red on the blackish cover of my grandmother's book: *Gribnik's Sputnik*. The two words sounded alike, toylike. I couldn't help but associate them with our Soviet Sputnik Number One, that bright, speedy red-hot dot in the sky of 1957, when I was two years old. It could be seen with the naked eye every night that October. But I don't remember actually seeing it then. I remember looking at the sky. I was standing on the kitchen windowsill, my plump feet clasped tightly by two old women from our communal apartment. I strained my eyes in a futile attempt to glimpse the pulsing Sputnik in the sky. Everyone else could see it. "Look, it's right there!" the old women said, pointing. Their heads shook with old age and wonderment. They were almost blind. Everyone was watching, either in the kitchen or in the courtyard six stories below. Our family was in the kitchen, but not my *gribnik* grandmother: it was early October and the woods around Leningrad were still teeming with late mushrooms. Everyone cheered and laughed. One of the hands squeezing my foot was ugly, covered with six furry moles. Slow transparent balloons soared and floated in the sky. Two jars with blackberry preserves sat on the windowsill to the left of my feet. Strings of dried mushrooms dangled above my head. "Can't you see it?" the old women kept saying. "It's right up there, on archangel Gabriel's wing!" They laughed, delighted. "Don't confuse the boy!" my mother said from the darkness behind. The women giggled. Down below, the invisible cheering crowd screamed, stomping their feet, pushing, shoving, squeezing, hugging each other. The air was thick with love. "Sputnik! Sputnik!" someone shouted. That couldn't have been long before a curly-tailed huskie named Laika (or was it Belka, or Strelka?) was shot into space. She never returned. I was three years old and learning how to read. I remember her pug-nosed profile on a soft white and blue pocket-size pack of cheap cigarettes; her name was printed beneath her picture in black letters. I remember wishing I were dead instead of that dog. I envied her fame. She was dead, but famous. She was Number One. The importance that people then attached to one's having done something first—coming in first, dying first—seemed to have deeply impressed me. It was like a deep thirst, this national quest for greatness.

In the summer of the year when smiling Yuri Gagarin was the first man to orbit the Earth, I was six and lived in Kavgolovo, twenty miles from Leningrad. It was a beautiful place. The grandmother-*gribnik* never traveled far away from Leningrad and couldn't stand suburban resorts like Kratovo, a quiet town near Moscow that I don't remember well. I know, however, that we rented a summer house there too, twice. But that's another story altogether. It has nothing to do with mushrooms, or with Gagarin's space flight.

There's a difference between the woods around Moscow and those around Leningrad. The former are less rugged and, like Anton Chekhov, more sadly joyous. Waking up near Moscow, first thing in the morning I would see the green wave of leaves casting uneven shadows on the bedsheets. Tiny, neatly carved, they trembled outside the open window, dripping with fresh green daybreak. Kavgolovo mornings, on the other hand, began with a long branchful of fir needles sharp against the blue sky and solemnly standing like the guards at Lenin's tomb in the Red Square. The moment I woke up I'd forget my dream. Sometimes it would repeat the following night, and then I would recall it, and, of course, forget it again. I developed a habit of screaming in my sleep, rousing myself with a thin wail early in the morning, even if my dream had been good. Everyone in the house would wake up too, shake their heads, and go back to sleep. At one point the doctor had to be consulted. He told my mother that there was nothing wrong with me: unconscious screaming seemed to be my way of coping with growing up. "Sounds fancy," the *gribnik*-grandmother's brother said disapprovingly. For a six year old, I was extremely high-strung.

People lived in every room of the Kavgolovo house: an old unmarried woman who owned it, my mother, my grandmother, her older brother, my toddler brother, and my cousins, Grandmother's brother's two adult sons. My father came down from Leningrad every Sunday (Saturday was still a working day). At night, they all gathered for tea in the living room. The house was full of people. And yet, it was surprisingly silent. Of all the people who were there that summer, I most clearly remember myself.

It was the end of August, days before what is called in Russian "womenfolk's summer"—Indian summer, autumn. Grandmother and her brother had been waiting for rain. They kept looking at the sky, but it was as blue as ever. Then, one morning, the rain began, a sudden shower, full of light; it continued through the afternoon. It was a "mushroom rain": golden threads ran smoothly along the beams of sun. It was, I already knew, a good omen. Russian tradition would expect you to dance barefoot in such a rain. I was sitting in the room I shared with Grandmother, looking out the window at the owner of the house's barking dog, Zhuk, who was four years younger than me. I was six. I knew that everyone expected me, the child, to rush out into the yard, so I decided to stay inside.

"Aren't you bored in there? Come outside!" Grandmother beckoned to me from the yard. She was looking up, smiling. I shook my head, but she wasn't looking at me. The dog kept barking. My mother put aside the magazine she was reading, left the porch and cautiously stepped into the rain. She laughed.

Grandmother's brother, chuckling, walked outside too, stretching and yawning, pretending that he had business to attend to in the yard. My cousins were playing with the dog. The owner of the house brought out two empty buckets to fill with rainwater. Soon everyone was outside. The rain, still benevolently sun-streaked, grew stronger. "Where's Zheka?" my mother asked. Then she saw me in the window and waved. "Come dance with us!" she called. Grandmother turned to her brother and his sons: "Tomorrow? What do you think?" They thought for a moment and seriously nodded their heads.

"Take him with you," my mother said.

Everyone looked up at me. "If he promises not to get lost," Grandmother said.

"Don't scare the boy!" said my mother.

"If he doesn't step on an old German mine and get blown up!" my cousins added, laughing.

"If he doesn't get scared and start screaming and ruin everything," Grandmother's brother said.

"I'm never scared!" I shouted back.

"Well, then, get a good night's sleep," Grandmother told me. Everyone smiled at me. I thought...but I don't remember what I thought. Then I thought: "How can one not get a good night's sleep?" It was pleasant to be a child and feel smug. I imagined the quiet, giant, slippery mushrooms secretly growing deep in the woods, under wet layers of old pine needles.

It was still early; too early to start thinking about night. There were many long days in each day. The day between dinner and supper was a day. Evening was a day, too. Grandmother would usually go to bed very late.

That Kavgolovo afternoon, 1961, there was a sharp smell of damp hay in the air. Thick light, the color of warm tree sap, poured into the room. The rain dragged on, the yard now empty. I was reading and writing. My room was cozy and austere, like a chronicler's cell: a chair and a table, an open window. Nestor (d.o.b. unknown–died c. 1115), a Russian monk who reputedly wrote the Chronicles of Nestor, must have seen the same serene presunset landscape from his monastery window: docile hills and green grass, smooth under the rain. I had read about him—and seen his picture: long sad nose, a black cassock, a skull-cap—in the *Abridged Soviet Encyclopedia* published in 1954. Its three black volumes now sat on the table in front of me, along with the notebook with my name written in angular block letters on the cover and a king-size, lemonade-stained book, *Masterpieces of the Italian Renaissance*, an incomplete collection of black-and-white reproductions. I had the first volume of the encyclopedia opened to the letter "A." With my father's fountain pen, I entered into the notebook the birthdates and deaths of the most prominent people. The fame of each was reflected by the size of the corresponding picture—or its absence. All of them had been involved in some undertaking of the creative spirit and had been known for their progressive ideas. They were revolutionary writers, philosophers, innovative and unorthodox thinkers—the immortals, like Abai Kunanbayev (1845–1904), prominent Kazakh storyteller *(akyn)* and educator, ardent proponent of closer ties between Kazakhstan and Russia; or Khachatur Abovyan (1805–1848), Armenian revolutionary pedagogue and writer; or Martin Andersen-Nekso̸ (b. 1869–still alive as of 1954), a writer of the Danish proletariat. I had been working on "A" for weeks. I was not a fast reader and writer.

I remember feeling good about myself—not just proud because I was the only six year old I knew who had been studying the encyclopedia. Of course, that, too, was important, but I remember thinking that my work had a purpose: to learn the names of all the great people who had ever lived, and to try to find a key to their greatness, or whatever it was that had enabled them to get their names and pictures printed in the encyclopedia. There was a pleasure in counting down the greats, drawing closer to the end of the first letter of the alphabet and—ultimately— to the end of the final volume. It was hard work, too. I wanted all those people sorted out and locked under the cover of my notebook. The dates of their births and deaths, their lives replaced by a short dash seemed to tell me reassuringly: "There's no rush! Relax! You've got all the time in the world!" But, of course, I didn't feel reassured. I didn't have all the time in the world. Time had no meaning whatsoever. Ever since I had learned how to read, I had become more and more frustrated by the sheer abundance of books sitting on the shelves in our Leningrad room. There were hundreds, thousands of them! I remember opening them at random, one by one. Their number seemed infinite. I was keenly aware of the fact that by the time I would be finished with one, there would be thousands of new books added to the number of those already existing in the world. It drove me crazy. How about the fifty-odd volumes of the *Great Soviet Encyclopedia?* How about the complete collection of Leo Tolstoy's works? How about Vladimir Ilyich Lenin's two shelves' worth? I was beginning to suspect that one could easily and forever drown in books and that life was too short for both reading and becoming as great and famous as, for instance, Nestor, who had chosen to write about his life instead of living it, or that poor old Kunanbayev with his goatee. Reading alone, I was afraid, couldn't make one great. What, then, was it good for? I didn't know. If someone had asked me if I'd rather be alive, knowing I'd never get into the encyclopedia, or die now and immediately be made immortally famous, I wouldn't hesitate to make my choice. And yet, it had already crossed my mind that the time would come when I would realize that the dead are always at a disadvantage.

Soon I got tired and put down the pen. The rain had stopped—and changed the view from my window. I started daydreaming. The empty yard, encircled by a black picket fence where an angry Kavgolovo raven grimly perched, gave way to a ravine. The wind was warm. Lamblike clouds, reflected in the silver river, moved across the timeless sky with considerable speed. Clusters of trees were scattered over the green hills. I was not imagining them. Imagining things was a waste of time. I was in my Kavgolovo room, looking at a picture in a book on the table in front of me. Then I looked up again. The view perfectly matched one of the reproductions from the *Masterpieces of the Italian Renaissance*—a heavy tome with the many pictures of naked men and women missing (Grandmother must have ripped them out)—namely, "The Old Man and His Grandson," by Domenico Ghirlandajo. In the background, behind the faces of an old man and a young boy, was a ravine and a silver snake of a river. Medieval Italy looked amazingly like Kavgolovo.

Whenever I opened that book, touching with my fingers the remaining fragile pages that were carefully separated by rustling rice paper, it occurred to me that I might be the only six year old in Kavgolovo who was enjoying the masterpieces of the Italian Renaissance. Time stood still and it seemed to me that I had existed forever. I leaned down to the small print in the parentheses to see how old Ghirlandajo (Domenico Di Tommaso Bigordi) was at the time of his death. Only forty-five! I was unnerved. 1449–1494: it was amusing that his life boiled down to a matter of inverted digits. It ended with the last two digits of the year of his birth, reversed. This could never happen to me. I was born in 1955. I was lucky.

That picture was a quiet joy to behold. The Renaissance old man resembled my grandfather: his nose was bulbous and his eyes seemed just as ready to well up with teary emotion. My grandfather was still alive. Five hundred years ago there was no Leningrad, no Lenin. The old man's grandson was my age, but he had been dead for the last five hundred years. Looking at that picture made me sleepy. I lay down on my bed and fell asleep, and my dream was pleasant. Then someone tapped me on the shoulder. I stretched and smiled, a child rising to the surface of his dream, and opened my eyes.

It was dark. Grandmother was standing over my bed. An enormous wicker basket with the mushroom knife rolling loudly across its bottom dangled from her elbow. "What time is it?" I asked. She said: "Three." I got up. She made me pull on two pairs of pants, knee-high rubber boots that an adder couldn't bite through, and a *budyonovka*, a flannel, pointed helmet with flapping ears named after the founder of the Red Cavalry, Semyon Mikhailovich Budenny, a silly-looking headpiece to protect my hair against ticks, the carriers of encephalitis. We walked outside. Grandmother's brother and his sons were waiting in the yard their faces serious. Zhuk, the dog, squealed thinly. The mist smelled of cold earth, worms, and fish. Grandmother took me by the hand and we set out for the woods. We went in silence. Then she looked at me and said: "Come on! Aren't you excited? Today's your big day!"
"Yes, yes, I'm excited!" I said, stifling a smile. Everyone seemed pleased with my answer. We walked along the railroad tracks, empty and stained with smelly grease. The woods on both sides of the tracks were two gray walls of trees. I had never been up that early—or that late. No other six year old could possibly be awake at this hour. After a while, we turned right and entered the woods.
Surprisingly, the woods were not as dark as the open space, but the infinity of the trees was overwhelming. They couldn't be counted, and even if I had spent the rest of my life here, I still wouldn't be able to touch the bark of each. There were just too many of them. Soon, after Grandmother had released my hand and everyone had wandered off and coalesced with the shadows of the trees, I got lost and found myself standing in front of a tall fir tree, staring at two mushrooms. I identified them as orange caps, or *podosinoviki*. They looked exactly like their pictures in *The Mushroom Gatherer's Guide*. "Not bad!" I thought. "But

what do I do next?" I knew, of course, how I should feel, being so much closer to the beginning of my life than to its end—as a natural part of nature which has no memory and survives by instinct: like a mushroom, a plant, or a grassblade. I was on my own in the woods. I smiled and hollered, but my voice sounded unconvincing and hollow. "I feel good!" I told myself, but I felt a little uneasy. Suddenly I knew that I had stood in this spot before. But when? I looked around. It was getting light. The moss under my feet was streaked by the sun. It was dry, despite the recent rain. Something rustled behind my back: a hare or a fox, or a snake. Birds were beginning to test their voices overhead. To my left was a thick aspen, a treacherous Judas of Russian trees, covered with black spots like a hyena. Its minute leaves shivered as though in fever. On its mossy lee side had to be a *chaga* outgrowth, a dark gray porous fungus—touchwood. According to *The Mushroom Gatherer's Guide*, drinking its extract could help one suffering from cancer survive. I squinted, peering through the dusk. There it was, *chaga*, a hundred years old. I stepped over to the tree and saw it. It seemed wet. I touched it. It was wet. Then I remembered that *chaga* was also called birch tree sponge—*beryozovaya gubka*—and that it didn't grow on aspens. I took another look at the tree and saw that I had been mistaken. It was a birch, the dear soul of Russia. When I touched it, its bark felt like onion peels. A sudden gust of wind set its leaves in motion. Then everything settled back into silence. I didn't know how much time had passed. It didn't really matter. Time had no meaning; not yet. Every minute for me was ten times longer than for my grandmother, and she was nowhere to be seen. I yanked the mushrooms from the moss and squeezed them to my chest. They were heavy. "I'm here!" I called loudly. No one answered. The sun kept rising and its light was familiar. "I have been here before!" I thought, frightened by the strangeness of recognition. It occurred to me then that maybe I was living someone else's life, which had already ended—and maybe (this made more sense) I was remembering things from my own future: that would explain why, finding myself lost in the woods, I kept doing the same thing every time, over and over again—running around in circles with my heart beating louder than the crackling of frail twigs under my feet or the warbling of wild birds overhead. I knew that this thought was too sophisticated for a six year old. I screamed tentatively. My voice boomed in silence; it boomeranged. Filled with my panting, the silence was no longer complete. I bolted. The forest darkened; I was breathing too deep, too fast. "Don't panic!" I shouted. The birds in the tree branches were full of indifference. I ran forever. Once or twice my foot slipped through windows of dangerous, deep mud thinly veiled by bright patches of decaying leaves. When, screaming, I jerked my foot out, the dirt gave with a greedy sigh and the greasy smacking of fat, disappointed lips. Soon, having completed a full circle, which could only mean that my right foot was stronger than the left one, I returned to the place where I had found the mushrooms. Then, too tired to scream, I remembered that real *gribniks*, so as not to scare away the mushrooms, communicated with each other by way of cautious hallooing. It was too late for me, though. I was lost for good.

"Halloo!" I hollered, and heard a dog's barking, and then a sweet and close "halloo" in response. A dog—it was Zhuk—cheerfully jumped at me from behind the nearest tree. Grandmother stepped out of the shadows. She stopped in front of two fresh black wounds in the moss. "Someone's beat us to two mushrooms!" she said angrily.

She didn't notice that I had been lost, which meant that I hadn't been lost. "Scared?" she asked, and I realized that she had been keeping an eye on me all along. She glanced at me and smiled. "You did all the right things," she said approvingly. "You were smart to start screaming. You didn't have to run, though. It always makes things worse. Next time stay right where you are and keep screaming."

"I knew I wasn't lost," I said sheepishly. "I was just teasing you."

She smiled again. I remembered the mushrooms that I had found. Running around, I had dropped one of them. I showed her the one that I still clutched to my chest. Her face brightened.

"Congratulations! Now you're a *gribnik!*" she said. Then her face took on a stern expression: "Don't you know you should have used the knife? Now you've destroyed the roots and there won't be any new mushrooms here next year!"

"But I don't have a knife!" I said.

She shook her head: "You should've called for me. I would've come over with my knife!" She grabbed my hand and slapped it. I started to cry. She hugged me. "I'm sorry, I'm sorry!" she said.

Her basket was full. There were all kinds of mushrooms inside. It was a shame, I thought, to leave so many mushrooms behind, in the woods, just because there was no more room in her basket. But we had to go. I was still looking around, remembering. On the way out of the woods, I spotted a colony of *lisichki*, or "little foxes," with their brilliant yellow cups, and an assorted bunch of gilled, pink and red and yellow *syroyezhki*, which can be eaten raw, as their name in Russian implies (of course, no one eats them raw). Later I saw a pale death cap, the destroying angel, more poisonous than cyanide and more lethal than the fancy scarlet, white-dotted fly killer—*mukhomor*. Redheaded *podosinoviki* grew under the aspens; prim *podberyozoviki* sprouted under the birch trees. The diminutive slippery jacks—*maslyata*, or "the buttery ones"—were covered with slimy film. "White mushrooms," or *boroviki*, were the kings of mushrooms. Grandmother would hang them on a thread over the stove to dry.

The woods were abundant with mushrooms that morning. It was sad to leave them all behind, unaccounted for. Indeed, if all I could do was to remember seeing them in the woods, I could just as well have imagined them, and then convinced myself, as I have often done since, that imagination is the best and most reliable source of recollections. I could have stayed home, waiting for Grandmother, for her brother with his sons, and for the dog to appear in our yard with their baskets full of the Kavgolovo mushrooms. At times I even seem to remember standing next to my mother in the yard of the Kavgolovo house that morning, looking at the *gribniks* and exclaiming: "At last! How was it, granny? What took you so long? Why didn't you take me with you? Why didn't you wake me up?" Maybe I wasn't in the woods with my grandmother, after all. That was such a long time ago. Yet I clearly remember being there with her.

We all gathered together at the edge of the forest, the five of us—but the dog, Zhuk, was nowhere to be seen. "Zhuk! Zhuk!" I called out twice. Grandmother, radiant after a good mushroom hunt, hugged me and said: "Don't you cry, he'll be back! He's just a dog!" I wasn't about to cry, until she said it. Then tears appeared in my eyes. I turned away. She paid no attention to me.

"Zheka's found a huge mushroom!" she said.

Her brother and his sons nodded, wasting no words. They, too, were proud of me.

"Big deal!" one of my cousins said.

"I found *two* mushrooms!" I corrected Grandmother.

"Of course," she said.

Their baskets were full of mushrooms covered with fresh leaves, green needles, and ferns in order to protect them from the rising sun and from the stares and questions of other mushroom gatherers along the way. It was considered bad luck and bad taste to reveal one's mushroom-picking spots. On our way back, Grandmother suggested that we take the picturesque lakeside road. I wanted to stay and wait for the dog, but Grandmother, or maybe it was her brother, told me that he must have run into some of his friends back there in the woods. "What friends?" I thought. I hated it when grown-ups talked to me condescendingly.

"What friends? Are you out of your mind?" I said.

"Dog hunters," my cousins said, laughing, expecting me to start crying.

"Stop teasing him!" Grandmother said.

I began to weep softly.

"He's very tired," Grandmother said. "Let's go home."

They patted my head, but I kept crying. "Shut up!" Grandmother's brother said sternly, giving me an excuse to become confused and inconsolable. Tears were sweet. They had a life of their own. Overtaken by the mysterious process of dissolving into tears, I forgot the cause and purpose of my despair. I gagged and choked. Grandmother's brother picked me up and set me down on his shoulders. "Look, he's smiling through his tears, like Chekhov!" Grandmother said.

"What a pain!" one of my cousins said.

I smiled.

We walked down the green hills that Kavgolovo is so famous for, past the serene and blue Kavgolovo lake. The weather was good. Gently swaying brown pines and firs climbed up the hills that looked like an Italian picture. High in the sky, two slender white scars in the wake of two invisible planes grew rapidly and stretched across the deep blue altitude. They were the color of early morning snow outside the ice-bitten window of the tourist center, a log cabin with two rooms and two windows, not far from Leningrad.

That was a long time ago, before I started to scream waking up. It was January, or December. I awoke and looked around, feeling cold, and saw my mother sleeping in the bed across the room, her pink toes peeking out from under the maize-colored woolen blanket with the purple ink stamp of the tourist center. I considered falling back asleep and decided against it. Nothing was happening, nothing was going to happen. Once started, the day could neither stop nor end. Minutes passed. There was a brick stove in the far corner of the room. It was cold. Loud snoring came from another room. I was three, or two.

Now the forest, the Kavgolovo lake, and the sky, healed from the planes' invasion, were crisp and clear. I shuddered with the anticipation of memories to come; there was a firm and conclusive promise in my having been able, at age six, to recall what had happened to me three, or even four years before. I already had, at age six, a solid stock of memories to draw upon! I smiled at the thought that when I was ten or twenty I would have so many memories that I would be able to do nothing but reminisce, pondering and comparing the events of my life against one other.

Then we came close to our house. Grandmother's brother unsaddled me from his shoulders.

My mother was waiting for us in the yard. "At last!" she exclaimed. "How was it? What took you so long?" I told her that we had lost the dog. "He'll be back," she said. We put our baskets up on the table and began to sort the mushrooms, arranging them in separate piles on the newspaper that was spread out across the tabletop. "Let me do this!" I said. "Let me count them!" They stepped aside from the table and began to watch me. I was good with numbers.

It turned out that we had gathered 34 *syroyezhki*; 178 *lisichki*, already wilting and crumbling in their fragile yellow beauty; 102 *maslyata*, or slippery jacks; 52 *podberyozoviki*; 40 *podosinoviki*, good for pickling, their red caps clasping rough and rugged gray-streaked stems so tight that they looked like giant matches waiting to be struck; and 47 *boroviki*. It had been a great mushroom hunt.

When the baskets finally were empty, I felt disappointed, as though I had hoped to find something exceptional at the bottom of each. I had no idea what I was looking for: maybe a surprisingly huge, ugly mushroom, or a very tiny one. I stepped back from the table and wiped my hands on the front of my red checkered flannel shirt.

"This boy is destined to become a mathematician!" Grandmother said.

My mother nodded. "Remember when he used to spend hours by the highway?"

"Oh yes." Grandmother smiled. "Maybe you should send him to a special school for gifted children."

"Don't confuse the boy," said my mother.

They were recalling the summer before in Komarovo, near Leningrad, when I used to spend hours by the highway, counting the cars that sped by. There were few of them, headed toward Leningrad or—much less frequently—from Leningrad toward northern Karelia and the state border of another country. The cars were slick and mesmerizing, each unexpected, appearing out of nowhere. I counted them, though I wasn't interested in the total number as such. All I really wanted to know was that the total was finite. In one hour, twenty-five Pobedas went by, ten new Volgas, eight posh, raven-black ZIMs, and twenty old Moskviches. I paid no attention to trucks and vans. To sort them out and keep their respective quantities in mind was interesting, but less important than the hope of being able, provided I stayed right there by the highway long enough, to count all the cars in Leningrad, or in Karelia, or even in the entire Soviet Union. I knew that it probably couldn't be done, but I had a feeling that maybe it could. And of course, I was looking for something surprising and unusual. That was what kept me there in the first place. I wanted to witness something unexpected, like a foreign car on the road (Finland was not far away), or maybe a horsecart, or a car accident. That same anxious feeling of standing on the verge of a surprise propelled me through the pages of the encyclopedia in my Kavgolovo room. I knew that I might discover on the next page that some writer had lived for almost two hundred years. It was highly unlikely, but it could happen. And there was a sense of doing a job, too. The more I read and counted, and kept the faces and numbers in my mind, the closer I was to the end, and being closer to the end was a good feeling. That feeling was decidedly unmathematical and defied any attempt at common-sense calculation. I simply wanted to see the end of the book, the emptiness of the road. There were only so many cars in the country; only so many mushrooms in the woods; only so many people in the world; only so many famous names in the encyclopedia. I could talk with every man alive. In the end, I could get to know them all. I flipped through the pages, and if one was worth no more attention than the next, I sighed with relief: I was drawing closer to the end. In the end, I would do all right. I would survive.

After dinner, when the rain began again and everyone in the house was sleeping, I stepped out into the yard. The rain grew stronger and colder. Remembering that it was my birthday, I ran around the yard, filled with excitement, sloshing in the puddles, repeating my age—"Six-six-six"—until the words lost their meaning and fell into the black depths of the language. I liked to play with words that I knew, repeating them until they began to sound funny, then scary. "Mother-mother-mother," I would repeat rapidly. "Blue. Blue-blue-blue. House-house-house"—and in no time at all the word would be menacingly transformed into something new: what was "mothermo?" What color was "blueb?" "Househou?" Each time, the sudden disappearance of the word's meaning scared me: where did it go?

When I stopped running around, I remembered that it was, of course, not my birthday. My birthday was in July, and there are almost no mushrooms in the woods until late August. I was already six. I stopped and paused. A cheering crowd approached our house. People were dancing, laughing, and screaming. Yuri Levitan in his deep, sonorous voice that was used only for radio news of planetary importance was announcing the triumph of Soviet spirit and science. "His name is Yuri Alexeyevich Gagarin, he is twenty-seven years old!" he exclaimed. The crowd went berserk. Never before had I witnessed such undiluted joy, such selfless exhilaration, such shameless happiness. People beckoned to me. I made a timid step forward, toward another story, "A Fiery Engine."

Then it occurred to me that Yuri Gagarin was launched into orbit on April 12, 1961, not in August. The dancing and cheering crowd, chanting "We've Made It!" and "We're Number One!" might instead be celebrating Space Flight Number Two in August of 1961—but, of course, I wouldn't remember it. Number Two didn't count. It's the first time, no matter what, that is always memorable. In my mind, I was back in Leningrad. Yuri Gagarin had been launched into space.

The crowds cheered. Everywhere—in Moscow, in Leningrad—people rejoiced and took to the streets. As happy as if someone had promised to keep them alive forever, they were carrying huge pictures of Yuri Gagarin's typically Russian face—so fit for print in the *Encyclopedia*—with its multi-dimpled, frozen smile: it floated slowly through the pink air of April.

That day, April 12, 1961, so many euphoric people were in the streets that some of them got stomped and trod upon, crushed and squashed under hundreds of feet. There were casualties, just like in 1953, when Stalin died and crowds gathered in their immeasurable grief. I remember thinking that those who were killed in the mourning crowd passed away at the very depth of unhappiness, their eyes full of tears and their hearts filled with boundless sorrow. They stumbled and staggered along, and then they went down, still crying, unable to see anything, falling smoothly through one darkness into another, more permanent. But those who were squeezed to death in the happy crowd of Gagarin's great victory were happier than they were ever likely to be if they had had a chance to keep on living. They shouted and chanted at the top of their lungs, too excited to notice their own deaths. The song that they sang played on the radio day and night. It went like this:

We all were born to make the legend real!
To claim the space! To work and study hard!
Our mind has given us strong wings of steel!
A fiery engine to replace the heart!

In 1961, Gagarin himself had no more than seven years to live. The plane he piloted lost altitude and crashed into a Russian forest. That was in 1968. He was thirty-four. I was thirteen and in high school.

The news of his death was announced on the radio the next day, after I had left for school. Our literature teacher entered the class sobbing. By sheer coincidence, it was the same day that my story, "A Fiery Engine," was to be proclaimed a winner in the inter-high school competition. I already knew that it had won. It was supposed to be a big day for me. It was also the hundredth anniversary of the birth of Maxim Gorky, the most famous Soviet writer of all time, March 28. I remember thinking how symbolic it would be to have my literary career launched on the hundredth anniversary of his death.

Instead of congratulating me and inviting the class to give me a round of applause, as she had promised me she'd do, the teacher sighed deeply and said: "I want you all to stand up. I have devastating news. Yuri Alexeyevich Gagarin is dead!"

There was a pause. We didn't know what to say, how to mourn. Class was promptly dismissed. We poured out, laughing, full of plans. I was disappointed and sad that Gagarin's death had so crudely intervened with my own life. However, by that time he was no longer Number One, and I was no longer six years old, and I didn't wish that I was dead instead.

But back in 1961, all that was still a lifetime away. I was in Kavgolovo. The rain had stopped and, sure enough, there was a rainbow in the sky. I looked at it for some time. Its colors were: red, then orange, yellow, green, blue, indigo, and violet. This sequence was easy to remember once you memorized the sentence in which the first letter of each word was the first letter of one of the rainbow's colors: "Kazhdyi Okhotnik Zhelayet Znat Gdye Skryvayetsya Fazan": Every Hunter Wants To Know Where the Pheasant's Hiding. I always wondered who had come up with this idea first.

It was the hour of the day when the sun strikes the eye at a crimson angle and everything begins to look eerily intense, but serene: a late August afternoon the color of an April evening. I was in my room, watching. The trees and the hills were green, there were swallows in the sky, and Russia was joyous and looked eternal beyond my window.

Late at night, unable to fall asleep, I stepped out of my room and walked to the kitchen. There was a thick thread of drying mushrooms stretched over the stove. The stove was hot, the coals were still burning inside. To get perfectly dry mushrooms, an indispensable vitamin source during the winter, Grandmother would keep them hanging over the stove for several weeks.

I reached out and touched one mushroom with my fingers. Still wet, it was already shriveled. I squeezed it hard, imagining everyone's surprise next morning, when they discovered that one mushroom on the thread of forty-seven *boroviki* was prematurely perfectly dry and ready to cook. Drops of bitter-smelling mushroom juice fell on the oven. There was a loud hissing; a cloud of dark bitterness hit my nostrils. When I dropped the mushroom, my index finger brushed against the metallic oven top. I was more scared than hurt. I knew that everyone would wake up if I screamed, but I couldn't help it. I had no other recourse. I remember screaming. That was a long time ago.

NAHID RACHLIN

I find writing in English more liberating than writing in my native language, Persian. It frees me from viewing certain words and concepts as taboo or painful. In Iran, where I was born and lived until I was seventeen years old, words are taken very seriously, so much so that, before the publication of a book, it is reviewed by a government-appointed committee to make sure there is nothing in it that would influence the reader in the wrong way. Many writers who manage to publish outside of the censorship are jailed.

Freedom of expression was something I yearned for all my life and was what eventually brought me to the United States. While going to high school in Ahvaz, a town in northwest Iran, I was constantly aware of oppression. We could not read books that might possibly spread the "wrong" ideas. I managed to buy some books from a store that smuggled them in against censorship. (That store was eventually ordered closed and its owner was sent to jail.) I read them only in the privacy of my room.

Still I was not immune. My father, a lawyer, was suspicious and afraid of what the written word could do. Once he burst in on me when I was reading in my room, took away a novel by Maxim Gorky called *The Mother*, and tore it into pieces. "Where did you get that communistic filth? I could lose my license if my daughter was caught reading a book like that." Communism was considered the enemy of the country at the time (as it still is). One female teacher in my high school whom I admired was arrested on the charge that she was spreading "communistic" ideas in the school, the word also being a catch-all for anything even remotely progressive or liberal.

I also was drawn to writing. That too I had to do hiddenly in my room. Fearful of my father now, I was extra careful not to get caught.

If I had remained in Iran I would never be able to write what I write now in America. Although my books do not deal with politics, the slightest reference to anything negative is interpreted as anti-government propaganda. When I tried to get one of my novels translated and published in Iran, under the Shah, the committee said I would have to rewrite a great deal of it. They wanted a travelogue, with everything in Iran presented in perfect light.

In that respect things have not improved under the new regime. If anything there are additional elements in the censorship. There can be no reference to holding hands, kissing between a male and female, no references to sex whatsoever.

Our house overlooked a square with two cinemas in it. One of the cinemas always played foreign movies, mainly American and European. For some reason foreign movies were shown in the cinemas then, without being censored (now most of them are not allowed to be shown or if they are, it would be with many scenes cut out).

So I was exposed to the western world through those movies (and the books I managed to read secretly). I became aware of how young girls in other parts of the world lived, other realities, sets of belief and values. A restlessness had set in, making me question everything.

But although I find American culture to be liberating in many respects, I am still connected to my Iranian identity. It hits me at unexpected moments. During the hostage crisis, for instance, when Iranians were the target of strong prejudice in the United States, made into caricatures in the American media, I found myself identifying strongly as an Iranian. At the same time I identify as an American. When I am in Iran, visiting, I become upset when I encounter anti-American sentiments.

This preoccupation with identity is a major theme in many of my short stories and novels.

My first novel, *Foreigner,* is about a young Iranian girl who comes to America after high school to go to college. She marries an American and stays on. She feels she is perfectly adjusted to this culture but at one point a restlessness for her past begins to set in. She goes to Iran for a visit after many years. At first she feels like a foreigner there but then she gets involved in searching for her mother, whom she had lost as a child. She finds her mother and then she begins to question her happiness in the United States. By the end of the book she is not sure if she wants to go back to America.

By the title, *Foreigner,* I wanted to convey that the protagonist of the novel, Feri, at first feels foreign in her own country, Iran, when she goes to visit after being away for twelve years. Gradually though as she stays there she realizes maybe she was equally foreign in the United States, that she is not as Americanized as she had thought.

Fatemeh

Fatemeh put her *chador* on and left her room early in the morning. She had a lot to do that day. In the alley, sweepers were going around with brooms, cleaning. At the curb of the alley a *hejleh* was set up, a bunch of tiny bulbs lit inside its glass case and an enlarged photograph of a young man pasted on its front. "Gholam, 18, martyred in the holy war," was written in red ink beneath the photograph. Tears gathered in her eyes. Will I be able to get Ali exempted; will God pay back my prayers, the pilgrimages I went on for a whole year, she wondered. It was wonderful last night, staring at the face of the moon, as she lay under the mosquito netting on the roof, seeing something, a trembling light, which had made her feel God was showing a bit of Himself to her. That had excited her so much that she had sat up and stared for a long time at the moon, for more signs. The sky was dazzling, with all the stars, large and clear...

On Ghanat Abad Avenue there was another *hejleh* right next to the beet stall. The man in the stall was shouting, "I have the best, sweetest beets in town, they taste like sugar." Doesn't he see that *hejleh*, she thought indignantly.

She walked rapidly toward the bus station. In the station she bought a ticket and got on the bus which was about to leave for Ghom. She sat by the window looking out but her mind was filled with all those weeks of going from office to office until she had gotten an appointment with Ayatollah Masjedi about Ali, then the meeting they had in the mosque.

"Don't you want your son to give himself up to the holy cause? His soul will directly go into heaven, if he's martyred. All the sins either one of you might have committed will be forgiven by God. What is the brief, wretched life we lead on this earth compared to a blissful eternity in heaven?" the ayatollah had said.

"Ayatollah Masjedi, he's my only son. I have a daughter, but I haven't seen her since she was eight years old, her father took her away from me...I had two other sons, they died. I can't let this one go. I have no one else in the world. Anyway he supports me. I do all I can cleaning house for rich people, but it only pays for our rent."

"Well then," he said. "Do you have proof that he's your only son?"

His tone was mild but Fatemeh was cut by an expression of utter disgust on his desiccated face.

"I can get proof," she stammered.

He waved his hand stiffly, dismissing her. The veins on his neck were drawn taut, his eyes were stony.

Am I going to be able to get proof today from that man in the morgue? Who knows if he is still there, or if he remembers anything. Would he have a record of my two little boys' deaths after all these years? All the possible complications...

"I'm really running away from my husband," she heard the woman sitting on the seat in front of her saying to another woman next to her. "He's truly frightening, the way he goes into a rage and starts throwing things at me..."

I was so frightened of my husbands, Fatemeh thought, of all three—Majid, Bahram, Khosro. Bastards. One she had left, giving up all claim to money; another all claim to money and worse—he had taken her only daughter, Nasrin, with him, had hidden her from her, forbidden visits, and then vanished leaving no trace. And of course the law was on his side. She was the one who had left. Ali's father, her first husband, was not such a bad man, only he was a drug addict, and though he had never abused her, he was useless. At least she had managed to get her son back from him. But first the poor boy had had to put up with the two stepfathers, then his half-sister to whom he had grown attached was taken away. The most joyous moments of my life were when I was pregnant, she thought. And how magical it was when the midwife would hold up the infant to her, then lay it into her arms. The feeling she had then was like looking at the moon last night and being aware of God. She would put her breast into the baby's mouth, hold its soft, small hand or foot, tickle its belly. Nasrin was a precocious baby, began to walk and talk early. On hot days she put her in a plastic pool and Nasrin splashed around or pushed the ball floating on its surface. What was happening to her now? She may be married, have children of her own...

She got off the bus in Ghom and after she had walked a few blocks she recalled where the mortuary was. She started in its direction. The streets were crowded and dirty, the trees and buildings dust-covered. Many *Aghounds* were passing by in their long robes and turbans.

The mortuary was a grim looking house on a quiet, rather deserted street. She knocked several times on the door and waited. There were tiny termite holes in the door. The few houses and shops on the street were in a bad state, some of their roofs or windows shattered. She heard footsteps from the inside and an old man opened the door.

"Yes," he said. He had yellowish crooked teeth. There was something deeply bitter in his expression.

"I have to talk to you about my two children I brought here."

"When was that?"

"It was years ago but..."

He seemed to be about to shut the door on her.

"Please, it's very important, I have to have proof that they died, please let me explain."

With a reluctant air he let her in.

Inside, in the dim light, she could see coffins lying around. There was a raised pool in the corner with several faucets and a cemented platform next to it, where they washed dead bodies before they wrapped them up in cloths and put them in coffins to be taken to the cemetery. She began to shudder—she could see so vividly the small bodies of her children being washed in that very pool, floating like dolls.

The man plopped himself on a wooden bench as if he were exhausted. She sat down also.

"What do you want *khanoom*, maybe you can tell me something to refresh my memory."

"What can I tell you. The last one I brought here was Mohsen; he was five years old; he got malaria. I had my little girl with me also when we came here. She was frightened and she clung to me the whole time and cried. Now I remember something. There was a fly buzzing around in the air. You told my daughter that the fly was the soul of her brother. She was startled by what you told her and stopped crying. Do you remember?"

He scratched his head, coughed. "Oh, Mohsen, sure, in fact not long ago, a man and a woman came here and asked me about him, they couldn't find the grave. They must have been your husband and daughter then. I told them where the grave was."

Her heart almost jumped out of her chest. "They were here? Where did they come from?"

He looked at her in a puzzled way.

"Do they live in Ghom? You see he's no longer my husband. He has kept my daughter from me."

"Oh, you poor woman."

"I have only one son living with me, from my first husband. He was a gift to me...and now they're going to draft him unless I can prove that I have no other sons or a husband who support me. Will you write a letter about my two sons being buried by you? If you would do me that favor, I'm sure God will pay you back. I can pay you with what I can, which is only some *tomans*." She fumbled in her purse and found the hundred *toman* bill which she had just gotten for some housework she had done. She needed it for her next month's rent but she could see him opening up to the idea so she gave it to him. He took it without hesitation and put it into his gray, frayed jacket pocket.

He got up slowly and went to the heavy wooden table in a corner and sat on a chair behind it. He began to write a letter with a pen he dipped in ink. After a moment he handed it to her.

"This is to certify that Mohsen..." He indicated both names, dated and signed it.

"I can't thank you enough," she said.

"I can tell you where the graves are. In fact there are fresh flowers on them. I do my duty—your daughter wanted me to put flowers on them every week. She's been sending me money for it. Go inside the cemetery and walk past the three graves with the very large, upright stones on them. Your sons' graves are just beyond them."

"Did my daughter or...her father...tell you where they were living right now, any addresses?"

He thought for a moment. "The money for flowers comes from Teheran."

They live in Teheran then, she thought. How incredible. She took out another bill, this time twenty *tomans*, and gave it to him. "Could you give me the address?"

He looked through some papers scattered on the top of the desk and in the drawers, and picked out one. He gave it to her. "Here, is this the name?"

"Oh yes, that's my daughter's name, how incredible." The address was the old house where they had all lived, a house Bahram had inherited from his parents. So he had returned there. Was Nasrin living with him, with a husband maybe?

After she left, though, instead of going to the cemetery she headed back home. It is more important to attend to those still living, she thought. If she went to the cemetery she would miss the only bus going back to Teheran today and she would have to stay overnight. She could not afford the money or the time. As she headed toward the bus she was elated—it seemed she had accomplished an incredible amount.

In the morning, she decided to go to the War-Related-Matters office first and submit the letter and her divorce documents and then from there go to see if she could track down Nasrin in the old house.

The office was teeming with people—parents, young men. Most of them seemed anxious. From what they were saying, some of the young men were there to enlist, some of the parents to collect compensations. Fatemeh was anxious too, aware of hot and cold flashes on her skin. A large bowl, filled with *sharbat*, was set in a corner next to some glasses and people went over and helped themselves to the drink. It was clearly going to be hours of waiting. She was such an insignificant figure, one among so many others, like a pale line on a white sheet of paper. The woman sitting next to her said, "I don't know what's happening to my son. I haven't heard from him for weeks and there are no reports on him. I haven't been able to find out anything about him."

A name was called and the woman jumped to her feet. "That's me." She walked away with choppy steps. Her black *chador*, which she held tightly around her, was too long, hindering her.

Finally, hours later, Fatemeh was called in. The man sitting behind the desk was short, bald, there was a pinched meanness about his face.

"Yes," he said curtly.

Fatemeh fumbled in her purse. She took out the documents and put them before him. "I had the privilege of meeting with Ayatollah Masjedi. He told me these are what I need."

"Your name?"

"Fatemeh Abbasi."

He began to look at the documents. She had a sinking, helpless feeling.

"We'll send you a letter about our decision," he said finally, after an eternity.

"Please, could you tell me now?"

"We'll send you a letter," he repeated impatiently.

What am I going to find, what can I expect from a child I haven't seen for so long, a woman now, but clearly a nice person to want to send flowers to her brother who died years ago. Has she been missing me? But if she hasn't contacted me all this time, living in Teheran, her mind must have been poisoned against me. The thoughts went around her head as she went toward the house in Varamin, where they used to live. What is Bahram like now? Is he as erratic, volatile as he used to be? He is capable of tender feelings toward his children, why not toward a wife? Bastard. As she reached Ghole Sar Lane, on which the house was located, she was so overwhelmed by contradictory feelings that she almost turned around and went back. She had to push herself to go on.

Then she was in front of the house and knocking. There were no sounds from the inside. Maybe no one was in. Bahram would be at his job, if he had one. Grape vines were hanging on the crude brick and straw wall. She knocked again. Then she heard footsteps in the hall and the door was opened by a woman. Nasrin. A grown woman, but she had the same features as the child she remembered.

"Do you know who I am?" Fatemeh asked through constricted throat.

Nasrin shook her head. "Can I help you?"

There was something sweet and kind in Nasrin's manner.

"Nasrin, my dear, I'm your mother."

"My mother?" A range of emotions passed over her face. "Really...my mother. Come in now, come in."

Fatemeh went down the two steps and they embraced, for a long moment. She wished she could hold her daughter forever. At some level she had a hard time believing it was really happening, that she was not merely dreaming it. How could she be holding her, finding her so easily, after years of having no idea where she was? Then in the midst of her emotions she felt a stab of guilt, thinking, maybe I really was not trying. Maybe I was afraid of encountering Bahram. But she said, "I thought you had moved away."

"We had. We came back here, this was rented until a few months ago. I'll tell you everything, if you come in and sit down."

Fatemeh followed Nasrin into the living room. They sat on a rug and talked. A few times they reached over and kissed each other. Once they both burst out crying.

The house was the same, only older, more run down. Just being there, being reminded of all the abuse Bahram had inflicted on her—she still had a scar on her chin from when he had thrown a plate at her—made her want to get up and leave but then there was Nasrin, sitting in front of her.

"My father told me you were dead," Nasrin said. "That you were buried in Zahra Cemetery but your grave was eroded or lost among all the new ones."

"How strange, cruel."

"I know he must have been cruel to you...but he has been kind enough to me. I live here now with my husband and children, two girls. My husband barely makes a living. My father stayed on in Kashan, where we lived all these years."

"How old are your children, where are they?"

"Heide is two and Fereshdeh is four. They're with my husband's sister today."

"You have to come over to my house soon and see your brother. Bring your children and husband," Fatemeh said. "I can't wait to see them." She could not take her eyes off her daughter. How pretty and kind she was, with her fine features, the wavy black hair, and no trace of bitterness. A nice human being. Just seeing her made her less angry at Bahram.

It was getting to be near dusk. "I should go back," Fatemeh said. The two of them got up and went to the door. They embraced once again before Fatemeh left.

Fatemeh sat with Nasrin and Ali on the rug she had spread by the pool, talking—easy conversation about this and that. Nothing serious or cumbersome. Nasrin was optimistic that her husband's lamp shop would begin to do better, was happy that Heide's smallpox had been cured without leaving marks. Ali mentioned the newspaper he was working for. It was so nice that there was this quick friendship between the two of them, Fatemeh thought. There was a definite resemblance in their looks and personalities too, though Ali had been on edge lately, naturally.

One of the women, living in the row of rooms opposite the ones she and Ali lived in, had watered the plants and splashed water on the brick ground to cool it off and the air was fresh and fragrant. Nasrin's two children, both lovely, with curly hair and plump cheeks were sitting by flowerbeds playing with marbles. Then they went inside, running around the two rooms, chasing each other. They paused to take a candy from a bowl or dress a doll with tiny clothes Fatemeh had sewn for them herself.

Then Ali said, suddenly somber, "What does it all mean? One day and then another passing?"

"Isn't it good enough for the three of us to be sitting together like this?" Nasrin said.

He whispered something strange, "Free your body, free your soul, die and be born again."

Fatemeh picked up her glass of *sharbat* and took a few gulps of it, her mind drifting to her main concern, that the letter about Ali's exemption had not arrived yet. Maybe it's better not to know, she thought.

Other tenants in the rooms around the courtyard were peeking out of the doorways of their rooms.

"Only beggars are benefitting from this war," one of the women said, addressing Fatemeh, Nasrin and Ali. "They go from one wake to another and fill up their stomachs."

"It has given me a job," Hamideh said ruefully. She came out and sat on the porch and began to sew buttons on army jackets, a job she had taken on to supplement her income.

An *aghound's* voice, amplified through a loudspeaker, flowed in from the mosque at the end of the street. "Gather your courage and fight on, we're near victory."

"I'm cowardly," Ali said.

"Please..." Fatemeh said.

"We are near victory, we are about to defeat the infidel enemy," the *aghound* said.

There was a knock on the door. Ali got up and went to get it. He came back with a letter in his hand. He gave it to Fatemeh. "It's to you, from the War-Related-Matters office."

Her hand was shaking as she opened it. She could feel Ali's and Nasrin's heavy gazes on her, could hear her own heart beat. Among all the words on it she could only see, "Not exempted." She felt a painful stirring inside her she had never experienced before. Was God really a just God? Did he exist at all or was he an invention? Or else why would he take away my son, just as I was happy finding my lost daughter? It was like she was falling into a dark, bottomless ravine.

Then she looked at the letter again and among all the words on it she saw only, "Exempted." She had the feeling she was in a dream, drifting through a maze of rooms she had once occupied, coming upon a famil-iar turn or looking out from behind a lacy curtain at a view, at events whose meaning was not quite clear to her. Then all she could see was a dazzling light, like looking into the full moon, with the face of God reflected in it.

THOMAS PALAKEEL

LANGUAGE ACTS

Malayalam language is my mother tongue, but now I write in English. I began to write in English long before I arrived in the United States to study creative writing. Although I promptly sensed America's tendency to erase other people's mother tongues, I always assumed that I would never abandon mine. Besides, I was so sure that the great Malayalam novels I was going to write would be enriched by my experience of English and America and the big world across the seven seas. For someone who had spoken Malayalam almost exclusively for the first twenty-six years life, I could feel my mother tongue slipping away as I quietly embraced English.

Whether English qualifies as my stepmother tongue or not, without a question "English" is the most substantial word characterizing my life. No other word encompasses so much of my personal history. Even now, when I get to ponder the word "English," at times the mere sound of it needles me deep within. For many "English" is simply the name of a language brought to our shores by a foreign people, the language of Lord Clive, Macauley, and "Rule Britannia" and Caliban's curses, and for many others, it is the language of King James Bible and Shakespeare. The language that overran Spanish and French and eventually came to dominate the New World. The language of Thomas Jefferson, Noah Webster, Emily Dickinson, the *New York Times*, Mahatma Gandhi, Salman Rushdie, CNN, and Yahoo! As ubiquitous all over the globe as mosquitoes and consumerism, spoken or attempted by nearly two billion human beings, the English language is indeed a stepmother to be reckoned with, and I, too, had to make my own private reckoning.

It's true. "English" is the word. Nothing else can be said to have tested me and tried me with such insistence. Not family. Not love. Not health. Not daily bread. Now, I am grateful that the English language brings me my daily bread, but every morsel has been earned with much anxiety and suffering, and I still have not grasped fully why all this happened to me, of all people.

Before I cast aspersions, I must make a personal confession: no one forced me to submit myself to the so-called tests. No colonial masters drew me into English. It was entirely my own handiwork. Even before I possibly could have understood the history and politics of the language, I desired to read English books and hoped some day to be able to write them.

Of course, I was one of those rural boys whom the family sent to an English medium school run by the Jesuits. This was where I started hearing about the wonders of the English language. Everywhere I turned I saw hints of the privileges bestowed upon those who mastered it. Of course, I knew I didn't have a chance, and I wasn't foolhardy enough to try, at least until the last few years at the school.

When I started writing and publishing a little here and there, I began to think that I wouldn't be cast into oblivion even if I didn't manage to learn the mighty language! My Malayalam prose possessed style and a quiet authority that many noticed, and very early in my life I started believing in my calling. Yet, I ended up abandoning my mother tongue and my style and my quiet authority in order to embrace somebody else's mother tongue, enduring in the process an endless and painful apprenticeship, and now I have begun to suspect that I may have already jeopardized my true calling.

Having insisted for years that my switch to English happened without a proper sociological reason, now I am convinced that I embraced English with a secret hope. A hope of flight. Of escape, exile. Yes, I thought I owed a self-exile to my land. The moment I understood the promise of English, I saw in it the shape of my wings, not the romanticized wings of Icarus, but wings with which I would fulfill my obligation. Few of us would admit it, but every young person in Kerala instinctively learns that he or she owes such an exile, without which our densely populated state would sink into the Arabian Sea. So it is necessary that some of us willingly backed away from our claims to our home, our mother tongue, our culture, becoming exiles, willing exiles, all in exchange for a foothold elsewhere on the planet. Most of us end up in the northern states, in the urban centers, in the far eastern islands, in Africa, in the Arabian Gulf, and of course, some in Europe and North America.

Once I unburden the economics and sociology of my story, speaking on a purely literary level, I must say that my desire for a stepmother tongue has nothing to do with the state of our mother tongue. I would have you know that my mother tongue is no dead language. Malayalam is alive and well in our small palace, too far away from New Delhi and the big world. This was where Vasco da Gama landed in 1498. Christopher Columbus had failed to make it to these shores, frequented for so long by the Babylonians, the Romans, the Chinese, and the Arabs, none of them making any hoopla about the traffic.

In spite of all the coming and going, all the flights, all the migrations, peregrinations, indentured sojourns across the oceans, nothing has dwindled the power of our mother tongue. Spoken by over 30 million people, almost all of them literate, Malayalam is flourishing in the breeze from the Arabian Sea and in the shades of the famed spice mountains. Although the geography of my mother tongue is meager compared to better know Indian languages, Malayalam leads newspaper circulation statistics of all 20 major Indian languages. She is as old and strong and nasty and ambidextrous as my stepmother tongue. She is good. She is a good mother, yet I allowed a foreign stepmother to lure me away from my true home.

My mother tongue has not abandoned me. I continue to dream in Malayalam. Although I tend to speak more often in English, the old scaffoldings show through. To illustrate how it feels to write in a stepmother tongue, allow me to describe how it feels to read a newspaper in my stepmother tongue. A Malayalam newspaper fully satisfies me. When I look at the pages of *Malayala Manorama* or *Deepika*, the whole universe leaps off the newsprint and enters my being. I do not have to decipher the gem-like print sown across the pages like rice on a Kerala paddy field, whereas, when I leaf through my beloved *New York Times*, the words still remain a tad distant, blurred. Even after all these years of reading and writing in English, I admit my stepmother tongue remains somewhat opaque. At a glance, what I first see on a printed page is a hazy mass of black ink, and then, of course, when I apply all my knowledge and intelligence on the page, the haze dissipates, and the act of understanding begins. And what an act it is, truly, truly, I tell you. The sad irony is that I keep telling everyone that very soon I am going to start writing again in my mother tongue.

Chocolate War

My friend Ommachan was sitting under the banyan tree at the center of our village some twenty years ago in the company of a goat and three fellow farmers, who were chewing betel leaves and tobacco. The next moment, Ommachan was trapped in a world conspiracy. For the five years that followed, he was held responsible for a revolution, botanical beheadings, floating love letters, heartbreaks, and for his own downfall from the famous Chocolate War of Thidanad.

Thidanad is small. You won't trace it on the map. A church, liquor shops, temple, post office, tea shops, school, and even a lady who offers professional happiness. Nothing else that could attract the big world. I must admit that my friend did have a predilection for the superpowers, especially America. And his late daddy, Inventor Esthappan, also possessed what we call the Moaning-Dog Syndrome. The dog wishes to moan and, boom, a coconut falls on its head. That's how the world conspiracy fell on Ommachan's head.

The day the big world was to collide with the small village, the three farmers were still chewing betel leaves and tobacco. The goat watched them and licked up an old newspaper from the street and started chewing herself.

"Cool day for a change, heh?" Ommachan said to the farmers, and he was met with silence. He hated these old-timers who quietly chewed like cows. Ommachan loved talking. None of the farmers could talk with their mouths full and leaking, not even the cantankerous Kanat Joseph, with his ancient rosary around his neck. Instead of joining them in the mastication, Ommachan took up the topic of the Green Revolution, which he had been reading about so much in the newspapers. Just like his father, Esthappan, who built the fateful automatic coffin, Ommachan was always enthusiastic about undertakings on the scale of the Pyramids and the Great Wall of China. Occasionally he came up with a massive project of his own like the Pickle Pond, in which all the villagers were to pickle their mangoes in a pond instead of little jars at home. Only the communists were moved by the idea. And the matchmakers crossed off his name from their lists of eligible bachelors.

"It's time we brought the Green Revolution to the South. Don't you think so? I think so," Ommachan said.

Kanat Joseph looked at his friends and shrugged.

"We're going to be rich. We'll get to eat four meals. We'll even have radios," Ommachan said.

His mouth still full, Kanat Joseph stared at Ommachan because he must have felt it rather expensive to spit out the betel juice just to express an opinion.

"The newspaper says we'll have electricity," Ommachan continued. This time Kanat Joseph did spit out. And Ommachan shouted, "What's the paper saying about rubber prices? 'Farmers Go Hang Yourselves!'"

"That's why we need the Green Revolution in our good old India country," Ommachan said.

"What's he talking about? Some communist stuff?" Kanat Joseph turned to his chewing friends.

"Wait and see. In five years we'll be like a little America." Ommachan raised his arms and counted the future on his fingers: "The Americans will send us everything. Fat cows, big tractors, new seeds, good electricity. I read it in the newspaper. I swear."

The goat bleated in agreement. A goat that eats newspapers should know. The goat also had some vested interest in the greening of the village, which was already quite green with the ubiquitous rubber trees, but all the animals had become contemptuous of the tasteless, indigestible, latex-oozing leaves of the rubber tree, which had killed off a generation of goats and cows when the white missionary brought the tree to Thidanad one hundred years ago.

"We'll cut down these stupid rubber trees and plant rice and wheat and sweet potatoes. Milk and honey will flow in Thidanad. Haha!"

"Milk and honey will flow and your pencil body will become fat. Haha!" Kanat Joseph laughed, showing his red teeth, and turned to his friends again: "I think he's a communist. You heard him talk of cutting down rubber trees. Tomorrow he'll want to cut our throats."

Traditionally the farmers had respected the durable wealth of the rubber trees. Even if the prices fell, some day they would come back up, they believed. The old adage is that a man gets to see rubber replanted only three times in a lifetime. For the fourth, he would either be dead or blind. Kanat Joseph had already seen rubber replanted three times and didn't appreciate what was in store.

Kanat Joseph brushed aside Ommachan and started talking about the weather. The goat reached out her nose to inspect all the spittle, which had begun to float in the dust like lava, but she had to withdraw her head and get up in obeisance to the arrival of the Government. Ommachan, Kanat Joseph, and the two other farmers also got up.

A rickety Jeep drove up near the banyan tree. A walrus-mustached agricultural officer stepped out, holding up some scrawny weeds. It was the famous cocoa plant from the Americas. The greening of the village was to begin right away. That moment.

For the five years that would culminate in the Chocolate War, whenever Ommachan remembered that moment, he would always invoke the divine powers, saying it was Providence. It had to be somewhat providential because just as Ommachan was discussing the arrival of better seeds from America, the Government officer appeared with the last four cocoa saplings left in his Jeep, searching for enthusiastic farmers to undertake some experimental farming.

Ommachan and the three farmers were chosen. They each received one cocoa sapling, a gift from the President of India, that was, in turn, a gift from the President of America, and the Green Revolution began. I was fifteen years old.

The Jeep spat out enormous quantities of nauseating smoke and drove away. The smoke delighted Ommachan because he saw progress in it. The three farmers sat down to chew another round of betel leaves. The goat also joined them after she noticed the cocoa saplings sitting at the foot of the banyan tree. The goat abandoned her newspaper and skillfully stuck out her long, pink tongue, and swallowed the delicious plants, leaf by leaf, making Ommachan the only surviving revolutionary. And I became his economic advisor.

Ommachan received his cocoa plant like the Olympic beacon and ran home. His lungi fell off on the way, but the beacon bearer proceeded in his underwear. The cocoa sapling was planted on the plot where he used to grow banana every year as a gift for St. George, the patron saint of farmers and damsels in distress.

Seeing the strange weed flourishing on the plot reserved for St. George, Ommachan's mother, Valia Mama, cried sacrilege because her son was depriving the saint of his bananas. The saint had to wait. I remember that year Ommachan showed up at the Feast of St. George without his annual offering. It was Kanat Joseph who won the prize for the best offering: a rubber sheet weighing eighteen pounds. Even the toothless vicar laughed, seeing the abnormal rubber sheet the size of a carpet. It had to be a dozen sheets sewn together. The relic was auctioned off for fifty rupees, double the actual price.

"How come you didn't bring your giant bananas, Ommachan? They would've fetched sixty," I said.

"I've planted a cocoa tree from America," he whispered in my ear. "Next year I will offer a giant cocoa pod. How about that?"

"Cocoa! My God! You will be the first to grow cocoa in this country," I said.

In fifteen months, Ommachan's cocoa plant blossomed. Ommachan fertilized the plant with eggshells and ashes and fish blood, and the legend is that one could actually see the plant grow. With bare eyes. Ommachan could even hear the sound of it.

That summer, half a dozen white flowers matured into pumpkin-yellow cocoa pods, and they hung from the tree, illuminating the dark green foliage, attracting the whole village to the glorious spectacle. The villagers shuttling between the church and the market and the liquor shop and the temple, and even the gentlemen on their way back from prostitute Ammini's house of joy, stopped by Ommachan's place to watch the magical tree. The tree acquired a historical dimension surpassing that of the arrival of Vasco da Gama and the departure of Lord Mountbatten. As the yellow fruit swelled up with the rich seeds inside, Ommachan veiled the whole tree with a quilt sewn out of gunny sacks and *lungis* and old shirts. That was to avert the evil eye of Mohammad Khader, the only Muslim in our village.

Mohammad Khader was responsible for the sudden fame of Ommachan's tree; he spread the word on his daily wanderings all over the seven villages in search of scrap metals. I remember the first time I saw Mohammad Khader, Mother whispered in my ear how everything Khader praised perished eventually and that I had to avoid him because of his black tongue. I often felt pity for Khader because the grownups blamed him for every misfortune. Sometimes he had to take the blame for national disasters. Barely a week after Khader had praised the beauty of Taj Mahal, the newspaper ran a story about how Taj Mahal had begun to sink into the ground. According to Thidanad folklore, when Khader praised a cow's udder, the poor creature was immediately run over by a bus, and just moments after he had complimented a nice lady about her beautiful long hair, the lady's hair started falling off and she went completely bald. I still liked him.

My friendship with Ommachan was based purely on our faith in the

Green Revolution. Mohammad Khader also supported it. Unfortunately, he couldn't participate; he owned no land. Though my father had plenty of land, he chose to ignore the movement as a low-class fad. And my own contribution was intellectual.

It was I who explained to Ommachan how farmers were harvesting cocoa gold in South America and West Africa and the Caribbean and how all the chocolate in the world was made of cocoa seeds, that the future of the Green Revolution rested on cocoa. Ommachan was the best target for practicing my knowledge of the high school botany text. I could call his plants *Theobroma cacao*, and he could comprehend the deep meaning in it.

As Ommachan himself resorted to the use of botanical and other names in many similes and metaphors, people began to run away. Those who saw him coming down the street turned back and fled, or they walked toward the riverside, pretending to take a leak.

Ommachan's early enthusiasm didn't get out of hand like his future frustration. The worst it ever got was when he metaphorically said that Rosamma, the daughter of Kanat Joseph, had breasts of pointed cocoa pods. One of her fellow beauties passed on Ommachan's bit of poetry to her. The next time Rosamma saw him under the banyan tree, she threatened to perform on him what his own father, Esthappan, used to perform on the animals of Thidanad: castration for free.

For the first harvest of cocoa, Ommachan invited the vicar to bless the tree and to receive the first fruit as a gift to St. George. And I was personally invited to the function. That evening while we waited for the vicar, Mohammed Khader and two dozen concerned citizens came self-invited. Leading the group was Kanat Joseph, the prize-winning rubber farmer and father of Rosamma.

The vicar and the sexton arrived. We stood around the tree in a circle. Mohammad Khader wiggled his way to the front as the vicar sprinkled holy water upon the tree and upon the gathering. A drop fell on Mohammad Khader. It was a great moment. I thought about God and Paradise and snakes as I watched the yellow cocoa fruits hanging on the main trunk of the tree. The holy water must have made Khader think of God. He exclaimed, "Allah, what a wonderful tree! God is great!"

"Shut up your black tongue," Kanat Joseph shouted.

"Out of here with your Allah. This is a blessing." The vicar's fierce admonition sounded mild as he gnashed his toothless gums. And Khader overestimated the goodwill and stayed on with a grin. It was a solemn moment. Ommachan seized the moment to pluck the first cocoa fruit. He looked like he was receiving holy communion.

And he proffered the fruit to the vicar: "The first cocoa fruit."

"You keep it. What'll the saint do with a useless fruit?" the vicar said. I still believe that if Khader had left the scene, the vicar would have received it.

"The first fruit, Father," Ommachan insisted. I pinched him on his wrist; he got the message and handed over the fruit to me, and the vicar and the people dispersed and the question "What'll the saint do with a useless fruit?" went down into history.

Ommachan didn't know where to sell the seeds of the first harvest. From a chocolate wrapper, I found out the address of the Bombay office of an American corporation and drafted my first English letter. Based on my vast research on cocoa, I advised him to keep the seeds sun-dried and to guard the ripening fruits from being drilled by beetles and squirrels and neighbors.

A month later, an agent of the multinational corporation arrived in Thidanad with his gold-trimmed leather suitcase. He wore the kind of jacket Nehru used to wear. He could barely speak the local language. That was a good sign. The visit is still remembered along with the visit of the Bishop. About the two crisp hundred-rupee notes that the man gave Ommachan, people said they were so warm and green that surely the man was just done printing them that morning.

When the man left, Ommachan treated me to tea and fried bananas and patted me on my back: "You most knowledgeable boy in the whole world. You run for Government." Sitting inside the tea shop, I suggested he start a nursery. To raise cocoa saplings for sale in the seven villages of the region.

Ommachan sprang up from his seat, glowing with a smile immortalized by his father, Esthappan. The old man smiled like that after an invention failed. Ommachan smiled before. Right away Ommachan wanted to undertake the nursery project, and he came up with a name for it: Inventor Esthappan Memorial Cocoa Nursery. The name worried me. Such was the colossal failure associated with Esthappan, whose best invention was his own coffin.

News spread that Ommachan could now live a whole week on the income from a single cocoa pod. It was true. People arrived from all the seven villages begging for a seed. The last one was Kanat Joseph. He brought a recommendation letter from the vicar.

"Come back in six months. I will give you saplings. As many as you want," Ommachan said.

One day Ommachan mentioned that he was selling off his two acres of rubber. To develop the first cocoa plantation.

"What if the prices came back up?" I asked.

"That's impossible," he said.

"Get your Mama to spend some of her moldy bundles and buy some cheap land," I said. We laughed. And I didn't think he was capable of chopping down the rubber trees until I heard that he had actually sounded it out to Valia Mama. She became angry and bit him; she could not find her torture weapon: the broom. A week later, while Valia Mama was at the church confessing the sin, Ommachan brought some lumbermen and chopped down the trees. Mama didn't faint when she returned to see the devastation. Ommachan did. Mama had found her broom.

Ommachan recovered and successfully planted three hundred cocoa saplings, and on the remaining little patch, he started the Inventor Esthappan Memorial Cocoa Nursery. Valia Mama went around the village broadcasting her intention to live as a nun for the rest of her life.

More gentlemen stopped by Ommachan's house to beg for a single cocoa seed. Ommachan repeated, "Come back in six months. Six months."

Many years after the Chocolate War had ended, I would find out how Ommachan had resisted the demands of the whole village, yet succumbed to a girl, Rosamma. One evening while Ommachan was shuttling between his nursery and the river, watering the saplings, he noticed a large round leaf floating down the river, carrying some kind of a payload. It was a letter. Ommachan remembered Rosamma's old threat, but Rosamma standing breast-deep in the water looked like a heroine out of a Bombay movie: bathing, smiling, soaping her famous body.

Ommachan looked around and quickly grabbed the letter and let the leaf float downstream. The letter read like this:

> My dear Ommachan to know,
>
> The person writing this letter is bathing right above the river where you are collecting water for your darlings. I am writing to you because I saw you looking at me. Please don't look at me like that. What will the world think of us? My friends say that you are working too hard and have become like a pencil. What's wrong with that? I heard what you had said about me. Two pointed cocoa pods, etc. I don't hate you for that. You know I was planning to become a nun, like Mother Teresa, and so I cannot hate anyone. Now I don't want to be a nun, though. My friends said you're bad and so I said something to you. I wasn't mad at you. But how can I say I love you? Shame, shame, isn't it? That's why I threatened to do to you your daddy's hobby but that was just to make you smile. Please smile. I am watching. Please tear up this letter. I will write again. Smile. Let me see.
>
> Your loving R
>
> P.S. Could you give my daddy some cocoa seeds?

That evening Ommachan personally delivered two dozen cocoa seeds to Kanat Joseph and thus one man came to have a head start into disaster.

By next year Ommachan had sold twenty-five thousand cocoa saplings. Valia Mama was pleased. The chocolate agent set up a collection center in Kottayam. I found out years later that every village had an Ommachan promoting the magic tree of the Green Revolution and that every village had a Chocolate War.

Ommachan started receiving floating-letter advice on personal habits. He started brushing his teeth on a daily basis. The traveling barber shaved him every morning, and he added two shirts to his wardrobe. The village worried about Ommachan becoming rich. The matchmakers put his name back on their lists. The rubber prices continued to decline; Ommachan's three hundred cocoa trees continued to grow and yield large quantities of cocoa pods. Every morning I saw Ommachan coming to the market with a cartload of cocoa, and he returned home with a bag full of money.

"Look at Ommachan's money bag. Fat and ugly and swollen like a pregnant buffalo's," Ouseph Sir, the retired schoolteacher, said at the tea shop.

"Thank God, he doesn't come here to yap about his Green Revolution." Kanat Joseph agreed. He, too, had begun to earn good money from his two dozen trees. But he was afraid to take the next step: to chop down ten acres of his rubber, which would have yielded latex for another twenty years.

Even the vicar started to mention the Green Revolution in his sermons. When parishioners didn't pay the tithes, he equated rubber trees with the barren oak in the parables, inspiring more people to chop down their plantations.

The first saplings Ommachan had sold in the region had already begun to yield fruits. Soon more bullock carts were coming out of the village roads with stacks of gunny sacks packed with cocoa. Every evening, trucks arrived in the market to transport the seeds to the collection center in the city.

Kanat Joseph was the first big farmer to cut down his rubber trees. Before making the decision, he did talk to the expert: "Imagine this. Me chop off all my rubber. Then the cocoa prices fall. Me left with no rubber! No cocoa! Will I end up begging in the streets, Ommachan?"

"Naaay," Ommachan said. "If they sent it from America, this plant got to have some nice future. Better than the goddamn rubber."

"How do you know?" Kanat Joseph rolled his rosary beads.

"Because the Americans make rubber from crude oil. Real cheap. And Europeans? Crude. Russians and Japanese? Crude. Cheap like cow dung. Then how do you expect our little rubber sheets to make money in the future?"

I had taught Ommachan this line of argument. Kanat Joseph was so impressed with Ommachan, he summoned his family matchmaker to discuss Rosamma's future.

From Rosamma's fifty-ninth floating letter, Ommachan received an intelligence report about her daddy's decision to replace all his rubber with cocoa. But daddy wasn't going to give him an order for ten thousand saplings. Daddy had grown them himself. In the postscript, she promised to marry Ommachan if he bought a car and drove her to the cinema every Saturday and to the church every Sunday. Ommachan would have to save up for three years to buy a car. He could have done it faster had he cultivated a larger plot. He didn't have any more land. And Mama wasn't willing to expend the large amounts rumored to have been stashed away in some mysterious clay pot.

Nineteen seventy-three. I graduated from high school and went away to the city to study economics at the University of Kerala: to be of service to my fellow beings. Kanat Joseph became the first big farmer to chop down his rubber trees. Ten acres of them. Then suddenly a war broke out between the Arabs and Israelis. I read in the newspapers that the Arab nations were cutting off the oil supply to America and Europe and that the rubber prices had started to shoot up.

Back home, the only buyer of the raw cocoa suddenly lowered the price from twenty rupees per kilogram to twenty-five rupees for a truckload.

The effect was quite palpable.

Ommachan was trying to send a floating reply to Rosamma, begging her to be patient about the car, consoling her that cocoa prices would rise again, that her daddy would stop breaking things at home, that the nasty rubber prices would have to hit the bottom, and that he would marry Rosamma without any dowry, as her father now wished.

Since the letter would not sail upstream, Ommachan walked up the strand as usual and sent the letter floating down the stream, on a ripe yellow cocoa leaf.

Ommachan watched the leaf slowly reach Rosamma's breasts as they emerged out of the soapy bubbles. She was angry. With a single swat she drowned the letter. Ommachan sat down in the sand and wept.

The chocolate company couldn't take any more cocoa, even for free. The trucks stopped coming to the market. A farmer threw a cartload of cocoa into the river. The cocoa pods floated like a yellow raft. Newspapers wrote that the Green Revolution was such a success in India that Harvard University was going to publish a book about it. The headlines raved that the rubber prices had been quadrupled in two months, and the Chocolate War broke out.

Ommachan took the first beating in the dark. He reached home bleeding from his nose. He did not know who did it. No voices. No faces.

The next week, Ommachan was found unconscious in a ditch. Another set of enemies had handled him in the dark. Again, no faces. Just plain beatings with green sticks and bare hands. When Ommachan was able to get out of bed, he went to the church to seek help from the vicar. A mob stopped him right in front of the church. And they started thrashing him. It was not even dark. Everyone in the mob lay hands on Ommachan, except three gentlemen farmers, one of whom was Kanat Joseph.

The mob left him bleeding in the street. Invoking the name of St. George, Ommachan begged for help. The three gentlemen offered help.

Two of the gentlemen held up Ommachan.

"Here is a final one for your Mama!" Kanat Joseph shouted, delivering a big one on Ommachan's navel. "And this one for flirting with my daughter." The second blow was harder. No wonder Rosamma had complained about her daddy breaking furniture and plates.

The three gentlemen left Ommachan right at the foot of the famous statue of St. George slaying the dragon.

Throughout the year, the Chocolate War raged in Thidanad. Father wrote to me not to return home for the vacation because I would be beaten up, too, for giving that kind of economic advice.

The nights were full of furious outcries against Ommachan. Then one night, it all ended. Rosamma had sent him her last floating letter: free advice for Ommachan, given with love, she wrote. He took the advice: that night as the whole village looked on, Ommachan mowed down his cocoa trees and piled them up and poured kerosene and set them on fire. Ouseph Sir reported that Ommachan had to rekindle the fire again and again because his tears kept extinguishing it.

Soon, the other green revolutionaries followed the good example. They threw the beheaded trees, complete with the glowing fruits, to the goats and cows.

No one beat up Ommachan anymore, and they even honored him with a nickname: Chocolate. The first thing Chocolate Ommachan did upon clearing the land was to plant a banana tree for St. George. Then he started planting the good old rubber trees again. This time the saplings came from the research laboratories of the Malay Peninsula.

Many years after the Chocolate War, we found out the true villain of the story: it was Mohammad Khader, with his wretched black tongue.

JAIME MANRIQUE

I've been writing all my fiction in English since 1984, but I've continued writing essays in both languages, and poetry almost exclusively in Spanish. I am still resistant to saying good-bye to the Spanish language when it comes to writing my poetry—I don't have the confidence that I'd like to have yet. And the truth be told, it seems to me that this would be the ultimate betrayal—which is not to say that someday I won't feel differently about it.

People find my bilingualism confusing, though I no longer spend time thinking about it. I've come to accept that I write in two languages and that sadly, because of the lack of commitment to just one language, I'll probably never achieve greatness as a stylist in either language. This is okay with me, because I'm more interested in substance than in form, in what's being said than in the way it is said. This does not mean that I don't appreciate the importance of style. On the contrary: I hope someday people will think of me as a graceful practitioner of the English language, as someone capable of musicality and even elegance—the qualities I strive to achieve in everything I write.

The Documentary Artist

I met Sebastian when he enrolled in one of my film-directing classes at the university where I teach. Soon after the semester started, he distinguished himself from the other students because he was very vocal about his love of horror movies. Our special intimacy started one afternoon when he burst into my office, took a seat before I invited him to do so, and began telling me in excruciating detail about a movie called *The Evil Mommy*, which he had seen in one of those Forty-second Street theaters he frequented. "And at the end of the movie," he said, "as the boy is praying in the chapel to the statue of this bleeding Christ on the cross, Christ turns into the evil mommy and she jumps off the cross and removes the butcher knife stuck between her breasts and goes for the boy's neck. She chases the screaming boy all over the church, until she gets him." He paused, to check my reaction. "After she cuts off his head," he went on, almost with relish, "she places his head on the altar." As he narrated these events, the whites of Sebastian's eyes distended frighteningly, his fluttering hands drew arabesques in front of his face, and guttural, gross croaks erupted from the back of his throat.

I was both amused and unsettled by his wild, manic performance. Although I'm no great fan of B horror movies, I was impressed by his love of film. Also I appreciated the fact that he wasn't colorless or lethargic as were so many of my students; I found his drollness, and the aura of weirdness he cultivated, enchanting. Even so, right that minute I decided I would do my best to keep him at a distance. It wasn't so much that I was attracted to him (which is always dangerous for a teacher), but that I found his energy a bit unnerving.

Sebastian started showing up at least once a week during my office hours. He never made an appointment, and he seldom discussed his work with me. There's a couch across from my chair but he always sat on the bench that abuts the door, as if he were afraid to come any closer. He'd talk about the new horror movies he'd seen, and sometimes he'd drop a casual invitation to see a movie together. It soon became clear to me that, because of his dirty clothes, disheveled hair, and loudness, and because of his love of the bizarre and gothic, he was a loner.

One day I was having a sandwich in the cafeteria when he came over and joined me.

"You've heard of Foucault?" he asked me.

"Sure. Why?"

"Well, last night I had a dream in which Foucault talked to me and told me to explore my secondary discourse. In the dream there was a door with a sign that said *Leather* and *Pain.* Foucault ordered me to open it. When I did, I heard a voice that told me to come and see you today."

I stopped munching my sandwich and sipped my coffee.

"This morning I had my nipple pierced," Sebastian continued, touching the spot on his T-shirt. "The guy who did it told me about a guy who pierced his dick, and then made two dicks out of his penis so he could double the pleasure."

My mouth fell open. I sat there speechless. Sebastian stood up. "See you in class," he said as he left the table.

I lost my appetite. I considered mentioning the conversation to the department chairman. Dealing with students' crushes was not new to me; in my time I, too, had had crushes on some of my teachers. I decided it was all harmless, and that as long as I kept at a distance and didn't encourage him, there was no reason to be alarmed. As I reviewed my own feelings, I told myself that I was not attracted to him, so I wasn't in danger of playing into his game.

Then Sebastian turned in his first movie, an absurdist zany farce shot in one room and in which he played all the roles and murdered all the characters in very gruesome ways. The boundless energy of this work excited me.

One afternoon, late that fall, he came to see me, looking upset. His father had had a heart attack, and Sebastian was going home to New Hampshire to see him in the hospital. I had already approved his proposal for his final project that semester, an adaptation of Kafka's *The Hunger Artist.* I reassured him that even if he had to be absent for a couple of weeks, it would not affect his final grade.

"Oh, that's nice," he said, lowering his head. "But, you know, I'm upset about going home because I'm gay."

"Have you come out to them?" I asked.

"Are you kidding?" His eyes filled with rage. "My parents would shit cookies if they knew."

"You never know," I said. "Parents can be very forgiving when it comes to their children."

"Not my parents," he snorted. Sebastian then told me his story. "When I was in my teens I took one of those I.Q. tests and it said I was a mathematical genius or something. That's how I ended up at M.I.T., at fifteen, with a full scholarship. You know, I was just kind of a loner. All I wanted was to make my parents happy. So I studied hard, and made straight A's, but I hated that shit and those people. My classmates and my teachers were as..." he paused, and there was anger and sadness in his voice. "They were as abstract and dry as those numbers and theories they pumped in my head. One day I thought, if I stay here, I'm going to be a basket case before I graduate. I had always wanted to make horror films. Movies are the only thing I care about. That's when I announced to my parents my decision to quit M.I.T. and to come to New York to pursue my studies in film directing."

His parents, as Sebastian put it, "freaked." They were blue-collar people who had pinned all their hopes on him and his brother, an engineer. There was a terrible row. Sebastian went to a friend's house, where he got drunk. That night, driving back home, he lost control of his car and crashed it against a tree. For forty-five days he was in a coma. When he came out of it, nothing could shake his decision to study filmmaking. He received a partial scholarship at the school where I teach, and he supported himself by doing catering jobs and working as an extra in movies. He told me about how brutal his father was to the entire family; about the man's bitterness. So now, a year after he had left M.I.T., going back home to see his father in the hospital was hard. Sebastian wasn't sure he should go, but he wanted to be there in case his father died.

When Sebastian didn't return to school in two weeks, I called his number in the city but got a machine. I left messages on a couple of occasions but got no reply. Next I called his parents. His mother informed me that his father was out of danger and that Sebastian had returned to New York. At the end of the semester I gave him an "incomplete."

In the summer I started a documentary of street life in New York. I spent a great deal of my time in the streets with my video camera, shooting whatever struck me as odd or representative of street life. In the fall, Sebastian did not show up and I thought about him less and less.

One gray, drizzly afternoon in November I had just finished shooting in the neighborhood of Washington Square Park. In the gathering darkness, the park was bustling with people getting out of work, students going to evening classes, and the new batch of junkies, who came out only after sunset.

I had shot footage of so many homeless people in the last few months that I wouldn't have paused to notice this man if it weren't for the fact that it was beginning to sprinkle harder and he was on his knees, with a cardboard sign that said HELP ME, I AM HUNGRY around his neck, his hands in prayer position, and his face—eyes shut—pointed toward the inhospitable sky. He was bearded, with long, ash-blond hair, and as emaciated and broken as one of Gauguin's Christs. I stopped to get my camera ready, and, as I moved closer, I saw that the man looked familiar—it was Sebastian.

I wouldn't call myself a very compassionate guy. I mean, I give money to beggars once in a while, depending on my mood, especially if they do not look like crackheads. But I'm not like some of my friends who work in soup kitchens or, in the winter, take sandwiches and blankets to the people sleeping in dark alleys or train stations.

Yet I couldn't ignore Sebastian, and not because he had been one of my students and I was fond of him, but because I was so sure of his talent.

I stood there, waiting for Sebastian to open his eyes. I was getting drenched, and it looked like he was lost in his thoughts, so I said, "Sebastian, it's me, Santiago, your film teacher."

He smiled, though now his teeth were brown and cracked. His eyes lit up, too—not with recognition but with the nirvana of dementia.

I took his grimy hand in both of mine and pressed it warmly even though I was repelled by his filth. At that moment I became aware of the cold rain, the passersby, the hubbub of the city traffic, the throng of New York City dusk on fall evenings, when New Yorkers rush around in excitement, on their way to places, to bright futures and unreasonable hopes, to their loved ones and home. I locked my hands around his, as if to save him, as if to save myself from the thunderbolt of pain that had lodged in my chest.

"Hi, prof," Sebastian said finally.

"You have to get out of this rain or you'll get sick," I said, yanking at his hand, coaxing him to get off the sidewalk.

"OK, OK," he acquiesced apologetically as he got up.

Sebastian stood with shoulders hunched, his head leaning to one side, looking downward. There was a strange, utterly disconnected smile on his lips—the insane, stifled giggle of a child who's been caught doing something naughty; a boy who feels both sorry about and amused at his antics. The smile of someone who has a sense of humor, but doesn't believe he has a right to smile. Sebastian had become passive, broken, and frightened like a battered dog. Fear darted in his eyes.

"Would you like to come to my place for a cup of coffee?" I said.

"Thanks," he said, avoiding my eyes.

Gently, so as not to scare him, I removed the cardboard sign from around his neck. I hailed a cab. On my way home we were silent. I rolled down the window because Sebastian's stench was unbearable. A part of me wished I had given him a few bucks and gone on with my business.

Inside the apartment, I said, "You'd better get out of those wet clothes before you catch pneumonia." I asked him to undress in my bedroom, gave him a bathrobe, and told him to take a shower. He left his dirty clothes on the floor, and, while he was showering, I went through the pockets of his clothes, looking for a clue to his current condition.

There were a few coins in his pockets, some keys, and a glass pipe, the kind crackheads use to smoke in doorways. The pipe felt more repugnant than a rotting rodent in my hand; it was like an evil entity that threatened to destroy everything living and healthy. I dropped it on the bed and went to the kitchen, where I washed my hands with detergent and scalding water. I was aware that I was behaving irrationally, but I couldn't control myself. I returned to my bedroom, where I piled up his filthy rags, made a bundle, put them in a trash bag, and dumped them in the garbage.

Sebastian and I were almost the same height, although he was so wasted that he'd swim in my clothes. But at least he'd look clean, I thought, as I pulled out of my closet thermal underwear, socks, a pair of jeans, a flannel shirt, and an olive army jacket I hadn't worn in years. I wanted to get rid of his torn, smelly sneakers, but his shoe size was larger than mine. I laid out all these clothes on the bed and went to the kitchen to make coffee and sandwiches. When I finished, I collapsed on the living-room couch and turned on the TV.

Sebastian remained in my bedroom for a long time. Beginning to worry, I opened the door. He was sitting on my bed, wearing the clean clothes, and staring at his image in the full-length mirror of the closet. His beard and hair were still wet and unkempt, but he looked presentable.

"Nice shirt," he whispered, patting the flannel at his shoulder.

"It looks good on you," I said. Now that he was clean and dressed in clean clothes, with his blond hair and green eyes, he was a good-looking boy.

We sat around the table. Sebastian grabbed a sandwich and started eating slowly, taking small bites and chewing with difficulty, as if his gums hurt. I wanted to confront him about the crack, but I didn't know how to do it without alienating him. Sebastian ate, holding the sandwich close to his nose, staring at his lap all the time. He ate parsimoniously and he drank his coffee in little sips, making strange slurping noises, such as I imagined a thirsty animal would make.

When he finished eating, our eyes met. He stood up. "Thanks. I'm going, OK?"

"Where are you going?" I asked, getting frantic. "It's raining. Do your parents know how to reach you?"

"My parents don't care," he said without animosity.

"Sebastian, I'm sure they care. You're their child and they love you."

I saw he was becoming upset, so I decided not to press the point. "You can sleep here tonight. The couch is very comfortable."

Staring at his sneakers, he shook his head. "That's cool. Thanks, anyway. I'll see you around." He took a couple of steps toward the door.

"Wait," I said and rushed to the bedroom for the jacket. I gave it to him, and an umbrella, too.

Sebastian placed the rest of his sandwich in a side pocket and put on the jacket. He grabbed the umbrella at both ends and studied it, as if he had forgotten what it was used for.

I scribbled both my home and office numbers on a piece of paper. "You can call me anytime you need me," I said, also handing him a $10 bill, which I gave him with some apprehension because I was almost sure he'd use it to buy crack. Sebastian took the number but returned the money.

"It's yours," I said. "Please take it."

"It's too much," he said, surprising me. "Just give me enough for coffee."

I fished for a bunch of coins in my pocket and gave them to him.

Hunching his shoulders and giving me his weird smile, Sebastian accepted them. Suddenly I knew what the smile reminded me of: it was Charlie Chaplin's smile as the tramp in *City Lights*. Sebastian opened the door and took the stairs instead of waiting for the elevator.

The following day, I went back to the corner where I had found him the day before, but Sebastian wasn't around. I started filming in that neighborhood exclusively. I became obsessed with finding Sebastian again. I had dreams in which I'd see him with dozens of other junkies tweaking in the murky alleys of New York. Sometimes I'd spot a young man begging who, from the distance, would look like Sebastian. This, I know, is what happens to people when their loved ones die.

That Christmas, I took to the streets again, ostensibly to shoot more footage, but secretly hoping to find Sebastian. It was around that time that the homeless stopped being for me anonymous human roaches of the urban squalor. Now they were people with features, with faces, with stories, with loved ones desperately looking for them, trying to save them. No longer moral lepers to be shunned, the young among them especially fascinated me. I wondered how many of them were intelligent, gifted, even geniuses who, because of crack or other drugs, or rejection, or hurt, or lack of love, had taken to the streets, choosing to drop out in the worst way.

The documentary and my search for Sebastian became one. This search took me to places I had never been before. I started to ride the subway late at night, filming the homeless who slept in the cars, seeking warmth, traveling all night long. Most of them were black, and many were young, and a great number of them seemed insane. I became adept at distinguishing the different shades of street people. The ones around Forty-second Street looked vicious, murderous, possessed by the virulent devils of the drugs. The ones who slept on the subways—or at Port Authority, Grand Central, and Penn Station—were poorer, did not deal in drugs or prostitution. Many of them were cripples, or retarded, and their eyes didn't flash the message KILLKILLKILLKILL. I began to hang out outside the city shelters where they passed the nights. I looked for Sebastian in those places, in the parks, along the waterfronts of Manhattan, under the bridges, anywhere these people congregate. Sebastian's smile—the smile he had given me as he left my apartment— hurt me like an ice pick slamming at my heart.

One Saturday afternoon late in April, I was on my way to see Blake, a guy I had met recently in a soup kitchen where I had started doing volunteer work. Since I was half an hour early and the evening was pleasant, the air warm and inviting, I went into Union Square Park to admire the flowers.

I was sitting on a bench facing east when Sebastian passed by me and sat on the next bench. Although it was too warm for it, he was still wearing the jacket I had given him in the winter. He was carrying a knapsack, and in one hand he held what looked like a can of beer wrapped in a paper bag. He kept his free hand on the knapsack as if to guard it from thieves; and with the other hand, he took sips from his beer, all the while staring at his rotting sneakers.

Seeing him wearing that jacket was very strange. It was as though he were wearing a part of me, as if he had borrowed one of my limbs. I debated whether to approach him, or just to get up and walk away. For the last couple of months—actually since I had met Blake—my obsession with finding Sebastian had lifted. I got up.

My heart began to beat so fast I was sure people could hear it. I breathed in deeply; I looked straight ahead at the tender new leaves dressing the trees, the beautifully arranged and colorful beds of flowers, the denuded sky, which wore a coat of enameled topaz, streaked with pink, and breathed in the air, which was unusually light, and then I walked up to where Sebastian sat.

Anxiously, I said, "Sebastian, how are you?" Without surprise, he looked up. I was relieved to see the mad grin was gone.

"Hi," he greeted me.

I sat next to him. His jacket was badly soiled, and a pungent, putrid smell emanated from him. His face was bruised, his lips chapped and inflamed, but he didn't seem withdrawn.

"Are you getting enough to eat? Do you have a place to sleep?" I asked.

"How're you doing?" he said evasively.

"I'm OK. I've been worried about you. I looked for you all winter." My voice trailed off; I was beginning to feel agitated.

"Thanks. But believe me, this is all I can handle right now," he said carefully, with frightening lucidity. "I'm not crazy. I know where to go for help if I want it. I want you to understand that I'm homeless because I chose to be homeless; I choose not to integrate," he said with vehemence. Forcefully, with seriousness, he added, "This is where I feel OK for now."

The lights of the buildings had begun to go on, like fireflies on the darkening sky. A chill ran through me. I reached in my pocket for a few bills and pressed them in his swollen, raw hands.

"I'm listed in the book. If you ever need me, call me, OK? I'll always be happy to hear from you."

"Thanks. I appreciate it."

I placed a hand on his shoulder and squeezed hard. I got up, turned around, and loped out of Union Square.

Several months went by. I won't say I forgot about Sebastian completely in the interval, but life intervened. I finished my documentary that summer. In the fall, it was shown by some public television stations to generally good reviews but low ratings.

One night, a month ago, I decided to go see a movie everybody was talking about. Because it was rather late, the theater was almost empty. A couple of young people on a date sat in the row in front of me, and there were other patrons scattered throughout the big house.

The movie, set in Brooklyn, was gloomy and arty, but the performers and the cinematography held my interest and I didn't feel like going back home yet, so I stayed. Toward the end of the movie there is a scene in which the main character barges into a bar, riding his motorcycle. Except for the bartender and a sailor sitting at the counter, the bar is empty. The camera pans slowly from left to right, and there, wearing a sailor suit, is Sebastian. He slowly turns around and stares into the camera and consequently into the audience. The moment lasts two, maybe three seconds, and I was so surprised, I gasped. Seeing Sebastian unexpectedly rattled me so much I had trouble remaining in my seat until the movie ended.

I called Sebastian's parents early the next morning. This time, his mother answered. I introduced myself, and, to my surprise, she remembered me. I told her about what had happened the night before and how it made me realize I hadn't seen or heard from their son in quite some time.

"Actually, I'm very glad you called," she said softly, in a voice that was girlish but vibrant with emotions. "Sebastian passed away six weeks ago. We have one of his movie tapes that I thought of sending you since your encouragement meant so much to him."

Then she told me the details of Sebastian's death: he had been found on a bench in Central Park and had apparently died of pneumonia and acute anemia. Fortunately, he still carried some ID with him, so the police were able to track down his parents. In his knapsack, they had found a movie tape labeled *The Hunger Artist.*

I asked her if she had seen it.

"I tried to, but it was too painful," she sighed.

"I'd be honored to receive it; I assure you I'll always treasure it," I said.

We chatted for a short while and then, after I gave her my address, we said good-bye. A few days later, on my way to school, I found the tape in my mailbox. I carried it with me all day long, and decided to wait until I got home that night to watch it.

After dinner, I sat down to watch Sebastian's last film. On a piece of cardboard, scrawled in a childish, gothic calligraphy and in big characters, appeared THE HUNGER ARTIST BY SEBASTIAN X. INSPIRED BY THE STORY OF MR. FRANZ KAFKA.

The film opened with an extreme closeup of Sebastian. I realized he must have started shooting when he was still in school because he looked healthy, his complexion was good, and his eyes were limpid. Millimetrically, the camera studies his features: the right eye, the left one; pursed lips, followed by a wide-open smile that flashes two rows of teeth in good condition. Next we see Sebastian's ears, and, finally, in a characteristic Sebastian touch, the camera looks into his nostrils. One of the nostrils is full of snot. I stopped the film. I was shaking. I have films and tapes of relatives and friends who are dead, and when I look at them, I experience a deep ocean of bittersweetness. After they've been dead for a while, the feelings we have are stirring but resolved; there's no torment in them. However, seeing Sebastian's face on the screen staring at me, I experienced the feeling I've always had for old actors I love, passionately, even though they died before I was born. It was, for example, like the perfection of the love I'd felt for Leslie Howard in *Pygmalion*, although I didn't see that movie until I was grown up. I could not deny anymore that I had been in love with Sebastian; that I had stifled my passion for him because I knew I could never fulfill it. That's why I had denied the nature of my concern for him. I pressed the play button, and the film continued. Anything was better than what I was feeling.

Now the camera pulls back, and we see him sitting in a lotus position, wearing shorts. On the wall behind him, there is a sign that reads, THE ARTIST HAS GONE TWO HOURS WITHOUT EATING. WORLD RECORD! There is a cut to the audience. A woman with long green hair, lots of mascara, and purple eye shadow, her lips painted in a grotesque way, chews gum, blows it like a baseball player, and sips a diet Coke. She nods approvingly all the time. The camera cuts to Sebastian staring at her impassively. Repeating this pattern, we see a man in a three-piece suit—an executive type watching the artist and taking notes. He's followed by a buxom blonde bedecked with huge costume jewelry; she is pecking at a large box of popcorn dripping with butter, and drinking a beer. She wears white silk gloves. We see at least half a dozen people, each one individually—Sebastian plays them all. This sequence ends with hands clapping. As the spectators exit the room, they leave money in a dirty ashtray. The gloved hand leaves a card that says, IF YOU EVER GET REALLY HUNGRY, CALL ME! This part of the film, shot in garish, neon colors, has, however, the feel of an early film; it is silent.

The camera cuts to the face of Peter Jennings, who is doing the evening news. We cannot hear what he says. Cut again to Sebastian in a lotus position. Cut to the headline: ARTIST BREAKS HUNGER RECORD: 24 HOURS WITHOUT EATING.

The next time we see the fasting artist, he's in the streets and the photography is in black and white. For soundtrack we hear sirens blaring, fire trucks screeching, buses idling, huge trucks braking, cars speeding, honking and crashing, cranes demolishing gigantic structures. This part of the film must have been shot when Sebastian was already homeless. He must have carried his camera in his knapsack, or he must have rented one, but it's clear that whatever money he collected panhandling, he used to complete the film. In this portion he uses a hand-held camera to stress the documentary feeling. I can only imagine that he used street people to operate the camera for him. Sebastian's deterioration speeds up: his clothes become more soiled and tattered; his disguises at this point are less convincing—it must be nearly impossible for a starving person to impersonate someone else. His cheeks are sunken, his pupils shine like the eyes of a feral animal in the dark. The headlines read: 54 DAYS WITHOUT EATING...102 DAYS...111 DAYS. Instead of clapping hands, we see a single hand in motion; it makes a gesture as if it were shooing the artist away.

Sebastian disappears from the film. We have footage of people in soup lines and the homeless scavenging in garbage cans. An interview with a homeless person ends the film. We don't see the face of the person conducting the interview, but the voice is Sebastian's. He reads passages from Kafka's story to a homeless woman and asks her to comment. She replies with a soundless laughter that exposes her diseased gums.

I pressed the rewind button and sat in my chair in a stupor. I felt shattered by the realization that what I don't know about what lies in my own heart is much greater than anything else I do know about it. I was so stunned and drained that I hardly had the energy to get up and walk to the VCR to remove the tape.

Later that night, still upset, I decided to go for a walk. It was one of those cold, blustery nights of late autumn, but its gloominess suited my mood. A glacial wind howled, skittering up and down the deserted streets of Gotham. I trudged around until the tip of my nose was an icicle. As I kept walking in a southerly direction, getting closer and closer to the southernmost point of the island, I was aware of the late hour and of how the "normal" citizens of New York were, for the most part, at home, warmed by their fires, seeking escape in a book or their TV sets, or finding solace in the arms of their loved one, or in the caresses of strangers.

I kept walking on and on, passing along the way the homeless who on a night like this chose to stay outside or couldn't find room in a shelter. As I passed them in the dark streets, I did so without my usual fear or repugnance. I kept pressing forward, into the narrowing alleys, going toward the phantasmagorical lament of the arctic wind sweeping over the Hudson, powerless over the mammoth steel structures of this city.

MINFONG HO

Like so many stories, "The Winter Hibiscus" is a synthesis of the various linguistic and cultural strands of my own experience. Like Saeng in this story, I used to take refuge in greenhouses during winter afternoons while I was a student at Cornell University and, like her, I had the kind of bifocal sensibility that comes with growing up with one language and then being a grown-up in another.

I did not grow up hearing or speaking English. The voices of my earliest childhood speak to me in Chinese. My father, in his deep quiet monotone, would tell me wonderful bedtime stories in Cantonese. My grandmother, my aunts, my amahs too, spoke in Cantonese, teasing or scolding me, or laughing and whispering among themselves, in an easy conspiracy. My mother's voice was cooler, more aloof, as she taught us T'ang Dynasty poems in Mandarin, evoking through them images of misty mountains in an exquisite but remote China. As naturally as I absorbed the basic feelings of love and anger, praise and blame that my family poured over me, so I also absorbed these two Chinese dialects. Thus Chinese is the language with the deepest emotional resonance for me. It was the only language which mattered, and I think of it as the language of my heart. Perhaps that's why, even now, when I cry, I cry in Chinese.

If Chinese is the language of my heart, then Thai is the language of my hands, a functional language which connected me to the wide world outside my family. Growing up on the outskirts of Bangkok in Thailand, I absorbed the simple Thai spoken by peddlers as they walked down our lane, swinging their baskets of fruit from their shoulder poles. It was in Thai that I would ask for a ripe guava or pickled mango, mixed with sugar or salt or chili sauce. At the Sunday market at Sanam Luang, it was Thai that I bargained in, picking out a potted orchid or a new kite. And it was in Thai that I would play hide and seek, or kickball with the neighborhood children. This busy, tactile childhood world swirled with the light, nuanced sounds of Thai, and I had only to reach out to touch it, connect with it, hold it in my hands. I taste and touch in Thai.

English came only much later, when I started learning it in school, in about the third or fourth grade. For a long time it was confined to the classroom, separate from the Chinese and Thai of my immediate world. Learning English was a form of intellectual exercise, and so I think of it as a language of my head. With all its rules and regulations, its grammar textbooks and arcane tests, it was really more of a discipline than a language. No wonder that for me, English is a language of the head.

What happens when you have a different language for your heart, your hands, your head?

Fragmentation.

There is a strange split that takes place, as if one's head cannot express what one's heart feels, or what one's hands touch.

For me, writing has become a way to try and piece together the bits and pieces of myself, a kind of glue which could cement the separate languages of my head, my hand and my heart. And I write in English because ironically, through years of sheer academic pressure, that is the language I have become most proficient in, even though it is the one which evokes the least feeling and memory in me. I may cry in Chinese and taste in Thai, but I write in English.

In that sense, it is very much a stepmother tongue for me. I feel a certain uneasy self-consciousness when I use it, as if I must always be on guard against making mistakes, because under a stepmother's judgmental gaze, acceptance has to be earned rather than assumed. And sometimes, yes, I do feel like a kind of cultural Frankenstein, when those who speak only English regard my fluency in "their" language as freakish, an interesting but somewhat grotesque mimicry of a language which belongs to them but was only lent to me.

Still, to be fair, this stepmother tongue has been good to me: it has allowed me to bring back what is gone, to relive what is lost, to make a mosaic out of fragments. And to feel—head, hands and heart—whole again.

The Winter Hibiscus

Saeng stood in the open doorway and shivered as a gust of wind swept past, sending a swirl of red maple leaves rustling against her legs. Early October, and already the trees were being stripped bare. A leaf brushed against Saeng's sleeve, and she snatched at it, briefly admiring the web of dark veins against the fiery red, before letting it go again, to be carried off by the wind.

Last year she had so many maple leaves pressed between her thick algebra textbook, that her teacher had suggested gently that she transfer the leaves to some other books at home. Instead, Saeng had simply taken the carefully pressed leaves out, and left them in a pile in her room, where they moldered, turned smelly, and were eventually tossed out. Saeng had felt a vague regret, but no anger.

For a moment Saeng stood on the doorstep and watched the swirl of autumn leaves in the afternoon sunlight, thinking of the bleak winter ahead. She had lived through enough of them by now to dread their greyness and silence and endless bone-chilling cold. She buttoned up her coat and walked down the worn path through their yard and toward the sidewalk.

"*Bai sai?*" her mother called to her, straightening up from neat rows of hot peppers and snow peas that were growing in the vacant lot next door.

"To take my driving test," Saeng replied in English.

Saeng remembered enough Laotian to understand just about everything that her parents said to her, but she felt more comfortable now speaking in English. In the four years since they had migrated to America, they had evolved a kind of bilingual dialogue, where her parents would continue to address her brothers and her in Laotian, and they would
reply in English, with each side sometimes slipping into the other's language to convey certain key words that seemed impossible to translate.

"*Luuke ji fao bai hed yang?*" her mother asked.

"There's no rush," Saeng conceded. "I just want to get there in plenty of time."

"You'll get there much too soon, and then what? You'll just stand around fretting and making yourself tense," Mrs. Panouvong continued in Laotian. "Better that you should help me harvest some of these melons."

Saeng hesitated. How could she explain to her mother that she wanted to just "hang out" with the other schoolmates who were scheduled to take the test that afternoon, and to savor the tingle of anticipation when David Lambert would drive up in his old blue Chevy and hand her the car keys?

"The last of the hot peppers should be picked, and the kale covered with a layer of mulch," Mrs. Panouvong added, wiping one hand across her shirt and leaving a streak of mud there.

Saeng glanced down at her own clean clothes. She had dressed carefully for the test—and for David. She had on a gray wool skirt and a Fair Isles sweater, both courtesy of David's mother from their last rummage sale at the church. And she had combed out her long black hair and left it hanging straight down her back the way she had seen the blond cheerleaders do theirs, instead of bunching it up with a rubber band.

"Come help your mother a little. *Mahteh, luuke*—Come on, child," her mother said gently.

There were certain words which held a strange resonance for Saeng, as if there were whispered echoes behind them. *Luuke*, or child, was one of these words. When her mother called her *luuke* in that soft, teasing way, Saeng could hear the voices of her grandmother, and her uncle, or her primary-school teachers behind it, as if there were an invisible chorus of smiling adults calling her, chiding her.

"Just for a while," Saeng said, and walked over to the melons, careful not to get her skirt tangled in any vines.

Together they worked in companionable silence for some time. The frost had already killed the snow peas and Chinese cabbage, and Saeng helped pluck out the limp brown stems and leaves. But the bitter melons, knobby and green, were still intact, and ready to be harvested. Her mother had been insistent on planting only vegetables that weren't readily available at the local supermarkets, sending away for seeds from various Chinatowns as far away as New York and San Francisco. At first alone, then joined by the rest of her family, she had hoed the hard dirt of the vacant lot behind their dilapidated old house and planted the seeds in neat rows.

That first summer, their family had also gone smelting every night while the vast schools of fish were swimming upriver to spawn and had caught enough to fill their freezer full of smelt. And at dawn, when the dew was still thick on the grass, they had also combed the golf course at the country club for nightcrawlers, filling up large buckets of worms that they would sell later to the roadside grocery stores as fishbait. The money from selling the worms enabled them to buy a hundred-pound sack of the best long-grained fragrant rice, and that, together with the frozen smelt and homegrown vegetables, had lasted them through most of their first winter.

"America has opened her doors to us as guests," Saeng's mother had said. "We don't want to sit around waiting for its handouts like beggars." She and Mr. Panouvong had swallowed their pride and gotten jobs as a dishwasher and a janitor, and were taking English lessons at night under some state program that, to their amazement, actually paid them for studying!

By the end of their second year, they were off welfare and saving up for a cheap secondhand car, something that they could never have been able to afford as grade school teachers back in Laos.

And Saeng, their oldest child, had been designated their family driver.

"So you will be taking the driving test in the Lambert car?" Mrs. Panouvong asked now, adeptly twisting tiny hot peppers from their stems.

Saeng nodded. "Not their big station wagon, but the small blue car—David's." There it was again, that flutter of excitement as she said David's name. And yet he had hardly spoken to her more than two or three times, and each time only at the specific request of his mother.

Mrs. Lambert—their sponsor into the United States—was a large, genial woman with a ready smile and two brown braids wreathed around her head. The wife of the Lutheran minister in their town, she had already helped sponsor two Laotian refugee families and seemed to have enough energy and good will to sponsor several more. Four years ago, when they had first arrived, it was she who had taken the Panouvong family on their rounds of medical check-ups, social welfare interviews, school enrollments, and housing applications.

And it was Mrs. Lambert who had suggested, after Saeng had finished her driver education course, that she use David's car to take her driving test in. Cheerfully, David—a senior on the school basketball team—had driven Saeng around and taken her for a few test runs in his car to familiarize her with it. Exciting times they might have been for Saeng—it was the closest she had ever come to being on a date—but for David it was just something he was doing out of deference to his mother. Saeng had no illusions about this. Nor did she really mind it. It was enough for her at this point just to vaguely pretend at dating. At sixteen, she did not really feel ready for some of the things most thirteen-year-olds in America seemed to be doing. Even watching MTV sometimes made her wince in embarrassment.

"He's a good boy, David is," Saeng's mother said, as if echoing Saeng's thoughts. "Listens to his mother and father." She poured the hot peppers from her cupped palm to a woven basket and looked at Saeng. "How are you going to thank him, for letting you use his car and everything?"

Saeng considered this. "I'll say thank you, I guess. Isn't that enough?"

"I think not. Why don't you buy for him a Big Mac?" Big Mac was one of the few English words Mrs. Panouvong would say, pronouncing it *Bee-Maag*. Ever since her husband had taken them to a McDonald's as a treat after his first pay raise, she had thought of Big Macs as the epitome of everything American.

To her daughter's surprise, she fished out a twenty dollar bill from her coat pocket now and held it out to Saeng. "You can buy yourself one too. A Bee-Maag."

Saeng did not know what to say. Here was a woman so frugal that she had insisted on taking home her containers after her McDonald's meal, suddenly handing out twenty dollars for two "children" to splurge on.

"Take it, child," Mrs. Panouvong said. "Now go—you don't want to be late for your test." She smiled. "How nice it'll be when you drive us to work. Think of all the time we'll save. And the bus fares."

The money, tucked safely away in her coat pocket, seemed to keep Saeng warm on her walk across town to the site of the driving test.

She reached it a few minutes early and stood on the corner, glancing around her. There were a few other teenagers waiting on the sidewalk or sitting on the hoods of their cars, but David was nowhere in sight. On the opposite side of the street was the McDonald's restaurant, and for a moment she imagined how it would be to have David and her sitting at one of the window seats, facing each other, in satisfyingly full view of all the passersby.

A light honk brought her back to reality. David cruised by, waving at her from his car window. He parallel parked the car, with an effortless swerve that Saeng admired, and got out.

"Ready?" David asked, eyebrow arched quizzically as he handed her his car keys.

Saeng nodded. Her mouth suddenly felt dry, and she licked her lips.

"Don't forget: step on the gas real gently. You don't want to jerk the car forward the way you did last time," David said with a grin.

"I won't," Saeng said, and managed a smile.

Another car drove up, and the test instructor stepped out of it and onto the curb in front of them. He was a pale, overweight man whose thick lips jutted out from behind a bushy mustache. On his paunch was balanced a clipboard, which he was busy marking.

Finally he looked up and saw Saeng. "Miss Saeng Panouvong?" he asked, slurring the name so much that Saeng did not recognize it as her own until she felt David nudge her slightly.

"Y—yes, sir," Saeng answered.

"Your turn. Get in."

Then Saeng was behind the wheel, the paunchy man seated next to her, clipboard on his lap.

"Drive to the end of the street and take a right," the test instructor said. He spoke in a low, bored staccato that Saeng had to strain to understand.

Obediently, she started up the car, careful to step on the accelerator very slowly, and eased the car out into the middle of the street. *Check the rear view mirror, make the hand gestures, take a deep breath,* Saeng told herself.

So far, so good. At the intersection at the end of the street, she slowed down. Two cars were coming down the cross street toward her at quite a high speed. Instinctively, she stopped and waited for them both to drive past. Instead, they both stopped, as if waiting for her to proceed.

Saeng hesitated. Should she go ahead and take the turn before them or wait until they went past?

Better to be cautious, she decided, and waited, switching gears over to neutral.

For what seemed an interminable moment, nobody moved. Then the other cars went through the intersection, one after the other. Carefully, Saeng then took her turn *(turn signal, hand signal, look both ways)*.

As she continued to drive down the street, out of the corner of her eye she saw the instructor mark down something on his clipboard.

A mistake, she thought. *He's writing down a mistake I just made. But what did I do wrong?* She stole a quick look at his face. It was stern but impassive. *Maybe I should ask him right now, what I did wrong,* Saeng wondered.

"Watch out!" he suddenly exclaimed. "That's a stop sign!"

Startled, Saeng jerked the car to a stop—but not soon enough. They were right in the middle of the crossroads.

The instructor shook his head. An almost imperceptible gesture, but Saeng noted it with a sinking feeling in her stomach.

"Back up," he snapped.

Her heart beating hard, Saeng managed to reverse the car and back up to the STOP sign that she had just gone through.

"You might as well go back to where we started out," the instructor said. "Take a right here, and another right at the next intersection."

It's over, Saeng thought. *He doesn't even want to see me go up the hill or parallel park or anything. I've failed.*

Swallowing hard, she managed to drive the rest of the way back. In the distance she could see the big M archway outside the McDonald's restaurant, and as she approached, she noticed David standing on the opposite curb, hands on his hips, watching their approach.

With gratitude she noticed that he had somehow managed to stake out two parking spaces in a row so that she could have plenty of space to swerve into place.

She breathed a deep sigh of relief when the car was safely parked. Only after she had turned off the ignition did she dare look at the instructor in the face.

"How—how did I do, sir?" she asked him, hating the quaver in her own voice.

"You'll get your results in the mail next week," he said in that bored monotone again, as if he had parroted the same sentence countless times. Then he must have seen the anxious, pleading look on Saeng's face, for he seemed to soften somewhat. "You stopped when you didn't need to—you had right of way at that first intersection," he said. "Then at the second intersection, when you should have stopped at the stop sign, you went right through it." He shrugged. "Too bad," he mumbled.

Then he was out of the car, clipboard and all, and strolling down the curb to the next car.

It had all happened so quickly. Saeng felt limp. So she had failed. She felt a burning shame sting her cheeks. She had never failed a test before. Not even when she had first arrived in school and not understood a word the teacher had said, had she ever failed a test.

Tests, always tests—there had been so many tests in the last four years. Math tests, spelling tests, science tests. And for each one she had prepared herself, learned what was expected of her, steeled herself, taken the test, and somehow passed. She thought of the long evenings she had spent at the kitchen table after the dinner dishes had been cleared away, when she and her mother had used their battered English-Lao dictionary to look up virtually every single word in her textbooks and carefully written the Lao equivalent above the English word, so that there were faint spidery pencil marks filling up all the spaces between the lines of her textbooks.

All those tests behind her, and now she had failed. Failed the one test which might have enabled her to help her parents get to work more easily, save them some money, and earn her some status among her classmates.

David's face appeared at the window. "How'd it go?" he asked with his usual cheerful grin.

Saeng suppressed an urge to pass her hand over his mouth and wipe the grin off. "Not so good," she said. She started to explain, then gave it up. It wasn't worth the effort, and besides, he didn't really care anyway.

He was holding the car door open for her and seemed a little impatient for her to get out. Saeng squirmed out of the seat, then remembered the twenty-dollar bill her mother had given her.

"Eh...thanks," she murmured awkwardly as she got out of the car. "It was nice of you to come here. And letting me use your car."

"Don't mention it," he said, sliding into the driver's seat already and pushing it back several inches.

"Would you...I mean, if you'd like, I could buy..." Saeng faltered as she saw that David wasn't even listening to her. His attention had been distracted by someone waving to him from across the street. He was waving back and smiling. Saeng followed the direction of his glance and saw a tall girl in tight jeans and a flannel shirt standing just under the M archway. Someone blond and vivacious, her dimpled smile revealing two rows of dazzling white, regimentally straight teeth. *Definitely a cheerleader*, Saeng decided.

"Hold on, I'll be right with you," David was calling over to her. Abruptly he pulled the car door shut, flashed Saeng a perfunctory smile, and started to drive off. "Better luck next time," he said as his car pulled away, leaving her standing in the middle of the road.

Saeng watched him make a fluid U-turn and pull up right next to the tall blond girl, who swung herself gracefully into the seat next to David. For a moment they sat there laughing and talking in the car. So carefree, so casual—so American. They reminded Saeng of the Ken and Barbie dolls that she had stared at with such curiosity and longing when she had first arrived in the country.

But it wasn't even longing or envy that she felt now, Saeng realized. This girl could have been David's twin sister, and Saeng would still have felt this stab of pain, this recognition that They Belonged, and she didn't.

Another car drove slowly up alongside her, and she caught a glimpse of her reflection on its window. Her arms were hanging limply by her sides, and she looked short and frumpy. Her hair was disheveled and her clothes seemed drab and old-fashioned—exactly as if they had come out of a rummage sale. She looked wrong. Totally out of place.

"Hey move it! You're blocking traffic!"

A car had pulled up alongside of her, and in the front passenger seat sat the test instructor scowling at her, his thick lips taut with irritation.

Saeng stood rooted to the spot. She stared at him, stared at those thick lips beneath the bushy mustache. And suddenly she was jolted back to another time, another place, another voice—it had all been so long ago and so far away, yet now she still found herself immobilized by the immediacy of the past.

Once, shortly after she had arrived in America, when she had been watching an absorbing ballet program on the PBS channel at Mrs. Lambert's house, someone had switched channels with a remote control, and it seemed as if the gracefully dying Giselle in *Swan Lake* had suddenly been riddled with bullets from a screeching getaway car. So jarring had it been that Saeng had felt as if an electric shock had charged through her, jolting her from one reality into another.

It was like that now, as if someone had switched channels in her life. She was no longer standing on a quiet street in downtown Danby but in the midst of a jostling crowd of tired, dusty people under a blazing sun. And it was not the balding driving instructor yelling at her, but a thick-lipped man in a khaki uniform, waving at them imperiously with a submachine gun.

Ban Vinai, Thailand. 1978. Things clicked into place, but it was no use knowing the name and number of the channel. The fear and dread still suffused her. She still felt like the scared, bone-weary little girl she had been then, being herded into the barbed-wire fencing of the refugee camp after they had escaped across the Mekong River from Laos.

"What're you doing, standing in the middle of the road? Get out of the way!"

And click—the Thai soldier was the test instructor again. Saeng blinked, blinked away the fear and fatigue of that memory, and slowly that old reality receded. In a daze she turned and made her way over to the curb, stepped up onto it, and started walking away.

Breathe deep, don't break down, she told herself fiercely. She could imagine David and that cheerleader staring at her behind her back. *I am tough*, she thought, *I am strong, I can take it.*

The sidewalk was littered with little acorns, and she kicked at them viciously as she walked and walked.

Only when she had turned the corner and was safely out of sight of David and the others did she finally stop. She found herself standing under a huge tree whose widespread branches were now almost leafless. An acorn dropped down and hit her on the head, before bouncing off into the street.

It seemed like the final indignity. Angrily, Saeng reached up for the branch directly overhead, and tore off some of the large brown leaves still left. They were dry and crisp as she crushed them in her hands. She threw them at the wind and watched the bits of brown being whipped away by the afternoon wind.

"Who cares about the test anyway," she said in tight, grim whisper, tearing up another fistful of oak leaves. "Stupid test, stupid David, stupid cars. Who needs a license, anyway? Who needs a test like that?" It would only get harder, too, she realized, with the winter approaching and the streets turning slippery with the slush and snow. She had barely felt safe walking on the sidewalks in the winter—how could she possibly hope to drive then? It was hopeless, useless to even try. *I won't, I just won't ever take that test again!* Saeng told herself.

That resolved, she felt somewhat better. She turned away from the oak tree and was about to leave, when she suddenly noticed the bush next to it.

There was something very familiar about it. Some of its leaves had already blown off, but those that remained were still green. She picked a leaf and examined it. It was vaguely heart-shaped, with deeply serrated edges. Where had she seen this kind of leaf before? Saeng wondered. And why, among all these foreign maples and oak leaves, did it seem so very familiar? She scrutinized the bush, but it was no help: if there had been any flowers on it, they had already fallen off.

Holding the leaf in her hand, Saeng left the park and started walking home.

Her pace was brisk and determined, and she had not planned to stop off anywhere. But along the way, she found herself pausing involuntarily before a florist shop window. On display were bright bunches of cut flowers in tall glass vases—the splashes of red roses, white carnations, and yellow chrysanthemums a vivid contrast to the gray October afternoon. In the shadows behind them were several potted plants, none of which she could identify.

On an impulse, Saeng swung open the door and entered.

An elderly woman behind the counter looked up and smiled at her. "Yes? Can I help you?" she asked.

Saeng hesitated. Then she thrust out the heart-shaped green leaf in her hand and stammered, "Do—do you have this plant? I—I don't know its name."

The woman took the leaf and studied it with interest. "Why yes," she said. "That looks like a rose of Sharon. We have several in the nursery out back."

She kept up a steady stream of conversation as she escorted Saeng through a side door into an open courtyard, where various saplings and shrubs stood. "Of course, it's not the best time for planting, but at least the ground hasn't frozen solid yet, and if you dig a deep enough hole and put in some good compost, it should do just fine. Hardy plants, these roses of Sharon. Pretty blossoms, too, in the fall. In fact—look, there's still a flower or two left on this shrub. Nice shade of pink, isn't it?"

Saeng looked at the single blossom left on the shrub. It looked small and washed out. The leaves on the shrub were of the same distinct serrated heart shape, but its flower looked—wrong, somehow.

"Is there—I mean, can it have another kind of flower?" Saeng asked. "Another color, maybe?"

"Well, it also comes in a pale purplish shade," the woman said helpfully. "And white, too."

"I think—I think it was a deep color," she offered, then shook her head. "I don't remember. It doesn't matter." Discouraged and feeling more than a little foolish, she started to back away.

"Wait," the florist said. "I think I know what you're looking for." A slow smile deepened the wrinkles in her face. "Come this way. It's in our greenhouse."

At the far side of the courtyard stood a shed, the like of which Saeng had never seen before. It was made entirely of glass and seemed to be bathed in a soft white light.

As she led the way there, the florist started talking again. "Lucky we just got through moving some of our tropical plants," she said, "or the frost last weekend would have killed them off. Anything in there now you'd have to leave indoors until next summer, of course. Next to a big south-facing window or under some strong neon lamps. Even so, some of the plants won't survive the long cold winters here. Hothouse flowers, that's what they are. Not hardy, like those roses of Sharon I just showed you."

Only half listening, Saeng wished that there were a polite way she could excuse herself and leave. It was late and she was starting to get hungry. Still, she dutifully followed the other woman through the greenhouse door and walked in.

She gasped.

It was like walking into another world. A hot, moist world exploding with greenery. Huge flat leaves, delicate wisps of tendrils, ferns and fronds and vines of all shades and shapes grew in seemingly random profusion.

"Over there, in the corner, the hibiscus. Is that what you mean?" The florist pointed at a leafy potted plant by the corner.

There, in a shaft of the wan afternoon sunlight, was a single blood-red blossom, its five petals splayed back to reveal a long stamen tipped with yellow pollen. Saeng felt a shock of recognition so intense, it was almost visceral.

"*Saebba*," Saeng whispered.

A *saebba* hedge, tall and lush, had surrounded their garden, its lush green leaves dotted with vermillion flowers. And sometimes after a monsoon rain, a blossom or two would have blown into the well, so that when she drew up the well water, she would find a red blossom floating in the bucket.

Slowly, Saeng walked down the narrow aisle towards the hibiscus. Orchids, lanna bushes, oleanders, elephant ear begonias, and

bougainvillea vines surrounded her. Plants that she had not even realized she had known but had forgotten drew her back into her childhood
world.

When she got to the hibiscus, she reached out and touched a petal
gently. It felt smooth and cool, with a hint of velvet towards the center—just as she had known it would feel.

And beside it was yet another old friend, a small shrub with waxy
leaves and dainty flowers with purplish petals and white centers.
"Madagascar periwinkle," its tag announced. *How strange to see it in a
pot*, Saeng thought. Back home it just grew wild, jutting out from the
cracks in brick walls or between tiled roofs. There had been a patch of
it by the little spirit house where she used to help her mother light the
incense and candles to the spirit who guarded their home and their family. Sometimes she would casually pick a flower or two to leave on the
offerings of fruits and rice left at the altar.

And that rich, sweet scent—that was familiar, too. Saeng scanned the
greenery around her and found a tall, gangly plant with exquisite little
white blossoms on it. "*Dok Malik*," she said, savoring the feel of the
word on her tongue, even as she silently noted the English name on its
tag, "jasmine."

One of the blossoms had fallen off, and carefully Saeng picked it up
and smelled it. She closed her eyes and breathed in, deeply. The familiar fragrance filled her lungs, and Saeng could almost feel the light
strands of her grandmother's long gray hair, freshly washed, as she
combed it out with the fine-toothed buffalo-horn comb. And when the
sun had dried it, Saeng would help the gnarled old fingers knot the hair
into a bun, then slip a *dok Malik* bud into it.

Saeng looked at the white bud in her hand now, small and fragile.
Gently, she closed her palm around it and held it tight. That, at least,
she could hold on to. But where was the fine-toothed comb? The hibiscus hedge? The well? Her gentle grandmother?

A wave of loss so deep and strong that it stung Saeng's eyes now
swept over her. A blink, a channel switch, a boat ride in the night, and
it was all gone. Irretrievably, irrevocably gone.

And in the warm moist shelter of the greenhouse, Saeng broke down and wept.

It was already dusk when Saeng reached home. The wind was blow-ing harder, tearing off the last remnants of green in the chicory weeds that were growing out of the cracks in the sidewalk. As if oblivious to the cold, her mother was still out in the vegetable garden, digging up the last of the onions with a rusty trowel. She did not see Saeng until the girl had quietly knelt down next to her.

Her smile of welcome warmed Saeng. "*Ghup ma laio le?* You're back?" she said cheerfully. "Goodness, it's past five. What took you so long? How did it go? Did you—" Then she noticed the potted plant that Saeng was holding, its leaves quivering in the wind.

Mrs. Panouvong uttered a small cry of surprise and delight. "*Dok faeng-noi!*" she said. "Where did you get it?"

"I bought it," Saeng answered, dreading her mother's next question. "How much?"

For answer Saeng handed her mother some coins.

"That's all?" Mrs. Panouvong said, appalled. "Oh, but I forgot! You and the Lambert boy ate *Bee-Maags....*"

"No, we didn't, mother," Saeng said.

"Then what else—?"

"Nothing else. I paid over nineteen dollars for it."

"You what?" Her mother stared at her incredulously. "But how could you? All the seeds for this vegetable garden didn't cost that much! You know how much we—" She paused, as she noticed the tear stains on her daughter's cheeks and her puffy eyes.

"What happened?" she asked, more gently.

"I—I failed the test," Saeng said.

For a long moment Mrs. Panouvong did not say anything. Saeng did not dare to look her mother in the eye. Instead, she stared at the hibis-cus plant and nervously tore off a leaf, shredding it to bits.

Her mother reached out and brushed the fragments of green off Saeng's hands. "It's a beautiful plant, this *dok faeng-noi*," she finally said. "I'm glad you got it."

"It's—it's not a real one," Saeng mumbled. "I mean, not like the kind we had at—at—" She found that she was still too shaky to say the words *at home*, lest she burst into tears again. "Not like the kind we had before," she said.

"I know," her mother said quietly. "I've seen this kind blooming along the lake. Its flowers aren't as pretty, but it's strong enough to make it through the cold months here, this winter hibiscus. That's what matters."

She tipped the pot and deftly eased the ball of soil out, balancing the rest of the plant in her other hand. "Look how rootbound it is, poor thing," she said. "Let's plant it, right now."

She went over to the corner of the vegetable patch and started to dig a hole in the ground. The soil was cold and hard, and she had trouble thrusting the shovel into it. Wisps of her gray hair trailed out in the breeze, and her slight frown deepened the wrinkles around her eyes. There was a frail, wiry beauty to her that touched Saeng deeply.

"Here, let me help, Mother," she offered, getting up and taking the shovel away from her.

Mrs. Panouvong made no resistance. "I'll bring in the hot peppers and bitter melons, then, and start dinner. How would you like an omelet with slices of the bitter melon?"

"I'd love it," Saeng said.

Left alone in the garden, Saeng dug out a hole and carefully lowered the "winter hibiscus" into it. She could hear the sounds of cooking from the kitchen now, the beating of the eggs against a bowl, the sizzle of hot oil in the pan. The pungent smell of bitter melon wafted out, and Saeng's mouth watered. It was a cultivated taste, she had discovered— none of her classmates or friends, not even Mrs. Lambert, liked it—this sharp, bitter melon that left a golden aftertaste on the tongue. But she had grown up eating it and, she admitted to herself, much preferred it to a Big Mac.

The "winter hibiscus" was in the ground now, and Saeng tamped down the soil around it. Overhead, a flock of Canada geese flew by, their faint honks clear and—yes—familiar to Saeng now. Almost reluctantly, she realized that many of the things which she had thought of as strange before had become, through the quiet repetition of season upon season, almost familiar to her now. Like the geese. She lifted her head, and watched as their distinctive V was etched against the evening sky, slowly fading into the distance.

When they come back, Saeng vowed silently to herself, in the spring, when the snows melt and the geese return and this hibiscus is budding, then I will take that test again.

SAMRAT UPADHYAY

I used to write both in Nepali and in English until my teenage years. But after coming to the United States at twenty one I gradually lost my facility in Nepali, which has been a considerable source of regret to me as I get older. I do wish to return to writing in Nepali, but I am afraid that I won't be as effective as I am in English.

All of my work is set in Nepal, so when I write a poem or a story I try to capture the emotional resonance of my characters first in Nepali (because they would be speaking Nepali), then use the English language to express that resonance. I constantly translate as I write, especially when I write dialogue: first imagine what a character would say in Nepali, then try to find an equivalent in English that retains the Nepali flavor but makes sense to western readers.

I love the English language. I am in awe of the ease with which it can adapt itself to various settings and characters.

This World

They met in New Jersey at a wedding party. Jaya knew the bride, a young Brahmin woman of twenty-four from Kathmandu, and Kanti was taking a course in economics at New York University with the bridegroom, a Nepali professor twenty years older than the bride. It was an arranged marriage, and Kanti had heard that the bride's parents had given away their beautiful daughter to the older professor for a Green Card.

On the professor's lawn, Kanti was in line at the buffet table that steamed with curries and rice, wondering whether she could slip out of there soon after eating, when she noticed the man in front of her. He was tall, with a sensitive, appealing face, and very fair, so fair that she thought he was a European. He saw her looking at him and said, in Nepali, "Yes, yes, I am a Nepali." The words tumbled out slightly thick, as if he didn't speak the language often. "Who did you come here with?" he asked with a familiarity that made it seem he'd known her before. When she said, "By myself," he said, "Then we should eat together. Over there." He pointed to a secluded corner. Their bodies touched as they scooped up the food, and he whispered in English, "Don't start hitting on me now."

She joined him in the corner, and they ate, standing. After some silence, he said, again in English, "Well, aren't you going to tell me about yourself? I thought that's what this is all about."

"This?" she asked.

"Yes, you and I are going to be lovers."

She wondered whether she should laugh or be angry, but she felt like laughing, so she did. "You are very arrogant."

"You'll come to like that about me."

She realized that they were conversing entirely in English, but it didn't seem odd with him, as it often did with other Nepalis in America. With them, even "how are you?" sounded rude, as the pronoun could be used unilaterally, with no regard for age and status.

He brought her a glass of wine, then another, then another, and every time she told herself that this was the last glass, that she'd leave his company and go talk to someone else, or leave the party as she'd originally planned. But as the evening progressed his face became even more arresting, and the conversation unlike conversations she had in Nepali gatherings, which she dreaded attending because they seemed laden with spices, nostalgia, incessant political chatter, and one-upmanship, with people vying to talk about how much land they owned back home. With Jaya, something inside her chest opened, and she could laugh and not worry about how loud it sounded, or whether some senior Nepali gentleman, a professor at a university or a consultant at a firm, would frown at her, and the women with their dark, critical eyes would talk about how she appeared like a "loose" woman. She couldn't tell how many glasses of wine she drank, but it didn't seem to matter because she forgot the loneliness that had been lying like a log in her stomach for years now. She told him then how she felt alienated in Kathmandu, how when she went there two years before, she felt like a stranger. She liked the sound of the words and repeated them, "I feel like a stranger in my own country." He put his arm around her and said, "Poor baby," and, her mind floating with wine, she thought that was funny.

Then someone came and took him away, and she was alone once more. She saw him several times in the evening, in different groups, his long arm visible in the brightness of the fluorescent lamps placed strategically throughout the lawn, his white shirt shining. Once their eyes met, he winked, and rolled his eyes at the Nepalis around him as if in exasperation. She kept wishing he'd come back, talk to her more, but he was laughing with some people he obviously knew. Realizing that all the wine had made her unsteady, she went to the bride and groom, seated on a couch inside the house, and said goodbye.

A few yards from the house he called her. "I thought we were lovers."

"But you abandoned me," she said.

He came closer. "Never again," he said, then kissed her lightly on the lips.

She was surprised by it, but more surprised that she hadn't resisted.

Later he gave her a ride to her apartment in his Volkswagen, his arm waving near her cheeks as he talked. He was fairly drunk, his eyes glassy. He was born in Nepal, he said, but grew up in Boston, then moved to New York when his parents moved back to Kathmandu a few years ago. His parents lost interest in the great American dream, he said. "But tell me," he asked her, "what's so great about Nepal except for the fact that it's your home country?" He visited Nepal every year, hung out with his cousins and friends. "Kathmandu is the garbage dump of the world. I hate the place, that country." He looked at her and smiled. "But I love to party there." The word "party" came out of his mouth like a celebration itself, as if merely uttering the word would bring forth a roomful of conversation, wine and dancing. She told him that she was going to Kathmandu during summer because her mother was insisting she come. Occasionally the car drifted to the side of the highway, and in the Lincoln Tunnel, he nearly rammed into a truck coming from the other side.

Outside her apartment he took her hand. He had soft brown eyes and bushy eyebrows, with two strands of white hair growing out of each in perfect symmetry. Her heart thumped, for she thought he was going to make a sexual move, and she didn't want to sleep with him, not yet. She found the American sexual mores a bit intimidating. She'd had only two boyfriends during her years here, a German guy she quite liked but who soon lost interest in her, and a Midwesterner from Ohio, who said he loved her "exotic" eyes. She had sex with both of them, but more out of a feeling of obligation than passion. In fact, she had a feeling her German boyfriend got bored because she didn't show enough excitement while making love.

But Jaya merely said, "Call me when you reach Kathmandu—I am also going there in May. We'll party together. My father is Somnath Rana." She recognized the name: a minister who was involved in a bribery scandal during the Panchayat era, absconded to the U.S., now back in Nepal working for a human rights group. He wrote down his phone number on the Upper West Side. "For rainy, lonely days."

The next morning she couldn't find the slip of paper with his number. She looked for his name in the phone book, but it wasn't listed. She contacted a few acquaintances from the party, but none knew him, and the bride and groom were already honeymooning in Hawai'i. She thought about him when she bought a hotdog at a stand in a corner of Times Square or when she went to the museums on weekends when the silence in her apartment made her stomach hollow or when it rained and the streets outside her Greenwich Village apartment glistened. She saw his face in the subway in the faces of other young men who were also fair and lanky, and arrogant. Once a young Italian saw her staring at him and came up to her, swaggering, and said, "Hey, you're cute. You Indian?"

In May she graduated with a master's degree in economics and made preparations to leave for Nepal. She left most of her belongings in the apartment with her Chinese roommate. "I don't think I can stay there too long," Kanti said. When the Chinese roommate asked her how she was going to get a new visa, she said, "I'm applying to Duke. Let's see what happens."

When her feet touched the tarmac of Tribhuvan International Airport in Kathmandu, the wind, coupled with the sight of her mother waving frantically from the terminal, brought back memories of how lonely she had felt the last time she was here, two years before. She felt the same loneliness descending upon her, just as the plane had descended from among the hills on the cramped city a few minutes ago. As soon as she and her mother reached the house in Pakanajol, she looked up Jaya's father's name in the directory. There it was. Somnath Rana, Jawalakhel. Her finger lingered at the name. Her mother, who set something to cook in the kitchen and came back, asked who she was looking for. "Just a friend," Kanti told her.

Her mother talked incessantly, as if she had been holding her breath till her daughter came home. Kanti watched her face, noticing new lines, the way her eyes had become smaller. Mother sighed every now and then, and didn't seem conscious that she was doing so. Kanti answered her questions, gave her the sweater and bracelets she'd brought as souvenirs, but her mind was distracted, as if she had just come back from a short journey, not a long one after two years. I'll call him tomorrow, she thought. Tomorrow.

They agreed to meet at a bar in a hotel.

She found him at a table drinking Jack Daniels. "I hate this place," he said. "I don't know why I came." He laughed as he said this, so she did not think he'd said it with bitterness. "Look at them, just look at them. Pathetic," he said, shaking his head slowly as his eyes surveyed the bar, full of Nepali men in business suits and young men and women in their jeans. Later, at the dance floor he kissed her impulsively, his drunken wet lips suffocating her, and she wondered if she had done the right thing coming to the bar to see him. But he danced crazily, and soon she found herself matching his movements, laughing, liking the way the colorful revolving lights cast patterns on his face.

He didn't drink anymore for the rest of the evening, and they left the hotel in his Suzuki to roam the city. They drove toward Ring Road, and he parked the Jeep in a secluded spot and turned to her. "I knew you would call me," he said. When she asked him how he knew, he said, "You are a lonely soul." When he embraced her and kissed her again, she didn't resist, and when he started caressing her breasts, she let him. They made love in the back seat, giggling when the headlight of an occasional car shone inside the Jeep. She cried out his name when he stroked her face.

They started spending long afternoons in expensive hotel rooms in the city. He had money—his father owned land all over the country—so she did not worry about how he opened his wallet.

Mother appeared perplexed. She'd heard rumors, Kanti was sure, that her daughter had relationships with boys in America. But perhaps she didn't think that she'd see someone so openly here. "What has happened to you?" she asked Kanti one afternoon, looking at her with eyes full of resentment. "You were not like this before. Mrs. Sharma from the neighborhood was asking me if having a boyfriend was all you learned in America."

In a hotel one drowsy afternoon lying next to him she played with the long grayish strand, sticking out from the thick black hair on this chest. She twisted it, caressed it, tugged at it, resisting the temptation to break it off. "Ouch!" he said, and it struck her that he didn't say "aiya" like a Nepali would. "You want to bring me bad luck, woman?" he said, laughing. When she looked at him in surprise, he said, "Who knows what could happen in this god-forsaken country." He climbed on top of her and unabashedly told her about his fantasies: standing by the door, watching her make love to another man; coming home to find her seducing another woman. She did not find these fantasies particularly exciting, but she willing responded when she felt him inside her. Soon after they made love, he fell asleep. She stood by the window of the hotel, figuring it must have been cold outside by the way the beggars were bundled up on the pavement. She imagined the city of Kathmandu, like New York, covered with snow, cars coming to a standstill, the Queen Pond frozen, the ice on top reflecting the lights that burned at its periphery all night.

Jaya stirred in bed and she went to him, arranging herself so her head rested comfortably on his long, bony chest, her palm flat on his stomach.

Kanti's mother did not like Jaya. "He is too much like those Americans."

Kanti's neighbors and relatives stared at Jaya when they saw them together, as if he were indeed a kuirey, a whitey. Kanti assumed that was because he walked with a swagger, chest spread out to challenge the world. And he went for days without shaving. Sometimes his jeans looked as if they had not been washed in months.

Jaya's friends in the city were richer than Kanti's friends. His cousins and best friends, Sunil and Vikas, copied Jaya's nonchalance, his accent, and the dreamy way he talked about himself and America. Unlike his cousins, his other friends were not from the fallen Rana aristocracy. One was the son of a big hotel owner in the city, another's father owned major sugar factories and a Honda dealership in the country. Often, sitting in an expensive restaurant in the Soaltee or the Yak and Yeti hotel, or watching Jaya and his friends play cricket in the gigantic compound of Jaya's house, Kanti could barely believe this world into which she'd stumbled—the world of upper class Nepalis. She liked the comfort with which they moved in their surroundings, the ease with which they traveled back and forth between America and Nepal, between Europe and Nepal. In parties at Jaya's house, she heard them talk about building new hotels in the city, or the new BMWs they'd bought, or how they'd just come back from a shopping spree in London. Jaya's parents barely spoke to her, not because they disliked her but because they didn't really sense her presence. Sometimes Kanti felt inadequate in these social events, as if she were a poor cousin, and she clung to Jaya. At a party one evening, while the monsoon rain fell like a riot outside, she was standing alone in a corner watching Jaya talk to his friends across the room when a middle-aged woman she recognized as Jaya's cousin came and spoke to her. "You take him seriously, don't you?" the woman asked Kanti, and before Kanti could respond, she said, "Be careful, Kanti. You don't know these people. Don't get attached to Jaya." Kanti wanted her to speak more, but the woman gave her a knowing look and moved away.

While the men played cricket, Kanti thought of her life in America, how in a small liberal arts school in Michigan she'd initially felt something break free inside her, away from the scrutinizing eyes of her mother and her relatives. She went to parties all the time, even experimented with cocaine. She told her American friends how, at the age of seventeen, she was walking the streets of Kathmandu holding a boy's hand, and an uncle had seen her. Her friends laughed when she mimicked the way he looked her up and down, then looked the poor boy up and down. "You're kidding me," they said when she told them that her mother didn't speak to her for three days.

By her third year in college, she pined for home, the food-smell of her mother, gossiping with childhood friends with whom she had already lost touch, the taste of hot-hot momos, Nepali dumplings that burst with spicy flavors inside your mouth. Her American friends didn't understand why she stopped trudging across the campus yard to go to classes, why she stayed in her room all day with the curtains drawn, why she stopped answering phones unless it was from her mother. One of her friends, frumpy Susan from Philadelphia, brought her a carrot cake in the middle of the night, and Kanti said, "I don't feel like eating."

"What has happened to you?"

Kanti couldn't tell her that she hated this country, the way people smiled too much, how everything was always "wonderful," how she didn't feel close to anyone, so she said that it was just a mild bout of homesickness.

"But you've been like this months now."

Kanti took a small piece of the cake and told Susan she had a headache and needed to sleep.

The day she finished her last exam, she flew back to Nepal, not even waiting to get her certificate. Within two weeks after she arrived, she

wished she were in America again. She couldn't understand why everything had changed so much. So much dust, so many houses with their
ugly television antennas shooting into the sky, the way people gargled
and spat on the streets, phlegm shooting out from their mouth, the way
they bragged about how much money they had, the way her relatives
constantly asked her when she was getting married, the way her mother
arranged for her to be "viewed" by dull-looking men, the way old men
and women stared at her when she walked down the street wearing
pants, the way her friends from college, married and with satisfied
smiles, carried babies in their arms, the way their husbands wore expensive but ill-fitting suits and ordered their wives about in sweet voices.
She felt that eyes followed her, watched her every move, ready to
pounce if she made a false move, didn't speak properly or addressed
someone the wrong way. She became convinced she couldn't live in this
country, and she despised this feeling, this constant critical attitude
toward her own people. I live in two worlds, she thought, perched
halfway in between, satisfied with neither. In her restlessness she
applied to the master's program at New York University and was accepted.

And now Jaya. He was giving instructions to a friend as he prepared
to bat. She caught his eye, and he winked at her, just as he had in New
York. She visualized them together, touring around Europe, or going
back to New York to visit old friends, and then later in Nepal with a
couple of kids. She wondered where they would live in their old age. In
Nepal? It didn't matter. With him, the city had become pleasant. The
only thing that worried her was Jaya's drinking. He always had a glass
of something or the other in his hand. He was indiscriminate when it
came to alcohol: wine, beer, whiskey, rum, even the strong local liquor.
Even now he had a glass of gin on the table where she sat.

Jaya and Kanti often went on excursions to the countryside. On his
Kawasaki motorbike he came by her house, sometimes deliberately having taken out the muffler, so that the noise of the engine shook her quiet
neighborhood. As the raucous motorbike stopped outside her house,
Kanti held her breath, a faint throbbing in her throat, and opened the
gate. Initially she'd wished Jaya wouldn't do that, but when she saw her
neighbors watching from their windows, she felt a strange sense of sat-

isfaction. Mother came to the porch with a frown on her face and nodded at Jaya, who gave her an exaggerated greeting, hands held high
above his head in namaste. Next day, her mother would inevitably mut-
ter to Kanti: "These Ranas. The way they flash their money, you'd think
they're still ruling the country. Someone needs to tell them that the
Rana rule was over when the people revolted centuries ago."

One afternoon they went to Gokarna with a picnic basket. Under a
large tree, they sat down and ate. Jaya drank beer, and after two bottles,
stroked her face and said, "I haven't felt like this with anyone else."

She called him a liar.

"Seriously," he said.

"So what does it mean?"

He shrugged. "It just means what it means. What are you looking
for?"

She shook her head. She didn't want to feel more vulnerable than she
already did.

"I have thought about a life with you," he said.

She waited.

"I've even thought of children," he said.

"I will die if we separate," she said. She swallowed so her voice wouldn't
break.

"Why would we separate?" he said. He held her, then they kissed. His
hands touched her breasts.

"What is this?"

Three men stood a few yards away.

"What do you think this is? Your bedroom?" one of the men said.

"What do you want?" Jaya said.

"Who is this?" the man said, pointing to Kanti. "Your sister?"

Jaya got up, enraged. Kanti asked him not to get involved.

"We like your sister, asshole," another man said. "She's sexy."

Jaya lunged at him, and Kanti started screaming. The three men
pummeled Jaya, who was valiantly trying to protect himself and strike
back at the same time. Kanti found a large stick, and rushed toward the
men. A Jeep appeared in the distance, on the unpaved road that led to
the gate. The three men ran away, laughing, shouting, "Your sister is

sexy." Jaya was bleeding from the mouth, and his lower lip and right eye were swollen. The Jeep came closer and a man got out.

They went to the park's office, where the man took out a first-aid kit and applied iodine to Jaya's wounds. "These hoodlums," the park official said. "Uncontrollable. Two months ago someone was murdered here."

"I remember their faces," Jaya said. "I'll take care of them."

Later, as they walked to the motorcycle, Kanti's heart was still thumping. "We're lucky the park official came when he did. Why did you have to fight? And what was that about taking care of them?"

"Hey, I have to protect my sister, don't I?" He started laughing. "My sexy sister."

As summer drew to an end, Jaya brought up the idea of staying in Nepal for another year or so. He had one more year to complete his graduate degree in business but, as he said, "I am absolutely in no mood to go back to the books now, Kanti." He wanted to stay in Kathmandu for another three or four months and then maybe go to Europe or even Africa before heading back to the United States. She had just received word from Duke that they were going to give her an assistantship for a Ph.D. in economics. The day Jaya told her about his decision to stay, Kanti became depressed. She really didn't want to stay in Kathmandu any longer. Mother was getting more and more critical of her relationship with Jaya. Kanti knew that Mother had her eyes fixed on another boy, a Brahmin from the city who had just come back from England with a degree in medicine. "Just have one look," Kanti's mother pleaded. "You'll like him. I don't know what you see in that hoodlum." The word hoodlum touched a nerve in Kanti, and she shouted back at Mother: "He's not a hoodlum. His life is more interesting than yours, you with your 'what will the neighbors say, what will the neighbors think.'" After some silence, she said, "I want to marry only Jaya, Mother. Don't look at anyone else."

Her mother didn't speak to her for the rest of the day. In the evening, as they ate separately in their rooms, Kanti felt a pang of guilt. She had never shouted at her mother before. She went into her mother's room and found her reading the *Bhagavad Gita*. She gently took the book from her mother's hands and put it aside. "I will see your man," Kanti said, "but you have to give me the option of refusing."

"I know you won't refuse," Mother said. "He's very attractive. Here, let me show you his photograph."

Kanti had to admit that the man was not bad-looking, with a faint mustache that ran all the way down to his chin. His eyes had a serious quality to them that she immediately liked. "He's okay," she told her mother.

Her mother squeezed her shoulder, saying that she knew her daughter would come around.

"Mummy," Kanti warned. "I told you—I might refuse."

"All right, all right," her mother said. "Just a look. After that, it's your decision."

Kanti told her then that she was thinking about taking a year off before starting school again, and staying in Nepal. Her mother said she thought this was a good idea, for she thought that Jaya would be leaving soon to resume his studies. "Once you get married to Prakash—" Mother started, then corrected herself, "if you get married to Prakash, then maybe both of you can go together to America."

Kanti walked into a bar in the tourist district of Thamel one afternoon to find Jaya kissing a woman wearing gaudy make-up and a skirt that revealed her thighs. The woman's hand cradled Jaya's neck while Jaya's right hand fondled her breast; their lips were glued together. There was no one else at the bar, except the bartender, who was looking out of the window. Kanti's eyes focused on Jaya's hand, the very hand that she had held, inspected, kissed, and traced with her finger. Dumbfounded, she walked out. She expected to feel angry, but she didn't. The only feeling she had was the urge to go and crawl into the earth so she wouldn't have to think. She walked the streets of the city for the rest of the afternoon, her body light with shock.

The next day news spread among people who knew them that Kanti had caught Jaya with another woman. In some versions of the rumor, the woman was a prostitute. Talk of the incident also reached her mother, who pounded on Kanti's door when she locked herself up in her room, "Kanti, open the door. You need to be with someone." But Kanti ignored her.

Jaya called later that evening but she wouldn't speak to him. He came by, this time silently on the motorbike, but her mother shouted at him from the gate. Kanti saw him from the window; his face was grim. Instead of anger, she felt like laughing at him. What was he thinking? In a short while he left, revving the engine to drown out her mother's voice.

Kanti avoided everyone for a few days, stayed in her room, listening to music or reading novels she'd already read. She brought out her old photo albums and went over the pictures, remembering friends she'd forgotten she once knew. One morning, she told her mother she wanted to go away. Her mother understood. Her daughter needed time, some breathing space to get over this unspeakable thing, and then she might agree to marry Prakash.

Kanti spent a month in India. First she went to Delhi, visited the Taj Mahal in nearby Agra. The history of the tomb, which housed the young queen of a Mogul emperor, saddened her. She thought of Emperor Shah Jehan, grief-stricken by the death of his beloved queen Mumtaz Mahal and wanting to create a grand monument of love in her memory. Kanti remembered what she'd read: it took twenty-two years for more than twenty thousand craftsmen to build the gently swelling marble dome. Kanti sat in the garden by the oblong pool that reflected the tomb and recalled a haunting song from a film chronicling the emperor's love for his wife. *Jo bada kiya wo nivana padega, roke jamana chahey roke khuda bhi tumko ana padega*: The promise you made, you have to honor, whether the world stops you or god himself, you have to come. But the dust and the dry, scratchy heat of Agra made her want to leave, so she took a train to Bombay. There she met her high school friend, Sushma, in a girl's hostel near Juhu. Sushma's eyes went wide when she saw Kanti, and especially when she learned that Kanti was traveling all by herself. "What? You think you've become an American now?" Laughing, Sushma added, "You want to stay in an ashram here? Search for your spiritual self?" The next day she went out by herself to

Juhu beach, felt the ocean air brush against her cheeks, looked at the grand houses of well-known actors and actresses. She took the bus to Colaba to see the India Gate, and in the evening strolled on the Marine Drive, watching big, expensive cars roll into the driveways of modern hotels. She went to the Hanging Gardens, its foliage obscuring the sight of the city below, and sat on a bench to watch pigeons grumbling from their chests, nannies strolling with small children, and bespectacled men reading thick books in the lawns. One evening while walking on the Marine Drive, with the ocean battering the rocks, Kanti decided that life was larger than Jaya, more expansive than the relationship she had with him, and that she needed to move on, despite images of Jaya crammed inside her head.

Back in Kathmandu Kanti pushed herself to find a job. Eventually, through an uncle in an engineering firm, she found work in a dilapidated office right in the center of the city. The salary was not large, but now she no longer had to turn to her mother for spending money. She started socializing again, going to a party in some hotel or spending an afternoon with friends on someone's balcony. Now that Kanti had recuperated, her mother wanted to fix the deal as quickly as possible. One night as Kanti was about to go to bed, her mother entered her room and told her that Prakash was coming to the house the following week with his two uncles. Kanti didn't protest.

Kanti sometimes thought of Jaya, his exaggerated sense of his own grandeur, and wondered what made him kiss that woman in a bar. How can you be sure, Kanti asked herself, that there is not something like that in every breathing person, an ugly facet that reveals itself unpredictably? How could she be sure that this doctor, this Prakash, did not also have a defect that would surface as soon as they got married?

She did see Jaya twice on social occasions, once at a party in a friend's house, and once in the lobby of the Soaltee Hotel, the very hotel where they'd spend long afternoons. They smiled at each other, both self-conscious. Each time she saw a different, heavily made-up woman draped around him. Jaya had lost weight and he looked haggard. She had heard that he had started drinking heavily. In the party she found him looking at her forlornly from across the room when he thought she couldn't see him.

On the morning Prakash was supposed to arrive, her mother handed her a Banarasi sari she had expressly ordered from India for the occasion. It was beautiful, purple with reddish border, and embroidered with golden thread. "Do I really have to wear that?" Kanti said, but before mother could answer, got up to try it on. The sari suited her, made her face brighter. "Prakash will be hypnotized," her mother said, eyes shining. As the afternoon approached, her mother became nervous and kept scolding the servant for petty mistakes. Kanti was amused watching her, and once she even joked, "Is he coming to see you now, Mummy?"

Prakash and his two uncles showed up at the door precisely at four o'clock. Both uncles were short, and on looking closer, Kanti saw that they were twins, although one had a mustache and the other did not. Prakash was taller than he had appeared in the picture, with a stoop that made him seem very interested in the person he was talking to. Her mother hurriedly invited them into the drawing room, where a tray of cut apples, bananas and guavas waited for them. "Why don't you talk with them, Kanti, while I get some food from the kitchen," her mother said.

There was some silence after her mother left, everyone waiting for someone else to initiate a conversation. Kanti knew that the burden fell on the man, so she smiled and kept her mouth shut. Finally, the mustached uncle, said, "Nice house you have here, Kanti."

Before the uncle could continue, Prakash said, "Is it a master's in economics you have?" His voice was deep and guttural, like that of Amitabh Bacchan, the Hindi movie star.

Kanti nodded.

"Plenty of jobs here with that degree," the mustached uncle said.

They talked about her studies for a while, neither party broaching the crucial question of whether she would indeed go back for her Ph.D. if she were to get married to Prakash, who had already opened a clinic in the city. Kanti knew that her mother hoped she would forget about the

Ph.D. once she got married.

Kanti found Prakash easy to talk to. He had a shine in his eyes whenever he said something, as if he, too, found this whole bride-viewing amusing. Soon, the uncles grew quiet and let Prakash and Kanti carry on the conversation. Prakash talked of his experiences in England, the craving for food from home, the loneliness in his dormitory in the evenings, and Kanti felt that he understood what it meant to live in two different, contending worlds.

After her mother brought hot puris and chana-tarkari from the kitchen, the uncles spent some time praising her culinary skills. "Our Kanti cooks even better than I do," her mother said, and Kanti looked at her sharply, for she only knew how to make a few dishes, and even for them had to ask for mother's guidance. When Kanti turned, she found Prakash looking at her, a smile on his lips to indicate he knew what she was thinking.

After they left, her mother praised Prakash so much that Kanti had to tell her to stop. "Well, what did you think?" her mother said. "You liked him, didn't you?"

"He's a nice man," Kanti said. "But I can't make such a momentous decision after just one meeting."

"How many meetings do you need?" Mother's tone became slightly harsh. "This is not America, you know, where you sleep together before marriage."

"That's not what I said. At least a few more meetings, alone, before I can make up my mind."

"You will come across as a very modern girl," her mother said. "They might not like that—the girl saying that she needs to meet the boy more. This doesn't happen here."

"If they don't, then maybe I am not right for him."

"Kanti, why are you being so difficult? Here I am trying and trying, and you never appreciate what I do."

Kanti went to her room, followed by her mother, whose voice had gotten louder, "You think you can do anything you like, come and go as you please, see as many boys as you want. And now, when such a good man is interested in you—"

"I gave you my decision," Kanti said.

Prakash came to pick her up the next evening in a taxi. She wore a simple salwar-kameez, one of her older ones from her college days in Nepal.

At the Indian restaurant of Hotel de la Annapurna, they sat near the window, from where they could see the main entrance of the hotel. The restaurant had very few people in it, which made Kanti slightly nervous. She would have preferred a crowded room, so the conversation would not be so intimate.

Prakash took in a deep breath and said, "You know, I agree with you. People shouldn't make hasty decisions about marriage. It's good you said that we should meet a few times more, although," here he smiled and played with the napkin, "I had already made up my mind."

"You shouldn't rush," Kanti said, worried that she sounded like a school madam.

"You're right," he said. "You're very right." His eyes dropped. "It's just that I'm a little lonely."

"All the more reason not to," she said.

As they ate, some men wearing traditional Indian salwar-kameez, tapered trousers and long, flowing shirts, set up musical instruments in a corner of the restaurant and started singing ghazals, their melancholy voices floating through the room, quieting conversations and the clatter of forks and knives. Once or twice when she looked at Prakash's face, she found him engrossed in the music, a sadness in his eyes that startled her.

The next morning during a walk she nearly bumped into Jaya turning a corner at Durbar Marg in front of the Royal Palace. He looked down and said "sorry," with a sulk.

She adjusted her shirt and, without thinking, said, "Can't you watch where you're going?" He looked at her with surprise, and they both burst out laughing. He turned his back to her, leaned his arm against a building, and placing his forehead on it, went through convulsions of hiccup-like laughter with which she was all too familiar. She stood there, on the middle of the sidewalk, holding her face, aware that people walking by were looking at them in curiosity and irritation. She could not make up her mind as to whether she should stay until Jaya turned around or she should stop laughing and move on. It was the first time since the afternoon in the bar that she had laughed so hard.

Finally Jaya turned to face her, his cheeks moist. He tried to frown and again broke into laughter. "Come on, don't embarrass me," she said, hitting him on the arm with her fist. Those words seemed to break whatever intimacy they'd just established, and he composed himself, a shadow slowly appearing on his face.

"How are you, Jaya?" she asked.

"Life continues," he said.

Standing there in front of Jaya she suddenly did not care who he had kissed and how many women he had slept with since they parted. And she wanted to say something more to him, comfort him, comfort herself, make plans to meet, but she swallowed whatever words and phrases formed in her throat.

He looked at her expectantly, and when she didn't speak he said, "I have to go. I have to meet someone."

She nodded, and he left.

At work that day Kanti found herself impatient with everyone and everything. "Are you ill, Kanti? Do you want to go home?" her supervisor asked, but she shook her head and pretended to be busy filing. When everyone left the office that evening she picked up the phone and dialed Jaya's number. The numbers came to her easily, ready on her fingertips. The phone rang for a long time. She wasn't surprised that Jaya was out, and his parents must have been on one of their trips abroad. She imagined the servants out in the garden, the setting sun lending a pink hue to all the flowers, the large stone Buddha in the middle, almost smiling, the servants laughing and joking, taking advantage of the freedom, the phone by the stairs, the sound carrying to the corners of the big empty house.

She and Prakash went out again a few days later, this time to a rooftop restaurant in the center of the city, where they sat under colorful garden umbrellas. Prakash ordered beer, which surprised Kanti because he hadn't drunk on the previous occasion. Was he another Jaya? He looked at her in embarrassment and said, "We need to celebrate. You liked me enough to come out for a second time." He persuaded her to order wine, which she barely touched all evening. She hoped he didn't think she was going to say "yes" just because she was with him again.

But he didn't broach the subject of marriage at all. They talked about his work, and the kinds of problems he dealt with among his patients, his ambitions about the new clinic. She kept searching his eyes to see if she would encounter the same sadness she had seen last time, but today he seemed in a jovial mood, cracking jokes and asking her questions about America: Were Americans as wild as the Brits thought them to be? Did she see Nelson Mandela in New York after his release? He kept ordering more beer, and she became afraid that he would get drunk by the time dinner was over.

By the time they finished dinner, it was already dark and a light drizzle was falling from the sky. In slightly slurred speech, Prakash said, "I find rain romantic, don't you?"

"I don't know," she said, thinking, here it comes, so expected. "Perhaps we should go."

They stood under an awning, waiting for a taxi. Rain began to splatter against the asphalt, and people ran to whatever shelter they could find. All the taxis that whizzed by were occupied. Prakash went upstairs to the restaurant to call for a taxi, and when he came down, she could see that his movements were still not coordinated.

The rain continued, and dark clouds rumbled in the sky. Once in a while lightening streaked through the city, illuminating everything in sight. She caught Prakash's face, and saw that his eyes were far away.

The cab he'd ordered appeared nearly twenty minutes later. As they got in, the driver asked where they wanted to go.

"Where are we going?" Prakash said, his hand casually on her arm.

"I want to go home," she said, surprised he would think they would go anywhere else, in this rain, this late. She gave the driver her address.

After a few hundred yards, the cab stalled. The driver cursed, got out, and instantly drenched with rain, opened the hood and tinkered with something. Soon the car started, but stopped again after a few yards. This happened three or four times, and then the taxi finally refused to budge. Kanti asked the driver whether he could summon another taxi from the company, and the driver said, "How? I don't have a phone in here, and I don't see any shops around."

"We can walk," Prakash said. "It's not too far."

As they stepped out of the taxi, rain pelted down on them. Prakash linked his arm in hers, and she let him. They half ran, half walked to the house. Just as she reached for the front gate, Prakash said, "Kanti, could I tell you something, before you go?"

"Here, in this rain? Why don't you come inside?"

"No, your mother is inside," he said. "Besides, we're already thoroughly soaked."

She waited.

"I know how you feel," he said.

"I don't understand."

"I mean, about that Rana boy."

It took a moment for Kanti to realize who he was talking about; she had never thought about Jaya as a Rana boy. She felt annoyed. What right did he have to bring up Jaya? "I don't feel like talking about it," she said.

"I know how you feel," Prakash said as if she hadn't said anything. "I feel the same way. I understand you." His voice became strange, as if he was about to cry.

She looked up at the neighbor's house and saw a boy staring at them.

"I had a girlfriend," Prakash said. "In England." He looked down. "I miss her in my bones."

She didn't know what to do or say, so she remained quiet. A man walked by, holding a large umbrella, and looked at them curiously.

"Her name was Sandy. She was from Kenya," he said. He touched her hand. "She was as beautiful as you are, Kanti. But she went to Kenya and never came back."

"Family obligations?" Her voice sounded rational and cold to her.

"No, no," he said. "Her parents were dead. She had an elder brother who was already married. She left me. She just decided that she didn't want me."

"Why wouldn't she want you?"

"Who knows? Maybe she didn't love me. Maybe she realized the difficulty, I mean, getting intimate with someone from a different culture. Maybe she's happily married now to a black man, has kids. I don't know why she left me." Prakash seemed to realize that he sounded pathetic, for he straightened his shoulders and said, in a controlled voice. "Why am I saying this to you? I guess I just wanted to tell you that I know the feeling."

"Relationships are not the same, Prakash-ji," she said, hoping he'd notice the distance the "ji" brought.

"I apologize," he said. "I didn't mean to probe."

"Good night," she said. She opened the door, went inside and closed it firmly behind her.

Inside, she leaned against the door and held still, water running down the outside of her thighs and forming a pool around her feet. She looked toward her mother's room, and saw, through the narrow gap between the door and the floor, that the lights were off. Kanti felt that her mother was lying awake in bed, listening to sound of the rain and the creaking of the door. Kanti slid down and sat on the floor. A weight seemed to tug her, and she wished the cold cement would open up and swallow her.

Kanti wondered where Jaya was right now—probably in bed with some awful woman in some hotel. But then again, Kanti herself had been this woman for a while.

Kanti got up from the floor and went to her room. "Kanti, is that you?" Mother's voice rang faintly, but Kanti didn't respond.

The next morning Kanti gave her mother her decision about Prakash.

"But what happened? What's wrong with him?"

"Nothing is wrong with him," she said.

"Then?"

"I'm just not ready, Mummy."

"Not ready," her mother said, nodding her head slowly. "I understand. You want to remain an old maid."

Mother remained cold after this, replying to Kanti in monosyllables.

On the day she was to leave for North Carolina, Kanti tried calling Jaya. A servant answered and told her Jaya had left the country. He did not know where. "India perhaps? Maybe America?" He sounded as if the two countries were so similar. Kanti remembered the fight in Gokarna. Did Jaya seek out those men? Take his revenge? Right then, Kanti's aunts came into the room, carrying with them gifts for her journey.

At the airport Kanti smiled and talked with her relatives, telling them she would be back right after finishing her Ph.D. Her mother would not even look at her.

When the time came for her to go to her gate, Kanti faced her mother, who was now looking at a poster of Thai Airlines.

"Talk with your daughter, Nirmala," one of the uncles said. "Don't do this. Who knows when you will see her."

"Mummy, I will go now."

Her mother didn't turn.

"Mummy."

She turned, and Kanti saw that her eyes were moist. Her mother took out a handkerchief, dabbed her eyes and said, "All right."

As the plane lifted from the ground with a thundering noise Kanti noticed a man across the aisle who looked like Jaya—black hair curling at the neck, broad sulky forehead.

Clasping the sides of her seat as the plane tilted at a giddy angle, Kanti closed her eyes and, for a brief moment, an image flitted across her mind of another man, perhaps darker than Jaya, someone at Duke, or in New York, or in some other American city. The man had bright eyes, and his words were soothing, calming. And then she saw herself, studying until late at night in her room close to the university, walking across the campus grounds with new friends and professors, watching plays in the university theater and discussing them with her colleagues, looking into the mirror and noticing new lines under her eyes, and with them, a sense of how far she had traveled in this world.

Kanti opened her eyes and saw an elderly woman in the adjacent seat smiling at her. "Good, you're awake," the elderly woman said. "Someone to talk to."

SHIRLEY GEOK-LIN LIM

What does it mean to speak and write English as a second language? In truth, I cannot answer, for English has been my first language since I was of an age to choose—which would be about the age of six, when I began attending classes in a British colonial school. Memory of my speaking a different language as a child is dim; I would be making up stories were I to narrate this memory.

Perhaps this obscurity of remembrance has to do with the oppressive pressure of colonial education, a system of rote learning, fierce punishment, and seemingly tantalizing rewards that has successfully erased native cultures world-wide and over the millennia. Perhaps it has something to do with the fact that my childhood home possessed not one first language but multiple languages, many of them unintelligible to each other.

My grandparents, my father's brothers, and wives were Hokkien-speakers; my mother was a *peranakan* (a native-born Malay-speaker of Chinese descent) who spoke both Malay and Teochew. Although they were and are all viewed as of Chinese-descent, "Chinese" are not homogeneously one people. Language divides and unifies them. "Chinese" speak what some linguists call "dialects" that are so distinctly different that a Cantonese speaker will not understand a Hakka speaker, nor will a Shanghainese understand a Chinese from Fujien. In any other linguistic field, these so-called dialects would have been termed separate languages, the way that linguists attribute over 500 languages to Native American tribes in North America.

Despite these language differences, populations of "Chinese" descent are supposed to share a common language, the language of the book, Mandarin, now called Hanyu Pinyin. It was the language of imperial examinations, court edicts, poetry, and the elite. In China until the Revolution in 1949, only a tiny percentage of the population, which was composed chiefly of illiterate peasants, ever received this "common" language. My parents, in fact, never learned to read, write, or speak Mandarin, and as a family of dual Hokkien-Teochew speakers, with Malay as my mother's preferred tongue, English became our home language.

For many years I imagined I must have learned to speak English only from the moment I entered the gates of the Convent of the Holy Infant Jesus and came under the influence of the good Irish nuns from the county of Clare. Now I see this memory has been a personal myth. My two older brothers had been attending English-language schools a few years before me. More, my father had graduated from high school with a senior Cambridge certificate, a diploma that testified to his abilities in English, and my mother had studied for seven years at the Methodist Girls' School. As long as I can remember they had spoken to me only in English. I must have gone to my first day in the colonial school already an English-language speaker, if not a reader and writer of English.

I was conscious from the earliest years that my parents spoke in Hokkien, Teochew, Malay, and English to relatives, neighbors, shopkeepers, and strangers; and today, when I return to Malaysia and Singapore, I also switch from English to Hokkien to Malay, depending on who my addressee is. I carry the resources for a trilingual life and community from my childhood with me into America, resources that remain locked away, unexamined, untasted, except when I am back "home." Or when I write.

What is it to write from a multiply-tongued history and community? It is much more complicated than this statement suggests. Some of my characters speak only one language; they are limited in their ability to relate to others outside of their language circles and also in their ability to imagine these others. Other characters shift comfortably and mistressfully from one language to another; but I know that most of my readers will not be able to do so, and will be lost without translation. Interesting characters who speak only or chiefly in English play with English registers. These registers cover both Bakhtin's concepts of socio-dialects (the speech styles of lawyers, for example, against the speech styles of Hollywood-influenced teenagers or unschooled domestic help), and the speech patterns of speakers from these multilingual backgrounds. Malaysian Chinese characters, for example, often speak a pidgin whose syntactical play, word choice, tags, and so forth are recognizable as "Manglish" or "Malaysian English." In Singapore the state attempts to keep "Singlish" out of public television programs despite the intimacy of community identity it evokes, because Singlish is not universally understood or respected by international English speakers. In Hong Kong, linguists describe a unique combination of Cantonese and English called "Chinglish."

As early as the 1950s, young intellectuals in the British colonial territories that now comprise Malaysia and Singapore theorized a language creation termed "EngMalChin," a literary composite of English, Malay, and Chinese that would function as the identifying mark for a new community composed of Malays and Chinese unified under an English-language education system. "EngMalChin" was a failed vision from the outset, one of those dead-end avenues utopianist visionaries have turned to in the process of nation-building, in the hope of forming a national identity that would be inclusive, multicultural, heterogeneous, counter-hegemonic, and vibrant.

My writing comes from an age of disillusionment in nation-building that has deteriorated into the horrors of neocolonialism (as in Indonesia), ethnic-cleansing (Rwanda and Serbia), and late-capitalist corruption and depredation of the environment (almost everywhere). Through these late-twentieth-century political changes, I have remained faithful to writing in English, even as my reading has opened up to works in translation. The English I use is both deeply entrenched in the British literary traditions I was trained in: the novels of Jane Austen, George Eliot, Charles Dickens, Joseph Conrad, and D.H. Lawrence, for example; and reflective and operative in the English-language communities I grew up in and write about: Malaysia and Singapore, and now the United States of America.

Do I write in English as a second language? The answer is, No. English, as a "world englishes," has been my first language. Like my characters, my writing lives in a world saturated with multiple languages, one in which English is a nimble player, running across registers, an Asian and American bastard of British colonialism, and an inheritor of imperial wealth.

Sisters

When Yen was seven, she took Su Swee to the Methodist School playground and placed her on the swing. Su thought the swing was a dumb hairy animal, its plank seat hanging unbalanced on fraying hemp, a loose swinging head suspended by ropes of frizzy hair. "Swing, swing!" Yen chanted, pushing the dangling seat into the air, and Su felt the rush of a large animal against her cheeks. It rustled its mysterious paws in her hair. She smelled its breath up close in her nostrils—something sharp, ammoniacal, like the fumey air from the caustic soda bottles in Ah Voon's storeroom—before she wetted herself. "Aiiyah," Yen scolded, "good for nothing, scaredy cat!"

"Not so little, already five, how you marry if cannot keep your pee in?" Ah Voon grumbled when she changed Su out of her soiled clothes.

"Swing, swing," she mumbled, trying to keep the new word in her mouth a little longer. At five Su believed words were a kind of magic, conjuring ways to protect her from Ah Voon's rough caretaker's hands; when Yen and Su talked—Yen more talk and Su more ear—words invaded invisibly, placing unseen, powerful beings into their everyday life. Later, Su found that words could still the irregular mobile dancing visions that so terrified her, wordless, behind closed eyelids, and steady the motes into PRINT, which became STORY and MEANING.

Su remembered the day when Yen first came home from Methodist School speaking a strange new language called English. *Wah,* a new magic in this world, and one better for being black magic to Ah Voon, who could only scold them in noisy Hokkien, crackling like strings of firecrackers. Not listening, the sisters spoke more and more English—elegant, chirpy, difficult—to each other, leaving Ah Voon ignorant of their wicked ways.

Yen brought back new words for Su each day. Separate words like colored fragments, falling, shifting, breaking out in dreamy shapes inside a kaleidoscope. Or like dried plasticine figures, brittle, snapping as Su forced them out: *England. Asia. China. America. House. Father. Mother. Baby. Man. Woman. Brother. Sister. Dog. Cat. House. Tree. Bird. Aeroplane. Sky. See. Run.*

Yen laughed because the words scratched Su's throat and crumbled into messy pieces as she tried to repeat them. But Su didn't mind her laughter. Su liked the way the sounds scattered, pulling her out of Ah Voon's lap and into places Voon couldn't follow.

Su didn't mind Yen even when she kicked and bit, screaming no words until her face turned pink, then purple.

It was the wind entering into her, Ah Voon explained, a bad wind unbalancing her body's hot and cold and making her sick. Mama said she was just a no-good eldest sister.

Su knew Yen only wanted her to grow up faster so they could play better together.

Because of Yen's biting, Mama didn't send Su to Methodist School. Instead she went to the Government School. Su liked Government

School better because Yen had taught her English words and how to swing.

The earth under the school playground's ten swings was scraped hard by hundreds of pairs of canvas shoes bumping on it every day. At recess, Su's classmates crowded into the tuck-shop for curry puffs and sticky sweet orangeade. She planted her feet on the grassless dried hollow and pushed off alone on the swing. Once in the air she stood on the seat, pumping the swing higher and higher until it was flashing above the ixora bushes, higher than the young coconut palms by the toilets, until she was almost a bird rushing through the warm air, if she would only let go. Swooping up and falling down, hands gripping the woven hemp, air humming under feet, addicted to flying but more afraid of tumbling off—and so, at last, slowing down, out of breath and hungry.

Then the hot blue sky reeled by as she ran with the other children, without Ah Voon or Mama shouting, Don't be a tomboy! Don't get burned in the sun! Don't fall down! Don't get dirty! Don't sweat! She joined the other children singing and dancing. Marching with them down the lines of uniforms and chanting, "Oranges and lemons, say the bells of Saint Clemons," she shivered with delicious fright as they approached the executioner couple, fearing yet longing for her turn, yelling in one big voice, "Here comes the candle to light you to bed, here comes the chopper to chop off your head!"

Later Su found books. Neither Mama nor the teachers who were always lecturing her about running-around play said anything against hours of reading, although books carried her higher than the swings in the playground. Looking up from the page, her eyes saw teachers far, far, far away, inconsequential specks on a moonscape, through the reverse end of a flying telescope. Other characters in books—barbaric, hunchbacked, miserly, alien, all-familiar—she saw close, so close she whiffed their frightened sour-vinegar armpit sweat, the salt in their monstrous unwashed hair, as if holding her right up against them, chest to chest, they forced her to stare into their pained irises and breathe their choking, phlegmy, secretive breaths.

In this way Su became a good student. Taking in, learning, chewing, imagining words, words, words every day in Government School. Vocabulary lists, spelling lists, dictionary tests, adjectives and adverbs, synonyms and antonyms, prefixes, suffixes, roots, gerunds and participles, verbs and proverbs, nouns and pronouns, and pronunciation. Days filled with word-eyes, sprouted vines branching into paragraphs that rooted in her scalp and sent long-legged taproots into her brain, grew arteries shooting oxygen, life, blood into her frontal lobes. The months rustled in thickets of pages, clumps, whole strands of chapters and treatises, massive historical forests of books, shelves on shelves of paper, pulp and ink and paste, ancient timber to wander in, in the one-room library hardly anyone ever entered except her.

Of all the thousands of words she learned, she liked the words of her name best even though they weren't English words.

"Wing Su Swee" was the last name teachers called from their roll-books, like a favorite sweet kept for last, or an almost forgotten story.

Wing for Ah Kong and Mama. For Yen and herself. For Peik, so different that Yen and Su often forgot they had another sister.

Su, her name, like an ending sigh. Su-su, meaning "milk" in Malay, which the Malay girls, teasing, called her.

Swee, "beautiful" in Chinese, everything lovely and sweet to Mama.

Her name was both Malay and Chinese, and in Government School it became English.

She became possessive of her family name as she grew older and discovered no other Wings in town. There were hundreds of Wongs. Humdrum name. Wong, all wrong, Su hummed to herself. Thousands of Tans, Lims, Lees, Chins, Chans, Chias. But only one Wing family. Magic name, easy to associate with feathers and flutters and flight, bird freedom—starlings, magpies, kingfishers, ricebirds, even the grackles and crows that flew in and out of raggedy eaves in the narrow streets just before sunset, calling the sun down.

What was the good of magic if it didn't do something?

At seventeen Su became impatient for something to happen, something breaking out of the promise of their winged family name.

Then Ah Kong died. Hearing about it, Ah Voon, who did not attend the funeral in Singapore, said it was wickedly unnatural not to cry. Su supposed she would have cried monsoon rains if it had been Mama who died. Ah Kong was a different kind of family.

Pastor Fung used to tell his parishioners it was a fairy tale, Ah Kong having three daughters. Even what Mama asked them to call him was part of the fairy tale. Ah Kong. Chinese for royalty, king, your highness, the grand vizier in *A Thousand and One Nights*, patriarch, sir, grandfather, daddy, papa, father, all rolled into one name. Or King Kong, as Yen complained.

That was the creepy part of being a Wing. Ah Kong was old enough to have been their grandfather, so old he had hair growing out of every aperture—ears, nostrils, curling over his lips. Su sometimes wondered where else. The individual hairs grew longer and whiter year by year. They pushed out of his ears like white smoke, getting more solid every year. Or like long skinny ancient worms poking out to sniff the air.

Next to him Mama looked like a girl. He must have been seventy, and she only thirty or so, skin slippery soft, and dimples gently creasing her cheeks. Whenever she laughed, she looked like an older sister.

We must be grateful to the powerful for giving us life, she said.

But they didn't have to love him.

Every week, for Saturday nights and Sunday mornings, Ah Kong came to stay with them. His visits were short. The girls walked on his back with bare feet, pulled his toes till they crunched, and read their exercise books aloud until he fell asleep in the evenings.

Good girls did those kinds of things for their fathers, Mama said.

Ah Kong stopped talking to Yen one evening after he leaned close to her to say something and the white hair sticking out of his nose holes tickled her cheek.

"*Aiiyah!* Don't come so close, Kong-kong!" she cried out, slapping at her cheek. "Your hair is so itchy! Itchified!" She was fourteen.

He was offended. Girls must never call their fathers "itchified"; it means the wrong thing.

Yen was always getting into trouble with Ah Kong. It wasn't because she couldn't get her words right. They were right for her. But she didn't pay attention when she spoke, and words came carelessly out of her, sputtering hot oil that could hurt.

Ah Kong didn't speak to her again for a long time.

Mama said Yen was stupid all the time. Su disagreed. Yen had so many thoughts that she seemed forever mixed up, in one huge confusion.

About Su, Mama said she was too clever for her own good, because Su could see and be two ways at the same time, like the little girl in the poem Yen read to her from her first-year English book: "And when she was good, she was very, very good, but when she was bad, she was horrid." Whenever Mama reminded Su of the poem to shame her, Su thought she was better off being two ways than being like Yen, who seemed only one way.

Ah Kong liked Little Peik the best because she had the sweetest tongue of them all. By the time Peik was three, she knew when to be quiet and exactly what to say to him.

Take the last Saturday Ah Kong came home. When he came out of the shower, Peik had the Tiger Balm by his chaise longue. "Ah Kong, you so tired, I massage you now."

Peik was the one whose feet pattered on his back most often, kneading him with clean bare soles. Ah Kong lay groaning while she pounded his shoulders, double-fisted.

Then she brought out her best class drawings, papers smoothly encased in plastic folders. "Ah Kong, see, I keep these pictures for you!"

She copied photographs of American cars and cities that appeared in *Life* and *National Geographic*, the only magazines that Ah Kong subscribed to for the girls. Yen and Su saved their money for *Seventeen* and *Vogue*, which they hid under their beds. Ah Kong hated to see pictures of modern women, actresses and models showing off lipstick and mascara and short skirts.

That Sunday morning, before Ah Kong drove back to Singapore, Peik gave him his glass of warm ginseng tea. "Kong-kong, come back next week," she repeated parrotlike, a tape recorder for a mouth.

The lawyer read the will Ah Kong had dictated: "To my daughter Peik Wing, who gave me twice the pleasure of her sisters, I bequeath a double share."

It didn't matter to Su, because he'd left each of them enough to be independent.

Besides, he had ten other children in Singapore, and they received much more than the daughters did. They were his first wife's children, the legal family, the Wings Su had hardly met, except at Jason's and Wanda's weddings and at Ah Kong's funeral.

Su wasn't sad when Ah Kong died. What was the good of being a Wing if you couldn't fly?

She had thought and thought so much about it.

The strangest thing about their family was the difference between their name and their lives. Ah Kong kept them tied to him. They were his fledglings, he the eagle with hawk nose and white hair feathers, driving his Mercedes SL 270 across the Johore Causeway between Singapore and Malaysia every weekend.

Ah Kong had more than two nests. At Jason's wedding, when Su and Yen and Peik met their sisters and brothers, the legal Wings, many of them older than Mama, one of their brothers told them Ah Kong had been called the Timber King of Indonesia. He had lived in Sumatra, Sarawak, and Borneo when he was younger and had minor wives in each place, but because he didn't marry these women, their children had never been introduced to his legal family.

Mama said she knew better. She held out for a Chinese ceremony even if a civil ceremony was impossible, so her daughters were Ah Kong's recognized second family.

At Jason's wedding they had to address Jason's mother as First Mother, but they kept forgetting to call Mama Second Mother. First Mother told Mama they were badly trained daughters.

"Imagine that!" Mama said. "With her younger daughter living with an American diplomat—unmarried!—imagine her saying my daughters are badly brought up!" Mama didn't like to gossip. Still, she had a way of making things known.

Yen and Su never told Mama how Ah Kong died. Because she was never suspicious, Mama forgot what were secrets and what were not, and she often got Yen and Su into trouble with Ah Kong. After Su confided in her about a boy she liked or about some poor exam results and she promised not to tell, she was sure to mention it to Ah Kong over supper on Saturday. One night when Ah Kong slapped Su for going to a dance without his permission and she complained Mama had broken her promise, he retorted, "Your mother is simple as rain water. I married her for one reason—for her virtue. You should learn from her if you wish to find a good husband." That terrified Su.

Ah Kong was the only person in their family who could fly. The sisters were allowed to leave Malacca twice—each time to travel to Singapore. A few years after they met Ah Kong's first family, they were told to come for their Seventh Sister's wedding.

Yen wore a new red dress for Wanda's wedding reception at the Equatorial Hotel. She had hemmed the pouf skirt up without telling Mama, and even in the expensive hotel lobby full of white women tourists in bare sundresses, she looked amazing, as if she was wearing a tutu and had wandered onto the wrong stage, or as if her legs had sprouted inches overnight.

Mama didn't show any embarrassment. Being the Second Wife, she had warned them, she was accustomed to mean gossip, and she had already anticipated rudeness from First Mother's children and grandchildren, some of whom were meeting them for the first time.

Yen was disgracing the Wing family, they said, pulling long faces at Mama.

The next weekend Ah Kong greeted them with a dirty face, white eyebrows scrunched up like dishrags. Peik showed off the pillowcase she was embroidering for him with peonies and phoenixes—Chinesey images he liked—but the fancy stitching didn't help improve his mood.

"Yen," he said after dinner. They were all surprised, for he hadn't spoken directly to her for years. "Yen," he repeated. "You are completing your exam this year?"

"Yes, Ah Kong." Yen looked at Mama for help.

"What plans do you have?"

"Plans?"

"Yes, what do you plan to do after sixth form?"

"Sixth form?"

"Don't repeat after me like an idiot! Your mother was already married with two daughters when she was your age. A woman cannot be too careful about her plans when the time comes. I was watching you at Wanda's wedding. It seems to me I should be making some plans for you if you haven't any of your own."

Yen gave Mama another look and opened her mouth.

Before she could speak Mama said, "Goodness, Ah Kong, of course you must make plans for Yen. She not yet nineteen and know nothing of the world, and her exam results maybe not successful, she maybe not lucky, able to continue in university, maybe a secretarial course in Singapore or even London the best thing for her, so hard three daughters, how to help them later in life—"

"I'm thinking of an arranged marriage for Yen," Ah Kong interrupted.

"What!"

"Don't be rude, Su," Mama said softly. "Apologize to Ah Kong."

"Sorry," Su mumbled.

Ah Voon padded to the table with a plate of gold-yellow sooji cake famous among Mama's friends. Su bolted a square down to comfort herself.

"Yen, thank Ah Kong for thinking of your future," Mama prompted.

Curious, Su stared at Yen. Yen never liked reading Barbara Cartland and Harlequin Romances. So sissy, she sneered at Su's taste, preferring Raymond Chandler and Mickey Spillane—tough guys. "I want to be tough," she said to Su one night when they caught each other sneaking into the kitchen for Ah Voon's love-letter biscuits.

"Yi, I don't care! I don't believe in love," Yen said. "Like you and

Mama, uh? You also had arranged marriage."

Mama kept her eyes down.

"If not love, what difference does it make? Anyone can do."

"We have a family reputation to consider. Not anyone can marry a daughter of mine." Su could see Ah Kong was steaming. "It may not be easy to find a husband for you."

"Will Yen be able to choose?" Su had to ask it.

"There will be no time." Ah Kong stared at her suspiciously. "The fortuneteller says Chap Goh Mei is the auspicious time for her to marry. That is in a few months. I have two prospects; the one from Sarawak is more willing."

"What's the hurry, Ah Kong? I'm not going to go bad, you know. *Hah hah!* Now I'm not so sure what my plan is. You have already made plans for me before you asked me. That's not right!"

Reading so many detective novels, Yen had grown an extra-vigilant mind. "What's behind all this?" she would nag, harassing Mama and Ah Voon after they had cleaned her room or rearranged her things. Once she asked the question there was no putting her off. It was as if she just set her mind down, went on strike.

"Right? Right? A daughter has no right. Ignorant girl! Have you done any work in your life? Made any money? You've been a parasite all your life, living off my body, this body that gave you life." Ah Kong smacked his chest. The liver spots on his cheeks throbbed like purple thumb prints.

"Now, Ah Kong, Yen not disobeying you, you know her tongue always put in wrong place, we talk more about it next week, Peik has letter commendation from Mrs. Winny Chew, you know, her Sunday-school teacher, she want you to read it."

Peik said Mama was truly the meek of the earth. But Su agreed with Yen that what Mama wanted was to inherit the earth. In Ah Kong's will he left her plenty of money. To my good and obedient wife, he said, even after death, and Mama was still obeying him, exactly the way she did when he was alive.

Su took her share of Ah Kong's money—blood money, she said to

Yen—and went to America.

Where should her wings carry her?

Mama said not New York and not San Francisco, because they were wicked cities—Sodom and Gomorrah, Pastor Fung called them when she went to him for advice.

"Only to study," he added. "A young girl must be protected. In a quiet college far away from big cities."

Su had thought all America was the same.

"You see Paul Newman in the East and in the West and he looks just the same," Yen agreed. "Boy oh boy oh boy! You're gonna have fun!"

They talked like Americans when they were alone together, a game they began after seeing *West Side Story* on television. A good movie; the actors talked with twisted mouths, and the boys and girls rumbled and kissed.

Su picked Colgate College because it was in New York. Besides, it was the only college to accept her application.

Mama and her friends thought she had done the funniest thing. Everyone they knew apparently had a tube of Colgate toothpaste in the bathroom. "Colgate! Ah, she learning to brush her teeth there?" Auntie Mei-mei asked, rolling her eyes. Her classmates thought Su was going to dental school. "Why you want to be dental hygienist?" they asked. "Lousy job, looking down people's stinky mouths. All those rotten teeth!"

Ah Kong had been prowling around the house that Saturday night, the week after he began arranging for Yen to marry a stranger in Sarawak. Yen had told Su she had seen him peeking into their bedrooms, but Su never believed her until that Saturday.

Su was angry that he was shipping Yen off like that, simply because she had worn a short skirt to Wanda's wedding. As Mama liked telling everyone, their half-sister Weena had been the mistress of a U.S. attaché to Singapore for years before he married his American fiancée. Ah Kong never made a stink about it. Being mistress to an American embassy official was acceptable to First Mother and her children—they were proud of Weena because Paul Frazer took her to diplomatic parties and she got to shake the hands of visiting dignitaries like the Sultan of Brunei and assorted rajahs. "Face clean, backside dirty," Mama giggled, explaining First Mother's attitude. Su couldn't understand why Ah Kong would act as if Yen's miniskirt episode had tarnished her virtue.

She could not rouse Yen to indignation.

"Oh, who cares?" she said chirpily. "Where am I going to meet a man anyway in sleepy old Malacca? I don't want to continue studying, and marriage must be OK. So many million women marry and do OK!"

Yen had no idea about herself and what she wanted. She was like Mama, but without the check on her tongue Mama practiced in front of Ah Kong.

When Su told Mrs. Brecker, her high-school English teacher, that her older sister was having an arranged marriage, Mrs. Brecker was horrified. "Why, that's like the Dark Ages!" she exclaimed. "You poor girls. Has your mother told your sister anything about sex?"

Sex? Poor Mama would have burst before she could pronounce the word. Su dropped her eyes in embarrassment that Mrs. Brecker would use the word in front of a student.

On Friday after class, flushed, determined, Mrs. Brecker gave Su a package for Yen. She had wrapped it in newspaper as if it were a fish from the wet market. "Tell your sister she should open this only in the privacy of her room!" she admonished.

Su's fingers traced the outline of a large oblong book beneath the newspaper wrapper. She stifled her curiosity until she and Yen were alone in the evening.

"Can I look?" she pleaded as Yen opened the package.

At first she was disappointed. It was an old book, more worn than even the books you could buy from the secondhand bookstalls along the Central Market alleyway that sold paperbacks the Australian backpackers left behind in the YMCA. The pages were yellow and frayed; the bent cover showed a boring black-and-white picture of women holding up a poster, WOMEN UNITE; and in red the title proclaimed *Our Bodies Ourselves.*

"It's a book by women," Yen said as she turned the pages, "so I guess it isn't a dirty book."

All through Saturday, with Ah Kong lounging around the house, Su could not talk to Yen about her book, although she was sure Yen was reading it in secret, quiet all day, a smirk appearing through supper hinting at some bubbling inside. Thinking of Yen reading the book, she couldn't sleep, and at about midnight she sneaked out of her room.

Sure enough, when she pushed open Yen's door, Su saw her sitting in bed, knees up, reading.

"Let me read a little," she whispered.

"No, no, I'm at an exciting part."

"It isn't fair! You have the book only because of me."

"Well, get into bed with me. We'll read together."

Yen was reading a passage about that part of a woman's body, the vagina. They stared at the photograph of a mirror reflecting a woman's bottom.

"Hey, let's do an examination!" Yen said, excited. "We can use the reading lamp instead of a flashlight, and a compact mirror."

"I get to look first." Su wasn't going to be the shy one.

"Cannot. I'm getting married first, so more important for me to know about the labia and all that. Here, you take the compact. Now, squat on the bed and open your legs wide. I'll bring the reading lamp close, and we can see what we look like there."

Would Su dare? She lifted the nightgown around her waist. Whichever way she turned, nervous, the cloth shifted, blocking the light, until she pulled it over her head and squatted on the bed.

It was difficult to see anything in the small compact mirror. She tried angling it in different directions, and Yen twisted the gooseneck so the lamp turned, shining upward. It came into view. Two pink things, frilled, a little tongue, as well as a small opening, an indentation in her bottom. It flashed in the mirror, a stranger's face, bearded, with lips and mouth, having hidden down there all her life.

"Let me see, let me see," Yen urged, craning her head down. Then Su looked up and saw Ah Kong at the door.

How to gauge how long he had been watching them? She wanted to dive under the blanket, her flesh suddenly rising in hard, cold pimples. Yen raised the lamp to shine on his face, the white hairs in his nostrils moving because he was breathing hard.

"Filth!" His mouth was shaping rather than speaking sounds, English Chinese sounds Su had never heard him make before. "Sisters sluts perverts mother...you have no shame no fear...I..."

Grabbing her nightgown, Su pulled it down over her head just in time to see Yen sticking out her tongue at him. That must have done it because he left at once, and they could hear him stumbling against something in the kitchen.

Su wanted to run to Ah Kong to beg his forgiveness. She wanted to show him the book, to show him they were simply learning about their bodies. But she didn't move. Ah Kong would never understand such a book. For him it could only be a dirty book.

"Go away!" Yen ordered, irritated. "If you hadn't come into my room, we wouldn't be in this trouble. Just wait. Ah Kong will find a way to punish you also."

A faint light glowed where Ah Kong had opened the refrigerator door. Su thought of going into the kitchen to say something, then remembered he had just seen her squatting naked, breasts tingling with cold, bottom raised, an ugly, abnormal frog. Covering her face with the bedsheet, she knew she would stay awake all night wishing she were dead. But she must have slept, because she didn't hear Ah Voon screaming until Mama shook her.

At her usual time, 5 A.M., Ah Voon went to the kitchen. There she found Ah Kong lying beside the refrigerator. Standing in front of the open door, he had had a massive heart attack. *Myocardial infarction*, Dr. Hong told Mama, what you expect in a man his age, except he had seemed healthy—particular in diet, regular in habits, someone who took care of his body.

Frigid air had been pumping out of the refrigerator all night, and Ah Kong's body was doubly cold and rigid when Ah Voon found him, the tiny fridge door light spotlighting his twisted face.

"*Aiiyah,* what an unlucky way to die! He didn't look like a man, more like a ten-thousand-demon," she repeated, "hard like wood, his eyes open, glaring at Tua Peh Kong, the Underworld God. I always say cold water is bad for the body. Why he want a cold drink at night?"

Mama never ever knew he had come to Yen's room. He hadn't had a chance to tell her what he had seen, and how were Yen and Su to say that Ah Kong died because he caught them looking into a mirror?

JULIA ALVAREZ

I never wrote in another language. English is, in fact, my "first language" if we are speaking of the books and writing. Spanish certainly was the language of storytelling, the language of the body and of the senses and of the emotional wiring of the child, so that still, when someone addresses me as "Hoolia" (Spanish pronunciation of Julia), I feel my emotional self come to the fore. I answer Sí, and I lean forward to kiss a cheek rather than answer Yes, and extend my hand for a handshake. Some deeper or first Julia is being summoned.

But in the writing, I want both present, and so I often say, "I write my Spanish in English." In one of my essays, "Family Matters" in *Something to Declare*, I address this:

> Indeed like any like any small tribe, my familia has its national litera-
> ture: the family stories. And, of course, so much of my material has been
> inspired by these stories [from my original language and country]. I don't
> mean that my fiction slavishly recounts "what really happened," but that
> my sense of the world, and therefore of the world I recreate in language,
> comes from that first encompassing experience of familia with its large
> cast of colorful characters, its elaborate branchings hither and yon to con-
> nect everyone together, its Babel of voices since everyone has to put his
> or her spoon in the sancocho. But it isn't only my material—even my man-
> ner of telling a story is muy familial, a bittersweet approach, the heart in
> turmoil but a twinkle in the eye, much like my grandmother winking at
> my "corpse," or a drunk uncle dancing flamenco on the dining room table
> with the secret police knocking at the door.
>
> But what most surprises me—especially since I am now working in
> another language—is to discover how much of my verbal rhythm, my word
> choices, my attention to the sound of my prose comes from my native lan-
> guage as spoken by *la familia*.

"When are you going to write shorter sentences?" one reader asked during the question-and-answer period after one of my book tour readings. I went back to my hotel room and counted words. The next day I bought a paperback of Raymond Carver's stories at the airport bookstore, and when I did the numbers, I saw what my questioner meant: Carver's sentences stayed at a ten-word average; mine were at least twice that. Carver favored simple sentences; I tended towards complex sentences with their subordinate clauses, their appositives, their balanced opposites. (I think you can count all the semicolons in a book by Carver on your two hands.) My sentences were lush, tropical, elaborate, like those of that other southerner, Faulkner, adding a phrase here, and then returning to the main point there, subordinating one clause to another, training the wild, luxuriant language on the trellis of syntax until a dozen bright blooms of meaning burst open for the reader.

In another instance, an editor who was working with me on a magazine story noted that I overused the word "little." A little coffee, a little dessert, a little cough. And sure enough with the computer word-finder I discovered a dozen more examples of my overuse. Then I realized, I was translating from the Spanish diminutive, so common in family usage, where nicknames and small versions of large versions are always being distinguished and derived from each other. Mamayaya, my great-grandmother, as opposed to Mamayoya, my great-aunt, as opposed to Mamita, my grandmother, as opposed to Mami, my mother. There was Julia, called Juyi, my prima-hermana (sister-cousin), to distinguish her from Julia, my mother, to distinguish her from Juliminga, that's me, who wrote that terrible book about the family.

As for why I made the switch [from Spanish to English]: it was made for me. I landed in this country and language at age ten in the days before bilingual education was even an option, when you were thrown into the deep end of the pool and had to learn the new language. I've also written about this experience: how in fact it made me into a writer. As for keeping my culture alive in my U.S.A. life, I travel regularly to the Dominican Republic. My husband Bill and I have started a farm/foundation in the mountains, modeling organic/sustainable agriculture (his passion) and addressing the rampant illiteracy there (my passion). I'm now taking Middlebury College students for a writing workshop, "Writing in the Wilds," to the farm. They will be working on their writing (in English) in a Spanish-speaking world. Perhaps I am trying to turn the tables on them? Or merely to combine the many worlds that all of us, writers and human beings, are part of even if we chose to ignore those that we find too painful or challenging to address.

P.S. I do hate the term "stepmother" tongue as it comes too loaded with the negative baggage of stepmothering. (Believe me, I am a "stepmother.") It is my *madrina* tongue, my godmother tongue. I've cried with its vowels, laughed with its consonants, made love in its silences, even buried some dead deep in its soil. So, no, it's not a stepmother, but a "second" mother tongue.

Joe

Yolanda, nicknamed *Yo* in Spanish, misunderstood *Joe* in English, doubled and pronounced like the toy, *Yoyo*—or when forced to select from a rack of personalized key chains, *Joey*—stands at the third-story window watching a man walk across the lawn with a tennis racket. He touches the border of the shrubbery with the rim of his racket and sets one or two wild irises nodding.

"Don't," Yo mumbles to herself at the window, outlining her hairline with a contemplative index finger. It is her secret pride: Her hair grows to a point on her forehead, arches up, semicircling her face, a perfect heart. "Don't disturb the flowers, Doc." She wags her finger at his thumb-sized back.

The man stops. He throws an imaginary ball in the air and serves it to the horizon. The horizon misses. He walks on towards it and the tennis courts.

He is dressed in white shorts and a white shirt, an outfit which makes him look like a boy...a good boy...the only son of monied, unloving tycoons. Both of them are tycoons, Yo posits. Daddy Coon is a Fruit of the Loom tycoon. The band on her underwear squeezes gently.

Mama Coon is—Yo looks around the room—*scarf, mirror, soap, umbrella*—an umbrella tycoon. A dark cloud rolls lazily towards her in the sky. The ghost of the tennis ball is coming to haunt the man. Yo smiles, appreciating her charms.

An umbrella tycoon will never do. One more turn around the room: *typewriter, red satchel*—nice sound to that. But he isn't a red satchel tycoon. A breeze blows the white curtains in on either side of her, two ghostly arms embracing her. A room tycoon ....

The world is sweetly new and just created. The first man walks in the garden on his way to a tennis date. Yo stands at the third-story window and kisses her fingers and blows him the kiss. "Kiss, kiss," she hisses from the window. She wishes: Let him rip off his white shirt, push back the two halves of his chest like Superman prying open a door and let the first woman out.

Eve is lovely, a valentine hairline, white gossamer panties.

"In the beginning," Yo begins, inspired by perspective. Four floors down, her doctor, shrunk to child size, sits on the lawn. "In the beginning, Doc, I loved John."

She recognizes the unmistakable signs of a flashback: a woman at a window, a woman with a past, with memory and desire and wreckage in her heart. She will let herself have them today. She can't help herself anyway.

In the beginning, we were in love. Yo smiles. That was a good beginning. He came to my door. I opened it. My eyes asked, *Would you like to come in out of the rest of the world?* He answered, *Thank you very much, just what I had on the tip of my tongue.*

It was at the beginning of time, and a river ran outside Yo's window, bordered by cypresses, willows, great sweating ferns, thick stalks and palms. Huge creatures of the imagination scuttled across the muddy bottom of the river. At night as the lovers lay in bed and connected the stars into rams and crabs and twins, they heard the barks and howls of the happy mating beasts.

"I love you," John said, rejoicing, tricked by the barks and the howls.

But Yolanda was afraid. Once they got started on words, there was no telling what they could say.

"I love you," John repeated, so she would follow suit.

Yolanda kissed each eye closed, hoping that would do.

"Do you love me, Joe? Do you?" he pleaded. He wanted words back; nothing else would do.

Yo complied. "I love you too."

"I'll always love you!" he said, splurging. "Marry me, marry me."

A beast howled from the river. The ram galloped away from the sky, startled by human sound.

"One." John bowed Yolanda's thumb towards him. "Two." He folded up the index finger. "Three." He kissed the nail.

"All you need is love," the radio wailed, as if it were hungry.

"Four," she joined in, bending her fourth finger. "Five," they chimed in unison.

His hand met hers, palm to palm, as if they were sharing a prayer.

"Love," the song snarled, starved. "Love...love..."

"John, John, you're a pond!" Yolanda teased, straddling him by Merritt Pond.

John was lying on his back; he had just said that when you look up at the sky, you realize nothing that you ever do really matters.

"John's a hon, lying by the pond, having lots of fun," Yolanda punned, nuzzling the hollow of his shoulder.

He stroked her back. "And you're a little squirrel! You know that?"

Yolanda sat up. "Squirrel doesn't rhyme," she explained. "The point's to rhyme with my name."

"Joe-lan-dah?" He quibbled, "What rhymes with Joe-lan-dah?"

"So use Joe. *Doe, roe, buffalo*," she rhymed. "Okay, now, you try it." She spoke in the voice she had learned from her mother when she wanted a second helping of the good things in life.

"My dear Joe," John began, but put on the spot, he was blocked for a rhyme. He hemmed, he hawed, he guffawed. Finally, he blahhed: "My dear, sweet little squirrel, you mean more to me than all the gold in the world." He grinned at his inadvertent rhyme.

Yo sat up again. "C minus!" She rolled away from him onto the grass. "Where'd you learn to talk, Hallmark?"

Hurt, John stood and brushed off his pants as if the grass spears were little annoying bits of Yo. "Not everyone can be as goddam poetic as you!"

She nibbled all up his leg in playful apology.

John pulled her up by the shoulders. "Squirrel." He forgave her.

She winced. Anything but a squirrel. Her shoulders felt furry. "Can

I be something else?"

"Sure!" He swept his hand across the earth as if he owned it all:
"What do you want to be?"

She turned away from him and scanned the horizon: *trees, rocks, lake,
grass, weeds, flowers, birds, sky....*

His hand came from behind her; it owned her shoulder.

"Sky," she tried. Then, the saying of it made it right: "Sky, I want to
be the sky."

"That's not allowed." He turned her around to face him. His eyes,
she noticed for the first time, were the same shade of blue as the sky.
"Your own rules: you've got to rhyme with your name."

"I"—she pointed to herself—"rhymes with the *sky!*"

"But not with *Joe!*" John wagged his finger at her. His eyes softened
with desire. He placed his mouth over her mouth and ohhed her lips
open.

"Yo rhymes with *cielo* in Spanish." Yo's words fell into the dark, mute
cavern of John's mouth. *Cielo, cielo,* the word echoed. And Yo was running, like the mad, into the safety of her first tongue, where the proud-
ly monolingual John could not catch her, even if he tried.

"What you need is a goddam shrink!" John's words threw themselves
off the tip of his tongue like suicides.

She said what if she did, he didn't have to call them *shrinks.*

"Shrink," he said. "Shrink, shrink."

She said that just because they were different, that was no reason to
make her feel crazy for being her own person. He was just as crazy as
she was if push came to shove. My God! she thought. I'm starting to
talk like him! Push comes to shove! She laughed, still half in love with
him. "Okay, okay," she conceded. "We're both crazy. So, let's both go
see a shrink." She winced, taking on his language only to convince him.

He shoved her peacemaking hand away. She was the one who was
crazy, remember? No way he was going to go be shrunk.

She kissed him in silent persuasion, but she could tell he wasn't convinced.

"I love you. Isn't that enough?" he resisted. "I love you more than it's good for me."

"See! You're the one who's crazy!" she teased.

Already she had begun to mistrust him.

Because his pencils were always sharpened, his clothes always folded before lovemaking. Because he put his knife between the tines of his fork between mouthfuls of the dishes she made that were always just this side of not tasting like they were supposed to—the lasagna like fried eggs, the pudding like frosting. Because he accused her of eating her own head by thinking so much about what people said. Because he believed in the Real World, more than words, more than he believed in her.

But this time it was because he made for-and-against lists before doing anything, and she had discovered the *for-and-against-slash-Joe-slash-wife* list. Number one *for* was intelligent; number one *against* was *too much for her own good.* Number two *for* was exciting; number two *against* was *crazy,* question mark.

"What does this mean?" She met him at the door with the sheet of his calculations in her hand.

"What's that, Violet?" He had named her Violet after *shrinking* violet when she had started seeing Dr. Payne. John balked the first time Yo told him the doctor's name and fees. "A pain in the bloody pocket all right!" His name became a joke between them. But secretly for luck, Yo called Payne, Doc.

"What the hell you have to make a list of the pros and cons of marrying me for?" Yo followed John into their bedroom, where he began to undress.

"Come on, Violet—"

"Stop violeting me! I hate it when you do that."

"Roses are red, violets are blue," he recited, instead of counting to ten so as not to have two lost tempers in one room.

"You really had to *decide* you loved me?" She read the pro and then the con list out loud, shaking her head as she did so, ducking whenever John grabbed for his list. "Looks to me like the cons have it. Why'd you marry me?"

"My way is to make lists. I could say the same thing to you about words—"

"Words?" She swatted him with his paper. "Words? Wasn't I the one always saying, *Don't say it. Don't say it?* I was the one who tried to keep words out of it."

"I made a list because I was confused. Yes, me, confused!" John reached for her arm, more as a test of her temper than a touch of desire. She could tell the difference and pushed the hand away.

"Ah, come on, Joe," he said, his voice softening; he folded his tie ruler-size; he dressed the chair-back with his jacket.

She said *no* as sweetly as if it were *yes*. "Nooooh," the word opening her mouth, soft and ripe and ready for him to bite into it.

"Come on, sweetie, tell us what's for supper?" he coaxed. He took her hands and led her towards him.

"Sugared spaghetti with glazed meatballs and honeydew spinach. Sweetie," she taunted, tugging away in play.

He drew her towards him, in play, and pressed his lips on her lips.

Her lips tightened. She set her teeth, top on bottom row, a calcium fortress.

He pulled her forward. She opened her mouth to yell, *No, no!* He pried his tongue between her lips, pushing her words back in her throat.

She swallowed them: *No, no.*

They beat against her stomach: *No, no.* They pecked at her ribs: *No, no.*

"No!" she cried.

"It's just a kiss, Joe. A kiss, for Christ's sake!" John shook her. "Control yourself!"

"Nooooooo!" she screamed, pushing him off everything she knew.

He let her go.

John and Yo were lying in bed with the lights off because it was too hot to have them on or to be afoot. John's hand slipped down to her hips, beating a beat.

"It's too hot," Yo said, silencing it.

He tried to humor her, playing on a new nickname. "Not tonight, Josephine?" He turned on his side to face her and outlined her features in the dark. He traced the heart line from her chin to her forehead and down again. He kissed her chin to seal the valentine. "Beautiful. Do you know your face is a perfect heart?" He discovered this every time he wanted to make love to her.

The valentine was too hot. "I'm sweating," it moaned. "Don't."

The hand wouldn't listen. The middle finger traced a heart on her lips. The pinkie shaped a heart on the fleshiness above her right breast.

"Please, John!" His fingertips felt like rolling beads of sweat.

"John, please," he echoed. He printed J-o-h-n on her right breast with a sticky finger as if he were branding her his.

"John! It's too hot." She appealed to his common sense.

"John, it's too hot," he whined. The combination of heat and thwarted desire made him nasty.

She stoppered his mouth with her hand. He ignored the violence in the gesture and kissed her moist palm. His eyes lidded with hopefulness, he rolled towards her, his body making a sucking sound as it unglued itself from the bare mattress. The sheets had drooped from their hospital corners; they wilted onto the floor.

John's right hand played piano on her ribs, and his mouth blew a piccolo on her breasts.

"Shit!" she yelled at him, leaping out of bed. "Fuck!" He had forced her to say her least favorite word in the world. She would never ever forgive him for that.

"Ever?" he said, angrily grabbing for her arm in the dark. "Ever?"

Her heart folded, flattened, folded again. The halves fluttered, blinked and opened. Her heart lifted up to the cloud-flowers in the sky.

"Ever!" She slapped him with the sound. "Ever! Ever!" She wished she had her clothes on. It was strange to make absolute statements in the nude.

He came home with a bouquet of flowers that she knew he had paid too much for. They were blue, and she guessed they were irises. *Irises* was her favorite name for flowers, so they had to be irises.

But as he handed them to her, she could not make out his words.

They were clean, bright sounds, but they meant nothing to her.

"What are you trying to say?" she kept asking. He spoke kindly, but in a language she had never heard before.

She pretended she understood. She took a big smell of the flowers. "Thank you, love." At the word *love*, her hands itched so fiercely that she was afraid she would drop the flowers.

He said something happily, again in sounds she could not ascribe meanings to.

"Come on, love," she asked his eyes; she spoke precisely as if she were talking to a foreigner or a willful child. "John, can you understand me?" She nodded her head to let him know that he should answer her by nodding his head if words failed him.

He shook his head, *No.*

She held him steady with both hands as if she were trying to nail him down into her world. "John!" she pleaded. "Please, love!"

He pointed to his ears and nodded. Volume wasn't the problem. He could hear her. "Babble babble." His lips were slow motion on each syllable.

He is saying *I love you,* she thought! "Babble," she mimicked him. "Babble babble babble babble." Maybe that meant, *I love you too,* in whatever tongue he was speaking.

He pointed to her, to himself. "Babble?"

She nodded wildly. Her valentine hairline, the heart in her ribs and all the ones on her sleeves twinkled like the pinchers of the crab in the sky. Maybe now they could start over, in silence.

When she left her husband, Yo wrote a note, *I'm going to my folks till my head-slash-heart clear.* She revised the note: *I'm needing some space, some time, until my head-slash-heart-slash-soul*—No, no, no, she didn't want to divide herself anymore, three persons in one Yo.

John, she began, then she jotted a little triangle before *John. Dear,* she wrote on a slant. She had read in a handwriting analysis book that this was the style of the self-assured. *Dear John, listen, we both know it's not working.*

"*It's?*" he would ask. "*It's*, meaning what?"

Yo crossed the vague pronoun out.

We are not working. You know it, I know it, we both know it, oh John, John, John. Her hand kept writing, automatically, until the page was filled with the dark ink of his name. She tore the note up and confettied it over her head, a rainfall of John's. She wrote him a short memo, *Gone*—then added—*to my folks.* She thought of signing it, Yolanda, but her real name no longer sounded like her own, so instead she scribbled his name for her, *Joe.*

Her parents were worried. She talked too much, yakked all the time. She talked in her sleep, she talked when she ate despite twenty-seven years of teaching her to keep her mouth shut when she chewed. She talked in comparisons, she spoke in riddles.

She ranted, her mother said to her father. Her father coughed, upset. She quoted famous lines of poetry and the opening sentences of the classics. How could anyone remember so much? her mother asked her sullen father. She was carried away with the sound of her voice, her mother diagnosed.

She quoted Frost; she misquoted Stevens; she paraphrased Rilke's description of love.

"Can you hear me!" Doctor Payne held his hands up to his mouth like a megaphone and made believe he was yelling over a great distance. "Can you hear me?"

She quoted to him from Rumi; she sang what she knew of "Mary Had a Little Lamb," mixing it up with "Baa Baa, Black Sheep."

The doctor thought it best if she checked into a small, private facility where he could keep an eye on her. For her own good: round-the-clock care; nice grounds; arts and crafts classes; tennis courts; a friendly, unintimidating staff, no one in a uniform. Her parents signed the papers—"For your own good," they quoted the nice doctor to her. Her mother held her while a nurse camouflaged in street clothes filled a syringe. Yo quoted from *Don Quixote* in the original; she translated the passage on prisoners into instantaneous English.

The nurse stung her with an injection of tears. Yo went quiet for the first time in months, then burst into tears. The nurse rubbed a tiny cloud on her arm. "Please, honey, don't cry," her mother pleaded with her.

"Let her cry," the doctor advised. "It's a good sign, a very good sign."

"*Tears, tears,*" Joe said, reciting again, "*tears from the depths of some pro-found despair.*"

"Don't worry," the doctor said, coaching the alarmed parents. "It's just a poem."

"*But men die daily for lack of what is found there,*" Yo quoted and mis-quoted, drowning in the flooded streams of her consciousness.

The signs got better. Yo fantasized about Doc. He would save her body-slash-mind-slash-soul by taking all the slashes out, making her one whole Yolanda. She talked to him about growth and fear and the self in transition and women's spiritual quest. She told him everything except that she was falling in love with him.

Was she ready for her parents? he asked.

Ready for her parents, she echoed.

Her parents stepped into the room, staging happiness. They tested her with questions about the food, the doctor, the weather, and the tile ashtray she had made in arts and crafts therapy.

She offered it to her mother.

Her mother cried. "I shouldn't cry."

"It's a good sign," Yo said, quoting Doc, then caught herself. Quoting others again, a bad sign.

Her father moved to the window and checked the sky. "When are you coming home?" the back asked Yo.

"Whenever she's ready to!" Her mother parted the hair from Yo's forehead.

And the valentine appeared again on the earth.

"I love you guys," Yo improvised. So what if her first original words in months were the most hackneyed. They were her own truth. "I do, I do," she singsang. Her mother looked a little worried as if she had bit-ten into something sour she had thought would be sweet.

"What happened, Yo?" her mother asked the hand she was patting a little later. "We thought you and John were so happy."

"We just didn't speak the same language," Yo said, simplifying.

"Ay, Yolanda." Her mother pronounced her name in Spanish, her pure, mouth-filling, full-blooded name, Yolanda. But then, it was inevitable, like gravity, like night and day, little applebites when God's back is turned, her name fell, bastardized, breaking into a half dozen nicknames—"*pobrecita* Yosita"—another nickname. "We love you." Her mother said it loud enough for two people's worth. "Don't we, Papi?"

"Don't we what, Mami?" Yo's father turned. "Love her," his wife snapped.

"There's no question at all." Papi came towards Mami, or Yo.

"What is love?" Yo asks Dr. Payne; the skin on her neck prickles and reddens. She has developed a random allergy to certain words. She does not know which ones, until they are on the tip of her tongue and it is too late, her lips swell, her skin itches, her eyes water with allergic reaction tears.

The doctor studies her and smells the backs of his fingers. "What do you think it is, Joe? Love."

"I don't know." She tries to look him in the eyes, but she is afraid if she does, he will know, he will know.

"Oh, Joe," he consoles, "we constantly have to redefine the things that are important to us. It's okay not to know. When you find yourself in love again, you'll know what it is."

"Love," Yo murmurs, testing. Sure enough, the skin on her arm erupts into an ugly rash. "I guess you're right." She itches. "It's just scary not to know what the most important word in my vocabulary means!"

"Don't you think that's the challenge of being alive?"

"Alive," she echoes, as if she were relapsing to her old quoting days. Her lips burn. *Alive, love,* words she can use now only at a cost.

Yo's finger traces Doc's body on the metallic screen of the window as if she were making him up. Maybe she will try writing again, nothing too ambitious, a fun poem in the limerick mode. She'll call it, "Dennis' Racket," playing on the double meaning of the word *racket* as well as on his last name, Payne.

Deep within her, something stirs, an itch she can't get to.

"Indigestion," she murmurs, patting her belly. Perhaps not, she thinks, perhaps it is a personality phenomenon: the real Yolanda resurrecting on an August afternoon above the kempt green lawns of this private facility.

Her stomach hurts. She strokes wide I-am-hungry circles on her hospital smock. But the beating inside her is more desperate than hunger, a moth wild inside a lampshade.

It rises, a thrashing of wings, up through her trachea—until Yo retches. How tragic! At her age to die of a broken-heart attack. She tries to laugh, but instead of laughter, she feels ticklish wings unfolding like a fan at the base of her throat. They spread her mouth open as if she were screaming a name out over a great distance. A huge, black bird springs out; it perches on her bureau, looking just like the etching of the raven in Yo's first English poetry book.

She holds out her hand to befriend the dark bird.

It ignores her, and looks philosophically out the window at the darkening sky. Slowly its wings lift and fall, huge arcs rise and collapse, rise and collapse, up and down, up and down. Her hair is blown about her face. Dust hurries to corners. Curtains set sail from their windows.

It flies towards the window. "Oh my God! The screen!" Yo remembers in a moment of suspension of belief. "Have a little faith," she coaches herself, as the dark shape floats easily through the screen like smoke or clouds or figments of any sort. Out it flies, delighting in its new-found freedom, its dark hooded beak and tiny head drooping like its sex between arching wings.

Suddenly—it stops—midair. Delight and surprise are written all over its wing grin. It plummets down towards the sunning man on the lawn. Beak first, a dark and secret complex, a personality disorder let loose on the world, it plunges!

"Oh no," Yo wails. "No, not him!" She had thought that alone at her window on an August afternoon she would be far from where she could do any harm. And now, down it dives towards the one man she most wants immune to her words.

Yo screams as the hooked beak rips at the man's shirt and chest; the white figure on the lawn is a red sop.

Satiated, the dark bird rises and joins a rolling cluster of rain clouds in the northern sky.

Yo bangs on the screen. The man looks up, trying to guess a window. "Who *is* that?"

"Are you all right?" she cries out, liking her role as unidentified voice from the heavens.

"Who is that?" He stands, grabs the beach towel. The blood congeals into a long, red terrycloth rectangle. "Who is it?" He is annoyed at the prolonged guessing game.

"A secret admirer," she trills. "God."

"Heather?" he guesses.

"Yolanda," she murmurs to herself. "Yo," she shouts down at him. Who the hell is Heather, she wonders.

"Oh, Joe!" He laughs, waving his racket

Her lips prickle and pucker. Oh no, she thinks, recognizing the first signs of her allergy—not my own name!

The lawn is green and clean and quiet.

"*Love*," Yo enunciates, letting the full force of the word loose in her mouth. She is determined to get over this allergy. She will build immunity to the offending words. She braces herself for a double dose: "*Love, love*," she says the words quickly. Her face is one itchy valentine. "*Amor*." Even in Spanish, the word makes a rash erupt on the backs of her hands.

Inside her ribs, her heart is an empty nest.

"*Love*." She rounds the sound of the word as if it were an egg to put into it. "*Yolanda*." She puts in another one.

She looks up at the thunderclouds. His tennis game is going to be rainchecked, all right. There isn't a sample of blue up there to remind her of the sky. So she says, "*Blue*." She searches for the right word to follow the blue of blue. "*Cry...why...sky...*" She gains faith as she says each word, and dares further: "*World...squirrel...rough...tough...love... enough....*"

The words tumble out, making a sound like the rumble of distant thunder, taking shape, depth, and substance. Yo continues: *"Doc, rock, smock, luck,"* so many words. There is no end to what can be said about the world.

KYOKO UCHIDA

English is a language I grew up with from early childhood, like a sibling, familiar yet foreign, my equal. Whereas Japanese belonged to my parents, with its filial duty to report itself and tangled umbilical density, in English I was free to experiment, neither owning it nor owned by it. In a world where my first and second languages each set me apart from the other, so that I belonged fully to neither, writing in English became a way to carve out a place for myself. It was what allowed me to negotiate a space in which I had control over events and landscapes, to shape the world according to private experience.

Once I learned the alphabet and could sound words out, I took great pleasure in spelling: I loved to puzzle out how each new word might be spelled, in my own flawed English logic. Letters were like colorful building blocks that I could line up and rearrange to create phrases and sentences, and from them, entire pictures, imagined countries, histories, songs, and silences. Writing created a space entirely of my own making, more my own than anything else I had known. These were the stories I told myself, yet there were always surprises at the end, open doors and music I hadn't known had been there all along, the pleasure of finding something you didn't know you had. It was the language of my private imagination made public through writing—no longer secret, but more my own for it, for others read it and recognized it as mine.

Upon returning to Japan, I learned that I did not belong there or to its language any more than in the English-speaking countries I had left. On both sides of the Pacific I was a foreigner, speaking both languages without an accent, without a home. As a teenager I found myself trying to write in Japanese about American or Canadian landscapes, writing toward a place that I had lost: writing in the language of the country but writing outside of it, of a landscape I inhabit between two places.

Writing in English is for me is an act of claiming a place for myself—of announcing myself and this in-between space I occupy. For the last ten years I have written very little in Japanese, yet in writing one language I am writing the other, its rich shadow in the contours and rhythms of each, a dialogue between languages and loves. With every word I name a place both mine and other, negotiating both arrival and departure, for I am writing myself into a place where I belong and don't belong, claiming it for myself. There I, too, become other to myself, yet more my own.

from
Mother Tongues and Other Untravellings: A Long Poem in Prose

Fed on American beef and milk, we were supposed to grow tall, big-boned as the blond people my grandmother sees on TV. At four-foot-eleven I have betrayed them all, with my little-girl rib cage and feet too small for American shoes, my hip bones exactly like my mother's. I was always the shortest one in my class, the slightest. No one even bothered to shove me around. The only black boy in my fourth-grade class asked if I was a midget. I think he was disappointed. My mother said, *In Japan, you'd be average.* I imagined a land of small people, a country the size of my parents.

Still, every summer she signed me up for swimming lessons, drove me to the YMCA and back. On the way home I sat in the back, sticking to the seat in my wet bathing suit and shorts, and ate ice-cream sandwiches that tasted of chlorine. The trouble was that I could swim, but not very far. *An eager learner, but has no stamina,* my report cards said. At ten I loved only the rush of diving: the rough tile beneath my toes, where my whole body waited for the spring up my spine, the arc forward into air, where for a moment I was no one between spaces; the noiseless contact with water, familiar again, and moving through it without resistance as if returning. I never wanted to come up. When I did, the task became something else: breathing, breaching the surface, reaching the other side of the pool and starting out again, counting, keeping score. All summer I kicked and splashed across the distance, the taste of salt in my mouth, my seaweed hair.

When I went back to Japan, I was the second shortest.

English was my brother tongue, the sound of school and driveways, of summer camp, the backyard pool. At home we were forbidden to speak it, for fear of losing our mother tongue, though our mother, too, spoke it, her tongue not quite fitting around the *th*, the *v*. My brother taught me the words we couldn't say at school or in front of our friends' mothers, words our mother wouldn't know. She'd studied Faulkner and Brontë, said *often* with a British accent. Its secret music I shared with my brother, though secret to no one else; from the beginning, I shared it with my mother, later my sister. Like all my childhood secrets, my mother and I told it to each other, a story she knew only the ending of. *They lived happily ever after—mother, other, brother, voice.*

Excused from Sister Mary's English class at the missionary school in Japan, I sat alone in the unlit language lab, rehearsing my tongue's confessions. On Saturdays I spoke English with others like me, so as not to lose my brother tongue. People stared at us in stores. *Speak Japanese, children. Can't you speak Japanese?*

Very, listen, never, prom. The last time she lived here, my sister and I tried to correct our mother's pronunciation. *Bitter, early, rather, love.* In silence she suffered our impatience, our unforgiving daughterhood, the hard candy arrogance of smooth *l*s and *r*s.

When I returned to Hiroshima at ten, I found that I did not speak the language, though I recognized its fast clanging sound, like rough salt from the harbor. I spoke instead a Japanese without dialect or accent, as my parents and the teachers at Japanese School did. My mother grew up one prefecture west, in Yamaguchi, where the vowels were softer, the lilt slow and round as the oranges my grandmother fed me. My father's family was from Himeji, but he spent his childhood north, where the steel mills were. And although our parents had lived in Hiroshima for years before we were born, they never spoke the dialect while abroad.

More than my clothes, than that I'd spent seven years abroad, than that I spoke English, it was my mother tongue that separated me: even in this language we shared, we were different. The sounds bore no resemblance: *Hiroshima-ben* is notoriously combative, its vowels and word endings harsh, jagged in their upward notes, everything sounding like a command or an insult. The consonants, too, are the hard noises of gs and ds, js and ks. It is the language of survivors, of those who have had to carve a city out of seven rivers, mountains on three sides and an inland sea, and later out of ash and rubble; who have seen battles over a moated castle, navy shipyards dominating the bay, where two *yakuza* groups spreading their turf north and south would meet. The tongue has become hard and rough as the oyster shells gleaming on the docks all winter. It is a hot, blunt language, honest and quick to forget. Although we did not understand one another at first, the children were kind to me, for I was a newcomer; I might as well have been blond and blue-eyed.

It wasn't until I'd moved to a new school in the suburbs that my speech was seen as a sign of snobbery. *You don't sound like us. You think you're better, you put on airs*, they said in the perfect standard Japanese they accused me of speaking, reserved for classroom manners. In their mouths, this was what you spoke to injure, to mark distance, to recognize some central authority. I'd moved to the suburbs from downtown Hiroshima, so they couldn't have guessed I couldn't speak the dialect.

Still, in three or four years I lost my mother tongue to a *Hiroshima-ben* as fierce as that of anyone who'd lived there all her life, and to my surprise, my mother did, too. The dialect was something we learned together, for the first time, like classmates, or sisters at the piano. It has become my sister tongue, what I speak with my sister, my mother, the dialect of my teenage years, of growing up, of leaving. It is the language of returning, of common knowledge, of fights and oranges and silver-green oysters.

And now when I call, it is the dialect I listen for, the hard, familiar ring in my mother's speech, the unmistakable music we learned together —immigrants in a foreign land.

SIMON J. ORTIZ

The only language I've ever written fluently in is English. Although my native language is Keres—since I'm a Native American of Acoma Pueblo—I've mainly written in English for three reasons: 1. it's the principal language that's recognized or "authorized" in the U.S. social and political system, and 2. it's the predominant language which is read and spoken by just about any literate person in the United States, and 3. it's the main colonial language (i.e., the language of colonization, settlement, conquest) that Native people face and have to deal with.

I do write in Keres from time to time, at least spelling phonetically (i.e., writing out sounds of words using the English alphabet and orthography), and sometimes, or usually, I include it in context with English. I strongly feel that Keres or any other Native American language must have equal standing and use along with English and other languages, and because it doesn't I feel somewhat awkward and uncomfortable as a writer who writes mainly in English even though it's not my native language. Why do I feel that way? Because my native Keres language is not "authorized" or officially recognized—or simply not accepted—as I say above. Although there are no outright prohibitions or laws against Native languages, their use and practice is also not really encouraged by the U.S. public education and social system—so the implication is that they're not allowed. In effect, the result is that Native languages do not in a sense exist, not even for normal and usual use by Native speakers.

Because I do write most of the time in English, not in the Keres language of my native community and culture, I feel somewhat awkward and uncomfortable like I said above. Although there's not yet an extensive amount of discussion and discourse about this as a whole by Native American writers and intellectuals whose native cultures and communities have their own native languages, I feel it is an important and significant matter that has to be considered since it is central to our continuing decolonization.

If we do not consider this matter to be important and significant, we will continue to wholly regard the use of English (and other European or Western cultural languages) to be correct, justified, and unquestioned. And in a sense, we would be agreeing with the non-use and perhaps nonexistence of our own Native languages. And we would be in agreement with the continued colonization of our Native lands, cultures, and communities.

Distance

George had been bought from Macario, a Mexican American farmer who lived five miles south of San Rafael.

"That goat is mean like Macario," the girl's father said, trying to soothe his daughter.

The little girl was crying. She had just been butted and knocked down by George, and her knee was scraped and bleeding. Her father was cleaning her scrape with a clean cloth and a basin of cold water.

"We'll get that old goat tamed down," her father said.

George was a lively two-year-old billy buck. He was boss of the other goats in the goat yard. He stood defiantly in a corner of the goat yard and watched the father and daughter.

The next day, the girl's father roped George and tied him to a sturdy wooden post just out of reach of the water trough. All the other goats, as well as the chickens and a couple of ducks, were able to get water. But George couldn't. It was a hot day.

At first George didn't seem to pay any mind to not having any water. He just ignored the trough. In fact, he seemed to ignore the hard, rough rope around his neck too. He lay down by the post and looked straight ahead. Once in a while, he would turn his head and look around very calmly. It grew hotter by midafternoon.

When late afternoon shadows began to fall longer, the girl's father put water in the trough for the other goats and filled the bowls for the chickens and ducks. George got up on his legs then and for the first time strained against the rope. He looked disdainfully at the post and shook his bearded head, and then he lay back down.

George watched the man for a moment and then ignored him. He lay with his slender legs and hooves drawn up under him.

"We're fixing that Mexican goat good," the girl's father said at supper. The little girl looked out the kitchen window, but she couldn't see the goat.

She had watched George during the day. She felt a twinge of pity for the goat, but her scraped knee still hurt and she remembered the cool water and her father's soothing voice.

The next morning when the girl saw George he was standing on his thin legs. And he was leaning, pulling at the end of the rope tied at the back of his neck. George pawed the ground as if he were trying to pull it like a rug toward him.

Her father let the other goats out of their shed. They drank water from the trough and ate, and then they wandered around looking for shade to lie in. George watched them enviously. He looked over at the man's house but no one was around. It was a very hot day again.

By midafternoon the goat was lying down again. He lay with his head in the narrow strip of shade made by the wooden post. His flanks were sunken and he was breathing rapidly. Once in a while, George raised his head and bleated forlornly, and then he was quiet.

When the little girl saw the goat, she wanted to tell her father that George looked sad and tired. But her father wasn't around just then and that morning he had said, "We'll teach that old goat something all right!"

The next day was the same, and this time by noon George was plainly in weak shape. His slick brown and gray coat was mussed, the stiff hairs lying every which way like a badly-wired bale of hay. The little girl had come to gather eggs from the chicken house at noon. She watched George looking at her. On shaky legs George bleated, and the sound was pleading.

At their noon meal the girl asked her father, "When are you going to let George loose, Daddy?"

The father looked at his little girl, and he smiled and said, "When

George learns, sweetheart, when George learns not to be so mean."

There was a very dry spell that summer, and the hot days that George was tied to the post were burning hot. Little white tufts of clouds started up at the horizon in the mornings, but they never drifted together to even promise rain. The wind blew hotly and even the shades of farm buildings were no haven.

George lay on the ground all the time now, his spine against the sturdy post like he was trying to draw some strength from it.

By the morning of the fifth day, George hardly moved at all. The goat was lying on its side, heaving great, weak breaths infrequently. There were shallow gnaw marks on the dry wooden post. The girl's father checked the rope that held the goat. The strong, hard rope still held George very securely.

The little girl watched her father as he watered and fed the other animals. For several moments she was hopeful he would turn from his duties and take his knife and cut the rope that held George. But her father walked away and began to do something else. He didn't look at George anymore.

When evening came, her father penned up the animals. He checked George and found the goat's eyes clear, not sickly. He even spoke to George. George's eyes stared straight ahead, not giving the slightest flicker of recognition.

On the night of the fifth day, there was a full moon. The girl could see very clearly out of the window of her bedroom because the moonlight was so bright. She could see the white flanks of the hills a mile away. She could see the dark tufts of trees on the hillsides.

She looked toward the goat yard and shed. She could see the post that stood in an open space in the yard. The bright moon made the post white and shiny. At the foot of the post, in the very clear light of the moon, was a shadow. The shadow was very still. And she grew afraid.

The girl crawled deep under her covers, but it was a hot and stifling night. So she threw back the covers and covered her eyes with her hands. But she couldn't sleep. She listened. Except for the crickets, it was a very quiet night.

Then the girl got out of bed and dressed quickly. She didn't put on her shoes, and pebbles on the ground made it painful for her to walk as she made her way hurriedly to George in the goat yard. When George weakly rolled his head and looked at her, the light from the moon slanted into his eyes and made them shine with an odd sorrowful light.

The girl gave a small anguished cry then, and she reached for the knot around the goat's neck. The hard rope was so tightly knotted it was impossible for her to undo. She tried the knot at the post until her fingers bled, but there was no way to undo it. Finally, holding the rope in her hands, she could only whisper, I'm sorry, I'm sorry.

In the morning, the girl's father said, "I'm going to let George go today and see if he behaves any better." His daughter was overjoyed. After helping her mother with the breakfast dishes, she ran to the goat yard.

George was still lying there. He wasn't tied to the post anymore. He was just lying there.

The goat's breathing was trembly and thin and very weak. It was like an empty wind, purposeless and uncertain. The goat's eyes were half shut.

"What's wrong with George? Why won't he get up?" the girl asked her father who was standing nearby, staring at the goat prone on the ground next to the post.

Then, not looking at his daughter, he said lamely, "George will get up when he gets thirsty and hungry." But there wasn't any hope in his voice. A pan of water stood next to George's head. Not moving, the goat just lay there.

The little girl began to cry aloud then. Her father went to her and began to wipe her tears from her face. As he looked into his daughter's eyes, he saw them looking fiercely into his eyes and past him and into a great distance beyond.

BIOGRAPHICAL NOTES

JULIA ALVAREZ is a poet and fiction writer, whose work is published in ten languages. She spent her early childhood in the Dominican Republic, the homeland of both her parents. She emigrated to this country and language at the age of ten, a watershed experience which she says made her into a writer. After completing Syracuse University's Master of Arts in Creative Writing, Alvarez traveled America as a "migrant poet," teaching writing workshops in schools, nursing homes, prisons, bilingual programs, church basements from Kentucky to California. She kept body and soul together with these writing jobs as well as grants from the National Endowment for the Arts, the Ingram Merrill Foundation, University of Illinois Research Foundation, and the unbounded support of her friends and compañeras, some of whom still have her books and papers in their attics and garages. In 1991, she published *How the Garcia Girls Lost Their Accents*, which won a PEN Oakland Award for works that present a multicultural viewpoint and was selected as a Notable Book by the *New York Times* and an American Library Association Notable Book, 1992. Her second novel, *In the Time of the Butterflies*, was a finalist for the National Book Critics' Circle Award fiction, 1995. She has also published two books of poems: *The Other Side/El Otro Lado* and *Homecoming: New and Collected Poems*. Her poetry was selected by the New York Public Library for its 100th anniversary exhibit, 1996, "The Hand of the Poet: Original

Manuscripts by 100 Masters, From John Donne to Julia Alvarez." A novel, ¡Yo! was published in January 1997. Alvarez has settled down in Vermont. Her new book, *In Your Name, Salome*, will be published in June 2000.

ANDREI CODRESCU has published poetry, memoirs, fiction, and essays. He is a regular commentator on National Public Radio, and has written and starred in the Peabody Award-winning movie *Road Scholar*. His novels, *The Blood Countess* (1995) and *Messiah* (1999), were national bestsellers. *Alien Candor: Selected Poems 1970–1997* was published by Black Sparrow Press. Mr. Codrescu is Professor of English at Louisiana State University in Baton Rouge, Louisiana, and edits *Exquisite Corpse: a Journal of Letters & Life* (www.exquisitecorpse.org). Mr. Codrescu is available for lectures. For a partial list of publications, media contacts, and recent essays, visit the author's website at www.codrescu.com.

JUDITH ORTIZ COFER is the author of a novel, *The Line of the Sun*; a collection of essays and poetry, *Silent Dancing*; two books of poetry, *Terms of Survival* and *Reaching for the Mainland*; and *The Latin Deli: Prose and Poetry*. Her work has appeared in *Glamour, Georgia Review, Kenyon Review*, and other journals. She has been anthologized in *Best American Essays, Norton Book of Women's Lives, Pushcart Prize*, and *O. Henry Prize Stories*. She was awarded a PEN/Martha Albrand Special Citation in non-fiction for *Silent Dancing*, and the Anisfield Wolf Book Award for *The Latin Deli*; her work has also been selected for the Syndicated Fiction Project. She has received fellowships from the National Endowment for the Arts and the Witter Bynner Foundation for poetry. Her most recent book is a collection of short stories, *An Island Like You: Stories of the Barrio* (Orchard Books 1995, Penguin U.S.A. 1996), which was named a Best Book of the Year, 1995-96, by the American Library Association. It was awarded the first Pura Belpré medal by REFORMA OF A.L.A.. in 1996. *La linea del sol*, the Spanish translation of *The Line of the Sun*, was published in 1997 by the University of Puerto Rico Press. In 1998, Arte Publico Press published *The Year of Our Revolution: New and Selected Stories and Poems*; the same press also published the Spanish translation of *Silent Dancing, Bailando en silencio*. She is the 1998 recipient of the Christ-Janner Award in Creative Research from the University of Georgia. A native of Puerto Rico, she now resides in Georgia and is professor of English and Creative Writing at the University of Georgia.

EDWIDGE DANTICAT was born in Haiti in 1969, and was raised by her aunt under the dictatorial Duvalier regime (her parents left for the United States when she was four). Danticat was reunited with her parents and brothers in America when she was twelve. She published her first writings two years later, many of them taking the "rich landscape of memory that is Haiti." She says, "I tend to define myself in terms of the women I knew growing up and the stories they told me." Ms. Danticat holds a degree in literature from Barnard College and an M.F.A. from Brown University. She was nominated for a National Book Award for her story collection, *Krik? Krak!*, and she is the recipient of a James Michener Fellowship, a Lila Wallace-Reader's Digest Writers' Award, the Italian Flaiano Award, and an American Book Award. She was also selected as one of twenty Best of Young American Novelists by *Granta* in 1996 and her story "The Book of the Dead" was in the "Future of American Fiction" issue of the *New Yorker* in 1999. Her first novel, *Breath, Eyes, Memory*, was an Oprah Book Club selection in June 1998; her second novel, *The Farming of Bones*, was published in 1998 and reprinted four times in hardback. She is also the co-author, with filmmaker Jonathan Demme, of two books on Haitian art, *Islands on Fire* and *Odillon Pierre: Haitian Artist*, and is now editing two anthologies, *The Butterfly's Way: Voices from the Haitian Diaspora in the United States* (Soho Press) and *The Beacon Best of 2000: Creative Writing by Women and Men of All Colors* (Beacon).

STELLA POPE DUARTE: I was born and raised in the barrio of la Sonorita in South Phoenix, second-to-the-last in a family of eight children. The compact world of the barrio offered me a daily cinema of characters who passionately expressed every emotion and behavior known to mankind. These characters later bloomed in my imagination, dictating their stories to me. I was a child who wanted someone to explain to me who created God. I was always asking questions that had no answers, searching for the castle of the king in a world of dirt roads and finite lines.

I went through the social system, at times fearing the outside world, at times afraid that if I didn't make it out of the barrio I would never really know who I was. I went on to Arizona State University, the only one to graduate from a university in my entire family. I excelled in my studies and eventually worked as an elementary school teacher and mental health therapist. I am currently head of counseling at a very busy high school in Phoenix and am also adjunct faculty for the University of Phoenix and Arizona State University, teaching ESL/Bilingual education classes and masters of counseling.

Fragile Night, my first collection of short stories, was released for publication by Bilingual Review Press in November 1997. In December 1997 I was awarded first place for my short story "Benny's Pinkie," in the 17th Annual Arizona Author's Literary Contest and in 1999 the same story was short-listed in the Fish Anthology, judged by Frank McCourt, out of more than 1,200 stories from around the world. In February 1998 I was awarded a $5,000 Creative Writing Fellowship by the Arizona Arts Commission on behalf of *Fragile Night*. I am the first Chicana writer to be nationally published from South Phoenix and the first creative writer from Phoenix to be published by Bilingual Review Press in twenty years.

My passion for writing has been with me all my life, as has my passion for literature and poetry. As a child I read the classics, then set up my own theater troupe by using neighborhood kids as actors, often doing spin-offs of the stories and creating my own endings. As a teen, I recall jumping over broken wine bottles in the alley next to our family home, reciting from Dickens: "It was the best of times, it was the worst of times, etc." I loved those words!

In 1995, shortly after my mother's death, I had a dream in which my deceased father appeared and led me to an enormous, spiral staircase. The dream led me to understand that my writing was the way up the staircase. It is with deep gratitude that I now write, honoring the lives of my four children and giving voice to the cries of the beautiful and fierce...mi raza!

MINFONG HO was born to Chinese parents in Burma and raised on the outskirts of Bangkok, Thailand in an airy house "next to a fishpond and in a big garden," she says, "with rice fields on the other side of the palm trees, where water buffaloes wallowed in mud holes." As a child, she spoke Thai and Cantonese, then learned English when she started primary school. At sixteen she left home and went to Tunghai University in Taiwan, where she mastered Mandarin, then continued her studies in English at Cornell University in Ithaca, New York. Since then, she has learned some basic Cambodian while working with refugees as a nutritionist and relief worker on the Thai-Cambodian border. She also learned some French in Geneva, Switzerland, where she lived with her American husband and their three young children.

Ho started writing while she was at college in the United States, to combat homesickness by weaving her own private, familiar world around herself. Her first book, *Sing to the Dawn*, was the result of notes and letters she wrote while sitting in the Cornell University greenhouse, which was filled with lush tropical plants, like those Saeng sees in "The Winter Hibiscus." *Sing to the Dawn* and her next two novels, *Rice Without Rain*, based on her experiences teaching in northern Thailand, and *The Clay Marble*, the result of working with Cambodian refugee children, have garnered numerous awards, among them the *Booklist* Editor's Choice Award, and a Best Book for Young Adults from the American Library Association and the South-East Asian Write Award. Among her other books are *The Two Brothers*, *Hush! a Thai Lullaby*, *Maples in the Mist*, and *Brother Rabbit*.

MIKHAIL IOSSEL emigrated to this country, from then-Leningrad (former Soviet Union), in 1986. He writes both in English and in Russian. He is the author of a collection of stories, *Every Hunter Wants to Know* (Norton, 1991), which has been translated into several languages. His work has been anthologized in *Best American Short Stories*, and he has won a number of awards for his fiction, including a

Guggenheim Fellowship and a National Endowment for the Arts fellowship. He is the writer-in-residence at Union College and lives in upstate New York.

HA JIN served six years in the People's Liberation Army in mainland China before coming to the United States in 1985. He earned his M.A. and PH.D. in English from Brandeis University. Since 1993 he has taught at Emory University, where he is an associate professor of English. He has published two poetry books, *Between Silences* (1990) and *Facing Shadows* (1996). He has also published two books of short fiction, *Ocean of Words* (1996), winner of the PEN/Hemingway Award, and *Under the Red Flag* (1997), winner of the Flannery O'Connor Award for Short Fiction. In addition, he has written two novels: *In the Pond* was published in 1998; *Waiting* won the 1999 National Book Award for Fiction. His stories and poems have appeared in *Atlantic Monthly, Harper's, Paris Review, TriQuarterly, Kenyon Review,* and elsewhere. They have been included in anthologies such as *Pushcart Prize* (17, 19, & 21), *Best American Short Stories* (1997 & 1999), and *Norton Introduction to Literature*.

ANDREW LAM is an associate editor with the Pacific News Service in San Francisco, a member of the World Academy of Arts and Sciences, and a regular commentator on National Public Radio's *All Things Considered*. He was born in Saigon, Vietnam and came to the United States at the end of the Vietnam war in 1975 when he was eleven years old. Lam is currently working on his first short story collection. His articles have appeared in several dozens of newspapers across the country including the *New York Times, Washington Post,* and *San Francisco Chronicle*; his essays have been published in magazines such as *Los Angeles Times Magazine, Mother Jones, In Context, The Nation,* and MSNBC.com. Many of his essays have been anthologized in books such as *New to North America, Writings by Immigrants and Their Children and Grandchildren; The Compact Reader; Visions Across the Americas; The Asian American Experience; Breaking Traditions: Stories for 2001; Cast a Cold Eye;* and *The Cultural Diversity Reader*. His short stories have been published and anthologized in *Mānoa, Amerasia, Transfer,* ZYZZYVA, *Asian American Sexuality, The Other Side of Heaven, Once Upon A Dream: The Vietnamese American Experience, Sudden Fiction (Continued),* and many other publications. He has also won many awards, such as the Society of Professional Journalist Outstanding Young Journalist Award (1993), the Rockefeller Fellowship in UCLA (1992), and the Asian American Journalists Association National Award (1993; 1995). He was honored and profiled on KQED television in May 1996 during Asian American heritage month.

SHIRLEY GEOK-LIN LIM's first collection of poems, *Crossing the Peninsula* (1980), received the Commonwealth Poetry Prize. She has published four volumes of poetry subsequently: *No Man's Grove* (1985), *Modern Secrets* (1989), *Monsoon History* (1994), which is a retrospective selection of her work, and *What the Fortune Teller Didn't Say* (1998). She was interviewed by Bill Moyers for a PBS special on American poetry, "Fooling with Words," in 1999. She has also published three books of short stories and a memoir, *Among the White Moon Faces* (1996), which received the 1997 American Book Award. Lim's co-edited anthology, *The Forbidden Stitch: An Asian American Women's Anthology,* received the 1990 American Book Award. She has published two critical studies, *Writing South East/Asia in English: Against the Grain* (1994), and *Nationalism and Literature: Writing in English from the Philippines and Singapore* (1993); has edited/co-edited six other volumes, including *Transnational Asia Pacific* (University of Illinois Press), *Power, Race and Gender in Academe* (MLA Press) and *Asian American Literature: An Anthology* (NTC/Contemporary Publishers). She is Chair Professor of English at the University of Hong Kong, and professor of English and Women's Studies at the University of California, Santa Barbara. The short story in this anthology, "Sisters," is an adaptation from the first chapter of her novel-in-progress, *Sisters Wing.*

JAIME MANRIQUE was born in Barranquilla, Colombia. In Spanish, he has published two volumes of poetry, a collection of essays, and a book of short stories. In English, he has published the novels

Colombian Gold, Latin Moon in Manhattan, and *Twilight at the Equator;* the volume of poems *My Night with Federico García Lorca;* and the memoir *Eminent Maricones: Arenas, Lorca, Puig, and Me.* Manrique teaches in the M.F.A. Program at Columbia University.

BHARATI MUKHERJEE is the author of two books of short stories, *Darkness* and *The Middleman and Other Stories,* and the novels *Jasmine, Wife, The Tiger's Daughter,* and *The Holder of the World.* She also is the coauthor, with her husband, Clark Blaise, of *Days and Nights in Calcutta,* a book of nonfiction. Born in Calcutta, she attended college. in India, earning two master's degrees at the University of Baroda, and then came to the United States to study creative writing at the University of Iowa. At Iowa, she received a master of fine arts degree in creative writing and, later, a double-doctorate in English and comparative literature. A winner of the National Book Critics' Circle Award for Fiction, she is currently professor of English at the University of California–Berkeley.

SIMON J. ORTIZ is a poet, fiction writer, essayist, and storyteller. He is native of Acoma Pueblo in New Mexico, where he grew up at Deetseyaamah, a rural village area in the Acoma Pueblo community. He is the father of three children—Raho, Rainy, and Sara—and is a grandfather. As a major Native writer, he insists on telling the story of his people's land, culture, and community, a story that has been marred by social, political, economic, and cultural conflicts with Euro-American society. Ortiz's insistence, however, is upon a story that stresses vision and hope by creative struggle and resistance against human and technological oppression. His previous works include *Speaking for the Generations, After and Before the Lightning, Woven Stone, Fightin', The People Shall Continue, Howbah Indians,* and others. He has received award recognition from the National Endowment for the Arts, the Lila Wallace-Reader's Digest Fund Award, a "Returning of the Gift" Lifetime Achievement Award, and a New Mexico Humanities Council Humanitarian Award. Presently he lives in Tucson, Arizona.

THOMAS PALAKEEL is an associate professor of English at Bradley

University in Peoria, Illinois. His work has appeared in *Mānoa, North Dakota Quarterly, Short Story International,* and the *Christian Science Monitor.* He is completing an autobiographical narrative, a personal history of English.

NAHID RACHLIN, born in Iran, came to the United States to attend college and stayed on. While a student she held a Doubleday-Columbia University Fellowship and a Wallace Stegner Fellowship (Stanford). Among her publications are three novels, *Foreigner* (W.W. Norton, 1978), *Married to a Stranger* (E.P. Dutton, 1983), *The Heart's Desire* (City Lights, 1995), and a collection of short stories, *Veils* (City Lights, 1993). She has published individual stories in many magazines, including *Redbook, Shenandoah, Four Quarters, Minnesota Review, Ararat, Fiction, Columbia Magazine, Stand Magazine* (England), *New Laurel Review, New Letters, Crosscurrents, Pleiades, Mississippi Mud, Crazy Horse, City Lights Journal, North Atlantic Review, Scholastic Voice, Confrontation, Literary Review, Vignette,* and *Hawai'i Review.* Several of her stories have been reprinted in anthologies such as *Matters of Gender,* McGraw-Hill Ryerson Limited; *Stories from the American Mosaic,* Graywolf Press; *Power Play: Individuals in Conflict,* Prentice Hall; *Arrivals, Cross-Cultural Experiences in Literature,* Addison-Wesley Publishing Company; and *A World Between,* George Braziller. Among her many grants and awards are the Bennet Cerf Award, PEN Syndicated Fiction Project Award, and a National Endowment for the Arts fellowship. She currently teaches at the New School University.

KYOKO UCHIDA was born in Hiroshima, Japan, and raised between Hiroshima and Houston, Vancouver, Toronto, and Southern California. Currently she lives in New York City, working as a translator/editor and researcher. Her work has appeared in *Black Warrior Review, Faultline, Georgia Review, Mānoa, New Letters, Northwest Review, Quarterly West, Phoebe, The Prose Poem,* and *Shenandoah,* as well as in *An Ear to the Ground: Introducing Writers from 2 Coasts* (Cune Press). "Mother Tongues and Other Untravellings" is a long poem in prose composed of thirty sections, of which three are excerpted here.

SAMRAT UPADHYAY likes to read contemporary fiction by authors from around the world, especially from South Asia. He has published stories and poems in several journals. His story "The Good Shopkeeper," originally published in *Mānoa*, appeared in the *1999 Best American Short Stories*. A story collection with the same title will be published by Houghton Mifflin next year. Currently he's co-editing, with Manju Thapa, a special issue of *Mānoa* on contemporary Nepali literature, a task that is opening up still another world inside him.

Printed in the USA
CPSIA information can be obtained
at www.ICGtesting.com
JSHW082158140824
68134JS00014B/302